"What's the matter, Reb?"

John asked, surprising himself at how kindly the question came out.

"Nothing," she answered.

Nothing. She was homeless. Wet. Shivering. Starved. She'd been stuck with him when he was more than half-crazy, and now she was an accomplice to murder. But it was still *nothing.*

She began to take the pins out of her hair and rake through it with her fingers. Her hair was thick and heavy, and quite beautiful, particularly when it was undone. He let his eyes travel over her face and drop to her breasts. She was still pretty, even ragged and travel stained the way she was now.

Sweet, pretty little thing.

Damn! he thought at the sudden urgent stirring in his groin. She had the power to affect him, and he was feeling better than he had thought. A lot better.

Dear Reader,

This month we are happy to bring you *Rogue's Honor,* a new book from DeLoras Scott. Those of you who have followed DeLoras's career since her first book, *Bittersweet,* will be delighted by this tale of the Oklahoma land rush and of partners each with their own dark pasts.

With *Heaven's Gate,* the writing team of Erin Yorke has created the dramatic story of a wayward English countess and the renegade Irish lord who is determined to force her surrender.

Lindsay McKenna's *King of Swords* is a sequel to her January title, *Lord of Shadowhawk.* Abducted and held for ransom, Thorne Somerset learns to love the bitter soldier who holds her fate in his hands.

A fugitive Union officer and a troubled Rebel girl overcome seemingly insurmountable odds to find happiness in *The Prisoner.* Set at the close of the Civil War, this tender story is the first historical by popular contemporary author Cheryl Reavis.

Next month look for titles by Maura Seger, Julie Tetel, Lucy Elliot and Elizabeth August from Harlequin Historicals, and rediscover the romance of the past.

Sincerely,

The Editors

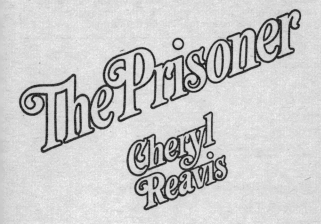

The Prisoner

Cheryl Reavis

Harlequin Books

TORONTO • NEW YORK • LONDON
AMSTERDAM • PARIS • SYDNEY • HAMBURG
STOCKHOLM • ATHENS • TOKYO • MILAN
MADRID • WARSAW • BUDAPEST • AUCKLAND

Harlequin Historicals first edition May 1992

ISBN 0-373-28726-7

THE PRISONER

CHERYL REAVIS,

public health nurse, short-story author and award-winning romance novelist, says she is a writer of emotions. "I want to feel all the joys and the sorrows and everything in between. Then, with just the right word, the right turn of phrase, I hope to take the reader by the hand and make her feel them, too." Cheryl currently makes her home in North Carolina with her husband and son.

To my agent, Maureen Moran,
for her unfailing support in the thirteen-year quest
to get an albatross to fly

Chapter One

Salisbury, North Carolina
January 1865

He was in total darkness. He couldn't see anything. He could only feel the tight wall of dirt that surrounded him and the roots that struck his face as he dragged himself forward. There wasn't enough room for him to bend his knees; he could barely get his shoulders through. His fingers dug into the ground in front of him for leverage. He was afraid to grab anywhere else, afraid he'd collapse the sides. It was getting harder to breathe, and he tried not to think of what he might encounter, what creature or what thing, in the blackness, or what he would do if Max had lied to him and there was no open end.

He jumped at a sudden noise behind him—collapsing earth. *Ah, God,* he thought. The tunnel behind him would be blocked. There was no going back for Max now. The decision had been made for him. He lay quietly for a moment, listening to the sound of his own labored breathing.

Go on! he berated himself. *Go on!* He was supposed to be the Pride of the Regiment. He could get a woman on her back in half the time it took to tell it. The best whores in

Washington would go into a decline if he never came home again.

He pulled himself forward, his arms trembling with the effort. His elbows and knees were rubbed raw and burning. His fingernails were torn. He could feel the warmth of his own blood on his hands. He had no idea how far he'd come or how far he had to go. There was only the darkness and the fear, ahead and behind, suffocating him....

I can't breathe!

A trickle of dirt poured down on his head and face. He hugged the ground with his body, trying to fight down the panic, the overwhelming urge to try to stand up, to run. It was all he could do not to tear at the walls with his bare hands. He was going to die in here!

"Easy," he whispered, taking comfort from the sound of his own voice. "Easy. Just go on. That's all you have to do. Go on. Go on...."

He inched forward, causing another shower of dirt.

"Go on!" he repeated, his litany of survival. How many times had he said the words in the past eight months? *Go on!*

He reached ahead of him, his hand striking dirt where there should have been open space. Did the tunnel angle? He reached farther, trying to find the way. There was nothing but dirt.

Frantic now, he began to claw at the wall of dank earth, trying to fling handfuls back over his shoulders. It got into his mouth and eyes, but he didn't stop. He had to get out. He had to get *out!*

His hand suddenly poked through into nothingness. He could feel a rush of cold night air. He crawled forward, digging as he went until he had the way open. He could see light; he could feel the outside. He pulled himself along until his head emerged from the hole, then he collapsed on his arms, sucking in great gulps of fresh air.

Outside! Ah, God!

"Pride...of the...regiment," he whispered, fighting down a ridiculous urge to cry. "And a damn sorry sight you are, too."

He abruptly lifted his head. Why was it so bright? He could smell smoke. He crawled the rest of the way out on his hands and knees, shivering as the cold wind hit him. Ahead, the sky was a brilliant orange.

The town was on fire.

Amanda Douglas moved to another window, looking out across the moonlit yard to the red glow in the sky. From time to time she could see a great shower of sparks whipped high in the wind. She didn't envy the fire brigades. It was so cold tonight. The wind moaned in the chimneys and banged an upstairs shutter. She couldn't hear the garrison bell ringing, and that was some comfort, but she knew that there wasn't a person in town who didn't believe that the fire in the Brick Row stores had somehow been caused by the captured Union soldiers in the prison. Barely two months ago they had tried to get out, and now there were supposed to be more of them locked up in that place than there were guards and townspeople put together—desperate men, vengeful men, who'd been left out in the cold too long, starved too long.

"Verillia?" she called out suddenly, because she was afraid and because she hoped that the source of the rustling at the end of the upstairs hallway might be her stepmother. There was no answer.

An oak tree branch, she decided, dragged against the house in the wind. Her stomach rumbled at the aroma of boiled cabbage that came from the kitchen. The last cabbage in Christendom, Verillia had called it, but Amanda would have no chance to eat it. The reverend would be home soon, fire in the Brick Row stores or not, escaping Yankee prisoners or not, and he believed that the sinful should fast.

"What are you doing home?" Verillia said behind her, making her jump.

"I didn't hear you come in," Amanda said, to keep from answering the question. Verillia still had on her bonnet and shawl, and she was carrying the wooden case of dried herbs she hardly went anywhere without. There was no medicine in town these days, and someone was always sick or hurt.

"I'm not coming in, I'm going out. They got people burned at the fire. That there boy the doctor sent to fetch me got me so addled I forgot my herb tins. One of them Wood boys, high-strung, just like his mama, hurrying me around—"

Verillia suddenly stopped talking, and Amanda could feel her scrutiny. She was so tired suddenly, tired of everything. Of war. Of being hungry. Of trying to deal with the reverend and always being caught in the wrong. Of trying to keep sweet, kindhearted Verillia from worrying over something she couldn't do anything about.

"I was out yonder in the side yard speaking to one of the night patrollers," Verillia went on. "He said the Yankees are locked up tight. They ain't trying to get out again. I reckon it's the truth. I swear you can't get at the real goings-on around here for nothing if you're a woman. I couldn't tell if he was lying or not— What's wrong?" she asked abruptly.

"Nothing," Amanda said.

Verillia lit the lamp on the nearest table and turned the flame up high.

"What does your daddy think you done now?" she asked, watching Amanda carefully. She came closer, but Amanda moved away.

"He doesn't think. He knows— Verillia, don't," she said as the other woman came still closer. "Don't baby me. I'll cry if you do and I don't want to cry."

"You'd be a whole lot better off if you *did* cry. Your daddy wouldn't be near so hard on you. I ain't never in my life— What have you done?"

"He made me sit with one of the soldiers at the hospital," she said tonelessly. "I was supposed to call him before the boy died so he could make him repent. I didn't do it. He died before I—"

"Your daddy can't blame you for that, child."

"Yes, he can. The boy wanted to talk to me. He knew he was dying, Verillia, but he was pretending—you know how they do sometimes. He was pretending everything was all right—like we'd met at church or something. He was just lying there—he was holding a slab of wood somebody gave him with his name carved on it. His own grave marker. But he was talking about all the places he'd been and all the things he'd seen, and what he wanted to do when he got home to Virginia, as if he had all the time in the world. I waited too long—"

"Amanda, this ain't your fault. You got no business going in them hospitals in the first place and I told your daddy. It ain't right."

Verillia sighed heavily, and Amanda realized suddenly how often the Reverend Douglas made them both sigh.

"You can come with me then. You can help me with them burned people—"

"No."

"Amanda—"

"No, Verillia. I'm supposed to wait here."

"I wish I had the money to send you off someplace. I wish I had the money to send you to James and Rose in the mountains."

Don't! Amanda wanted to cry out. She didn't want to hear Verillia's wishful thinking. There was no money for any kind of escape to the mountains. There would never be any money. She was caught here. She was as much a prisoner in this house as any of the men were in the stockade, only she was too much of a coward to try to do anything about it. She was too afraid to make a run for it, to try to get to a place where the reverend couldn't find her.

"I have to wait here," she said quietly.

"Amanda—"

"Verillia, I have to. You know that."

"You ain't had nothing to eat. Go get you some of that cabbage at least."

"No," Amanda said, forcing a smile. "I don't think I'd better eat his cabbage, too." She abruptly looked away, feeling the sting of tears, avoiding her stepmother's eyes.

"You want me to stay with you?"

"You've got people to see about."

"I can go later—"

"Verillia, he'll think you're interfering."

"If you'd just tell him you're sorry. It don't matter if you mean it. Just satisfy him. Then it won't go so hard for you."

But Amanda wouldn't tell him she was sorry, and they both knew it. She was like the boy in the hospital. She'd rather die pretending everything was all right than repent.

Verillia stood awkwardly for a moment, then turned to go. "Come lock this door after me," she said in the hallway. "I won't stay no longer than I have to. I swear I don't know why your daddy treats you like he does."

Because old sins cast long shadows, Amanda thought as she locked the door. Only in this case the sins were her mother's and a well-kept secret until she lay on her deathbed. Her mother had been sick with the typhoid and addicted to laudanum; it had been then, when Amanda was twelve, that her mother had inadvertently made her understand the misery in both their lives.

"I was never afraid of the dark," Mary Douglas kept babbling. And then, at the last, pressing Amanda's hand against her cheek and staring at something only she could see, "My darling Kenyan, do you see her? Do you see Amanda? Do you see our beautiful child?"

Amanda had known immediately who Kenyan was. He was the Reverend Douglas's handsome younger brother—"the poet," the reverend always called him—who had romantically died young of the consumption, scribbling his love poems to the last. Amanda had watched the life leave her mother's body, and she had understood why the man she'd always believed was her father despised her. She was a love child; her mother and Kenyan Douglas had committed adultery. And whether the reverend actually knew or only suspected didn't matter. She had no doubt that his vindictiveness, in either case, would have been the same.

If she had any comfort in this, it was the realization that the reverend's misery had to be comparable to her own. She had no doubt that he would have considered himself the better of the two men, and that apparently he hadn't been able to convince her mother of it. He hadn't been able to father a child of his own. He hadn't been able to win her mother's heart. Unfortunately, it was she, Amanda, who would continue to pay for that fact. She suspected that even Verillia was supposed to have been part of her punishment, the stoic, uneducated mountain woman the reverend married so impulsively and brought home to take her mother's place. He had met Verillia at a summer revival meeting in the mountains and married her within the week, his hastiness giving him no time to fully assess his second wife's true nature. He was in such a big hurry to bring home a wicked stepmother that he'd missed altogether Verillia's great compassion for the orphaned and the persecuted.

Amanda wished she had let Verillia hide her just for a moment in her warm arms. She was so tired!

She crossed the downstairs quickly and blew out the lamp, shivering again in the cold and feeling her way up the stairs in the darkness to the door to her room at the front of the house. The door was ajar, and she pushed it inward, the dread of the reverend's return sitting like a great iron weight on her chest. He had never physically harmed her; it was her sense of how badly he wanted to that frightened her. She understood him, and he knew it. She understood why he took her with him into the hospitals and the houses with the smallpox and the typhoid. She understood why he'd sent her home alone on the streets tonight with the town on fire and no one knowing if the Yankee prisoners were loose. He wanted her in harm's way. He was another Abraham, piously offering up his child in the name of charity, but thus far God had not seen fit to accept his sacrifice. The reverend wanted to be rid of her, but for all his determination she remained unscathed. She was well and healthy, and no escapee, as yet, had tried to murder her on the street.

She moved carefully in the darkness to the front window to look at the fire again. She couldn't tell if it was coming in her direction or not. She could see the moon through the oak tree branches, and there were voices in the yard below—patrollers coming in to trade the freezing cold of night watch for the warm excitement of the downtown fire. She leaned her head against the windowpane, her breath immediately icing on the cold glass. She was shivering again, as much from the memory of that boy's death tonight as from the cold.

You will sit with him, the reverend said. *You will sit with him and you will not touch his body.*

She closed her eyes. If only she could get away from here. There had been a time when she had thought it might be possible. On a warm spring night last year, well out of the reverend's hearing, Thayer Giffen had promised to marry her. She had admired—loved—Thayer for as long as she could remember. He had been her friend, her teacher, her confidant. There was nothing he hadn't known about her, even that the reverend was not her father. And if she *had* married him, she would have gone to live in his house with his mother and his sister Anne, and she would have been free.

But then Thayer had abruptly married someone else, some stranger from Tennessee neither Amanda nor his family had ever heard him mention. Amanda had seen him only once since his hasty wedding, when he'd gotten home from the fighting in Virginia long enough to try to apologize, to try to assuage his guilt and her injured pride with still more promises.

If you ever need anything, he'd kept saying, but it had hurt too much for her to listen. She had believed in him; she had loved him, and in the presence of that girl from Tennessee, it hadn't mattered. Even now she could close her eyes and remember the night he'd asked her to marry him. Thayer, close and warm and holding her fast, near tears because he had to go and he might never see her again. His skin had smelled of soap and leather and the out-of-doors. His kiss had tasted of whiskey and cloves. He had been too bold that night, with his mouth and his hands, and she hadn't cared. She had known how badly he wanted to take her, but it was he who had been strong. Strong enough to leave her a virgin. Strong enough to marry a stranger from Tennessee.

"Oh, Thayer," she whispered, fully aware that his name was the only prayer she ever said anymore.

She had no chance to say anything else. She was grabbed up off the floor; the hand was clamped so tightly over her mouth she was barely able to breathe. She clawed at it, at the arm that was crushing her in two, feeling, tasting the dirt on his hand grinding into her mouth.

"One sound," he hissed into her ear, "and I'll kill you."

She believed him. She believed him because of the smell. He reeked of damp wool and damp earth and the stench of the smallpox and a long time without soap and water. She could feel—smell—his greasy, matted hair against her cheek, and she clawed harder, struggling to reach the man's face.

"Stop it!" he hissed, dragging her back from the window. "Who else is here? Just the other woman?"

His grip tightened over her ribs enough to make her whimper.

"Well, nod your head or something, damn you!"

She nodded frantically. There was no sound in the room but the wind against the house and the both of them breathing.

"I know you're scared," he whispered, his breath hot against her face. "But you're not as scared as I am. I was told to come here—"

There were voices again in the yard below. He dragged her back to the window, standing in the shadows until he was satisfied that the commotion had nothing to do with him.

"You understand?" he asked.

Again, Amanda nodded, forcing herself to stop struggling. But she understood nothing at all—except that she had to get loose.

"I'm going to let you go now. You don't have to be afraid of me. Just tell whoever needs to know I'm here—"

She lunged backward, breaking his hold, but he grabbed her by her hair before she could get to the door. She had never in her life been a screamer, and that response came too late now. The noise she made was like the squawk of a stepped-on chicken, and she kept thinking in the middle of it that she should have been more like Anne Giffen. Thayer's sister would have had the Home Militia and half the prison garrison alerted by now. Amanda lunged backward again, knocking the man off balance. They both fell onto the foot of her narrow bed. He held her down, and she tried to bite him, to kick, but she couldn't get him off her. She had done more than make a sound, and she was about to die for it.

The man suddenly stiffened, and she knew immediately the cause—the sound of the hammer on a Colt revolver being dragged back.

"My God," he breathed onto her face, rolling off her to the floor on the other side.

"What is this?" the Reverend Douglas asked, his voice quiet but no less deadly. Amanda knew it, and so did the man.

"Tell me!" the reverend bellowed when she didn't answer, but he gave her no chance to explain anything. "Your stepmother is out and you thought I wouldn't come home tonight, is that it?"

The man began to edge around the foot of the bed.

"Stand where you are!" the reverend said sharply. "I am not so inexperienced with firearms as you might think. I advise you to consider your moves carefully." He reached out to grab Amanda by the wrist, dragging her off the bed and shoving her toward the door. "Get downstairs!"

She couldn't keep her teeth from chattering, and she went, pressing herself against the wall as the reverend forced the man ahead of her down the wooden steps. She hid her face when he hurried the man along—by planting his foot firmly into the man's back and shoving hard.

John Howe stayed on his knees at the foot of the stairs. He wasn't sure he could get up. He was shaking, and he couldn't stop. He clenched his fists against his thighs and looked up, trying to measure the distance to the barrel of the revolver, his eyes flicking to the girl and back again. She was scared out of her wits. She wouldn't be a problem, if the old fool would just come closer to him—

Damn! he thought suddenly, glancing at the girl again. *I've seen her before.*

She stood well away from him, but she met his eyes. Pretty enough little piece, he thought, wondering if he recognized her or the dress, a faded pink flowered thing with military CSA buttons sewed on the front of it. The females down here were nothing if not patriotic. All the young Reb women he'd seen seemed to wear dresses like that.

''Your name,'' the old man said.

He didn't answer, his eyes going to the girl again. If she'd just swoon or something—

''You want an unmarked grave then?'' the old man said, and John looked at him sharply. The old man certainly knew how to get a soldier's attention. He had known men to sew flower seeds into the linings of their clothes, so that if they were hastily buried in the field, their families would see some out-of-place flower growing and find them. He'd been in a living hell for the past eight months, where the dead were dumped into trenches, no names and no coffins, just a shovelful of dirt into open eyes and open mouths. And he didn't have any damn flower seeds. If he had, he would have eaten them.

He told the old man his name. ''Howe. Captain John D. Howe.''

''So tell me, Mr. Howe. How much do you pay the prison guards for this service?''

He stared back at the old man, his mind working hard to make some sense of the question. Thus far, it had been one hell of a night for an escape—a full moon and the town on fire and every man in the place out and about. He had known which house to come to; he'd unwittingly bought the information simply by offering a fellow prisoner a drink of water from his canteen. He'd even been able to locate the house once, when he'd been out of the stockade on a work detail—the same time he thought he'd seen this Reb girl. But he must have gotten turned around somehow. He was in the wrong house, or the old man wasn't taking any chances on getting caught giving aid to the enemy. The girl was no help. She seemed as baffled as he was.

"I . . . don't know what you mean," he said carefully.

"I mean it's apparent that my daughter is whoring for the garrison, Mr. Howe. I have asked how much you pay for it."

"No—" the girl protested, but she came too close, and the old man struck her full in the mouth with the back of his hand. Her head jerked backward, but she didn't cower. She held her body rigid, and her eyes flashed for a moment with something difficult to describe. Hatred? No, not quite that, John thought. Pride. Stiff-necked pride. The old man had hurt her. He could see her eyes watering, but she didn't make a sound. She wasn't going to give the bastard the satisfaction.

Well done, he thought with a certain admiration. His eyes locked with hers for a moment before she quickly looked away.

Amanda could taste the blood on the inside of her mouth. She kept her eyes averted until she could be sure that she wouldn't cry, focusing on the Yankee's knees. He was covered all over with dirt that must have come from tunneling. The Yankee tunnels were the topic of one of Charlie Wood's silly stories—how he could walk across the prison compound at any time and sink into some digging project, and how he was afraid some ignorant Yankee would dig straight down instead of toward the walls and end up in China.

She glanced up to find the Yankee watching her. She let her eyes hold his for a moment without apology, without shame. He was the enemy. She didn't care what he thought.

"My wife believes you are a good and dutiful daughter," the reverend said. "Good and dutiful. What do you suppose she will say about this?"

Amanda stayed silent. She could feel the Yankee's eyes on her, blue-gray eyes that stared out from under dirty, matted, no-color hair. She could almost feel sorry for him. He must be thinking that he was about to suffer the consequences of being in the wrong army, when his real misfortune was encountering her.

"You haven't fooled me," the reverend went on. "I have been right all along. I know—"

"Are you going to shoot me or what?" John interrupted. Whatever was going on here was making him damned nervous. He made an effort to get up off the floor, surprised that the old man let him do it.

"I haven't decided," the old man said. He waved the gun toward a doorway off the front hall. "Go in there—wait!" he suddenly commanded. "Amanda, bring in a lamp. And don't get close to him."

Amanda did as she was told, surprised that her hands were steady. She felt so strange now, detached, as if all this had nothing to do with her. She set the lamp carefully on the table the reverend indicated.

"Get down on the floor where I can see you," he said to the Yankee. "Not there! I don't want your vermin in my rugs. On the bare floor."

John sat down on the wood flooring well away from the somewhat threadbare carpet the old man was so worried about, his movements slow to give him more time to think. It was no warmer in this room than in the rest of the house— but it was warmer than the burrows in the ground where he and most of the prisoners in the stockade stayed for shelter. He kept glancing at the girl, still hoping she'd swoon. Anything to take the old man's attention.

God, what a fix!

"What do you want to let me go?" he asked abruptly. There was no use dragging this out. If he had a chance in hell to get out of here alive, he wanted to know it. "How much money?"

The old man laughed. "I hardly think one would be apt to get any kind of payment from the likes of you, Mr. Howe."

"I have been treated like an animal in this town. It doesn't necessarily follow that I am one—"

"Ah! A most interesting comment from a man I have just removed from my daughter's bed. Amanda! Get the Book! You're not a godly man, are you, Mr. Howe?"

"No," John said truthfully. He shifted his position a little. The old man was on guard instantly.

"Then you will not know Deuteronomy, chapter 22, verse 27. She will read it to you."

The girl hesitated.

That's it, John thought. *Don't do it. Stir him up again.*

But the girl abruptly went to a desk in the corner of the room and opened a Bible. She began to read quickly, her voice low.

"Not there!" the old man shouted. "The next verse!"

Amanda took a deep breath. The wind was coming in around the cracks in the window and causing the curtains to billow. The upstairs shutter still banged against the house.

"If a man find a damsel that is a virgin," she read aloud, her mouth hurting as she formed the words, "which is not betrothed, and lay hold on her, and lie with her, and they be found—" She stopped.

"Do go on," John prompted, because he thought she was going to cry after all. "If it's for my benefit, then I should certainly hear it."

Don't let the bastard make you cry, girl, he thought, surprised that it mattered to him when he'd been perfectly willing for her to make the old fool mad enough to hit her again.

"I have told you to read!" the reverend said.

She looked from one man to the other and then down at the page. She read quickly. "Then the man that lay with her shall give unto the damsel's father fifty shekels of silver...."

John nearly laughed out loud. God, his father would love this. He had accused him more than once of not being able to cross the street without getting into some kind of woman trouble. As it turned out, he couldn't make a decent military escape, either.

"I think you've overestimated my ability to perform, old man," he said. "She's comely enough, but my poor health of late has left me sadly lacking in—"

"Be quiet! Amanda, read!"

Amanda licked her lips and kept her eyes on the page. The sooner she read it, the sooner this would be over. "And she shall be his wife; because he hath humbled her, he may not put her away all his days—"

"Behold the humbled virgin, Mr. Howe," the reverend said.

"I told you, old man. I can't 'humble' anybody. If that's her state, it's through no fault of mine."

"Not so, Mr. Howe. Your fault is a matter of degree. And your duty now is to salvage her honor—as the Good Book says."

"And what honor is that, if you're convinced she's whoring for the garrison?"

"She is ruined! Do you think any man here will take your leavings!"

"I haven't done anything, old man!"

"Because I came back too soon!"

"My God, you people down here are crazy!" He was on his knees before he remembered that he was at the wrong end of a revolver. He sat back down, carefully, dropping his head because the exertion had taken its toll. He felt so *bad*. Weak and feverish and freezing, all at the same time. With some effort, he looked up at the girl.

Amanda stared back at him. He's sick, she thought. He drew a long breath, and his eyes held hers. She realized suddenly that he felt sorry for her. *He* felt sorry for *her*.

"Your immortal soul is in grave peril, Mr. Howe."

This time John did laugh. "You don't begin to know the truth of that, old man." He took another deep breath and rubbed his hand over his eyes. He had done what amounted to murder to get out of that hellhole of a prison and look where it had gotten him. "If I salvage this lady's *honor,* then what?"

"What do you mean?"

"I mean, what do *I* get out of it?"

"You go unimpeded from this house, just as you came into it. No more, no less."

"That smacks of treason, old man."

"I care nothing for your politics, Mr. Howe. Only your soul."

He stared at the old man. The son of a bitch had him over a barrel and knew it, but John asked the question anyway. "What...exactly constitutes 'salvaging'?"

"Why, the bonds of holy matrimony, Mr. Howe—"

"And where are you going to get a preacher crazy enough to marry us?"

"*I* am a minister of God, Mr. Howe. I will perform the ceremony."

"How convenient," John said sarcastically. The man *was* crazy!

He also had the gun.

"I have your word?" John asked. "I go free?" A few ceremonial words in front of a lunatic were nothing, he thought. He'd done a lot worse to get this far.

"I am a man of God, Mr. Howe. I have said you will go free. I trouble myself only with the condition of your soul. You are a sinner. She is a sinner. I do for you what I can."

"All right," he said, and the old man looked at him in surprise.

"You—agree?"

"Hell, I'll marry anything you've got, old man. Let's get on with it."

"You are as crazy as he is!" the girl cried out.

"No, I'm desperate," he told her. "There's a big difference."

He got slowly to his feet.

"We will pray," the old man said.

"I won't do this!" Amanda cried.

"Then you'll have another dead man on your conscience this night!" the reverend bellowed. "Another man lost before I can give him his salvation!"

"No!" she cried. She stepped forward, passing too close to the Yankee. His hand shot out to grab her, jerking her around in front of him, his arms clamping around her waist and neck.

"Put down the gun, old man! I'll break her goddamned neck!"

"God's will be done," the reverend said. "He will guide my hand."

Oh, God! Amanda thought as she looked into the reverend's eyes. The Yankee was dragging her with him toward the door. He didn't realize at all that she was no protection. She slumped against him as the reverend took better aim.

Oh, God!

The lamp on the table behind exploded in the roar from the Colt, just as the Yankee shoved her aside. She sprawled on the floor, lying in shattered prisms and green glass. She tried to roll out of the way as the two men struggled for the gun, but her skirts were tangled. The gun went off again; she could feel the impact of the ball in the floor near her head. She managed to get to her knees as the Yankee wrested the revolver away, and she gave a small cry as he brought the barrel down hard over the reverend's head.

"Come here!" the Yankee yelled at her.

She didn't move. The reverend fell heavily and lay so still; blood trickled over his forehead. The Yankee grabbed her by the wrist and jerked her upward, but her skirts were still tangled and she couldn't get to her feet. She dared a glance at him. He was looking around frantically, for what, she didn't know.

"Look, girl! I don't have time for this! Get up!"

She managed to get to her feet. "Is he—did you kill him?"

"Why, do you want me to?"

"No!" she said in alarm. She didn't want any more dead men on her conscience.

The Yankee suddenly made a decision. "Let's go!" he said, dragging her out of the room. "Half the town must have heard the shots. Hurry, damn you!" He pulled her along with him through the kitchen and out the back door of the house.

"Where are we going?" She couldn't keep up with him. She kept stumbling, nearly falling down the back steps. They crossed the moonlit yard, and the cold wind cut through her clothes. His stride was much too long for her, but he dragged her along anyway. "Let me go! You're hurting my arm!"

"Be quiet! I have to think!"

Clearly, he intended to do his thinking on the run.

"Where are we going!"

He jerked her around in front of him, grabbing her by both shoulders and shaking her hard. "Shut up! Do you hear me!"

"Please," she begged. "Let me go—I won't say anything!"

"No! You're not going to ruin my only chance to get out of here! Now you keep your mouth shut! One word, one sound, and I'll kill you!"

"I have to go back! I have to see about him!"

"That crazy old man was going to shoot you, girl! Don't you know that!"

She did know that. She had seen it in the reverend's eyes. She dropped her head.

There were voices nearby, and the Yankee dragged her into the shadows, pressing her against the trunk of a huge tree to keep her out of sight. His body leaned hard into hers; she could feel his heart pounding. She could hear footsteps passing very close, patrollers more than likely, she thought. She wanted to get away from him, but he had the Colt right by her ear.

The men walked on by, laughing from time to time, their conversation snatched away by the wind. The Yankee moved his grip to her wrist and suddenly bent over, the hand with the gun resting on his thigh. He gave a soft moan, and she thought he was going to fall.

"What's wrong?" she asked anxiously. "Are you going to be sick?" She wanted to know, because if he was, she was definitely in his way.

"Will you...shut...up!" he whispered between labored breaths. He had been grazed by the old man's second shot, and the pain in his side was excruciating. He ran his fingers up under his shirt, feeling for blood as well as he could and still hold on to the girl. It didn't seem too bad....

"What are you going to do?" she asked, and the question made him furious.

"I don't know! That's the goddamned problem!"

"You can't keep running around out here—"

"Oh, damn," he muttered, bending lower.

"What is it?" she cried, her anxiety making her put her hand out, because she was sure now he was going to topple over.

He thought she was reaching for the gun, and he forced himself upright. "Come on," he ordered, dragging her along. If he didn't find the right house soon, she'd be dragging him.

They moved quickly considering his indecision and her stumbling.

"Three streets," he said to himself. "Three—picket fence—"

"Wait, wait," Amanda said, trying to hold up her skirts so she could run. He didn't wait; he kept dragging. "Wait! That's not a picket fence! That's a pigsty!"

He altered their direction, surprised that, after the existence he'd led for the past few months, wading through a pigsty should bother him.

"Come on!" he said, but he still had no idea where. He hurried her along blindly, following a footpath he hoped went somewhere back in the direction he'd come. He suddenly stopped. There was a house ahead; a lamp burned in a lower-story window.

"That's it!" he whispered.

"That's not it!" Amanda cried. "You can't go in there." But he was heading directly for the Shanley house, and he was taking her with him.

There was no doubt that the two houses were similar. Amanda would concede that it would be easy for a stranger to make a mistake in the dark—except that Jacob Shanley's house was even less likely to be a haven for escaped prisoners than hers had been. Jacob Shanley was a prominent man in town, and he was a fiery Secessionist. At the beginning of the war, he had paid out of his own pocket to equip an entire company of soldiers. She tried to explain that to the Yankee as he dragged her along.

"You can't go in there!"

"I told you to be quiet! If it's full of humbled daughters, you tell them I'm already taken."

She faltered. He'd made a joke. He was running for his life and he'd made a joke.

But the joke was at *her* expense. It wasn't her idea to have him follow the laws of Deuteronomy. "Jacob Shanley doesn't have daughters," she tried to tell him. "He has sons—two of them dead at Gettysburg."

He wasn't listening to her at all, and there were riders coming down the road, pushing hard. The Yankee dragged her bodily up the back steps and into the alcove at the back door, hiding again in the shadows until the men had ridden past.

"Ah, God, they're looking for me," he said.

She thought that he was probably right. So many riders shouldn't be heading out of town tonight, not with the Brick Row stores on fire. He suddenly pounded on Shanley's back door.

"Don't!" she cried.

She tried to stop him, but it was too late. She pulled hard to get her wrist free, determined to make a run for it, but he slammed her against the alcove wall. He would have hit her if Shanley hadn't opened the door.

"What the hell is going on out here!"

"I believe—you are—expecting me," the Yankee said. He was winded from the struggle to keep her from getting away, but he carried off his meeting with Jacob Shanley with a certain aplomb. Shanley looked both of them up and down.

"Who are you? What are you doing with her?"

"John D. Howe—Captain, Sixth Pennsylvania Cavalry—and the rest is a long story."

"Get in here before somebody sees you," Shanley said, moving aside.

Amanda was perfectly aware of the Colt pressing into her back and of the fact that Shanley couldn't see it. The Yankee all but carried her in front of him, but Shanley didn't let them come inside very far. They were kept standing in the dark hallway, well away from what Amanda knew was a warm kitchen on the other side of the inner door.

"Who told you to come here?" Shanley said.

"A man I met on the train—he's dead now. We came to the prison in the same boxcar."

"And why would he send you to me?"

"I shared my canteen with him. He was grateful. He told me if I ever got out to come here. He said I could make arrangements with you."

"You have the money?"

"My family will get it. They'll arrange a draft at whatever bank you say."

John could feel the man smile in the darkness. There was nothing that warmed a profiteer's heart like the distinct possibility of getting paid.

"What did you say your name was again, Captain?"

"Howe. John D. Howe."

"How many of you got out this time?"

"Just me as far as I know. I'm traveling alone," he added, even though it was perfectly obvious that he had the Reb girl with him. But he wanted out of the cold before he got into that. "Could we go someplace warmer? I'm freezing."

He waited for Shanley to make up his mind, keeping the Colt out of sight, pressing it a little harder into the girl's back in case she'd forgotten that he had no qualms about using it. She was silent for the moment at least; she'd stopped fighting him. God, for a little slip of a girl, she was a handful.

"All right," Shanley said after a moment. He stepped back to let them into the kitchen, and John was back to pushing and shoving his captive, hiding the Colt under his shirt as he went. The kitchen was indeed warm, and apparently Shanley was about to have his Saturday night bath. A tin tub had been pulled in front of the stove, and several pots of water were boiling.

"You get over there and sit down in that chair where I can see you," Shanley said to Amanda. She went, grateful for the opportunity. She wasn't at all sure her legs would hold her anymore.

"And you needn't look so incredulous, miss," he said sharply. "We all do what we have to do."

"I am surprised, sir," she said quietly, "but not so surprised as James and Thomas would be."

John gave her a hard look. He had no idea who James and Thomas were, but he knew an insult when he heard one. This was no time for trading barbs.

Amanda stared back at him until Shanley took him aside, both of them standing between her and the back door. There was another door that led into the main part of the house, but Shanley made a point of suddenly locking it and putting the key into his pocket, as if he'd anticipated her interest in finding another way out. She shifted her position in the chair until she could just see both men out of the corner of her eye, and she did her best to eavesdrop.

"What are you doing with her?" Shanley asked again.

Their voices dropped, and Amanda couldn't hear the explanation, no matter how hard she tried, only a few words now and then—"old man objected" and "no time for murder."

Whose murder? she wondered. Hers? The reverend's? She closed her eyes at the image of him lying on the parlor floor.

"It's my hide, isn't it?" the Yankee suddenly said.

"And mine, you damn fool!"

"I get something for the hell I've been through—you'll get your money either way!"

"Of that you can be sure, Howe."

The Yankee stood there for a moment, then dragged another chair close to hers and sat down heavily. He was too close for her liking, and she pulled her legs back to keep their toes from touching.

"You shouldn't have brought me here," she said before he could say anything.

John looked at her, his eyes probing hers. By God, she'd hit the nail on the head with that observation. He shouldn't have brought her—except that he hadn't had time to do anything else. It was bring her along or shoot her. He hadn't wanted to shoot her. She *was* the girl he'd seen when he was out on the work detail. God, how he had stared at her that day. He hadn't been that close to a woman in a long time. He had stared and stared, until she elicited in him the welcome return of pure, carnal lust—when he'd thought that response lost to him forever. He had stared until Max Woodard had startled him out of his longing just in time to keep the guard from seeing his aroused state. He had stared until he had her image firmly committed to memory, so he could take her back into the stockade with him.

He let his eyes drop to her breasts, full, soft breasts under layers and layers of clothes. In his mind, for days and nights after he'd seen her, he'd taken away all those garments—every last one of them—and he'd slept with his head against her breasts. The mental pleasure she'd given had been quite unsurpassed.

He looked up at her. "I've spilled you out of the frying pan and into the fire," he said quietly. "It's up to you whether or not you get out of it."

"What do you mean?"

"I mean I'm going out of here tonight. He'll arrange it. You have to go with me."

"I'm not going with you!"

"Look!" he whispered fiercely. "This is not a parlor game. He'll kill you if you don't. You think he's going to let you run around town telling everybody he's been helping escaped prisoners?"

"Well, between you and the reverend, he'll have to stand in line, won't he?" she said sarcastically.

He had to fight down a smile. She was feisty, but he didn't want her to misunderstand the seriousness of the situation.

"You have to come with me," he went on. "I've already told him you're my—" He stopped. He didn't know how worldly she was. Not very, he suspected, regardless of her old man's accusations. He tried to think of a socially acceptable word for the kind of woman he'd led Shanley to believe she was. There wasn't one.

"I understand," Amanda said. She could see the smirk on Jacob Shanley's face. She had no doubt what the Yankee had told him.

"Come closer," John told her, and a look of panic filled her eyes. "Lean closer, damn it. He's watching. Do it now!"

She leaned forward, trying not to recoil when her face just brushed his.

"Tell me if he moves," he said. "Can you see him?"

"Yes," she answered, unable to keep the waver out of her voice.

"You don't have a choice. Do you understand? You go with me as far as northern Virginia. That's all I ask. I'll see you're looked after. I give you my word. I owe you that."

"You owe me?"

This time he did smile. He'd been thinking of the ribald fantasies she'd provided him when he said it. The smile faded. "Never mind. I want you to be careful what you say. If he thinks I'm lying, if he thinks I can't handle you, he'll kill you." He wasn't sure that Shanley wouldn't do it anyway, but he didn't say so. "Make up your mind. It's your old man, or Shanley, or me."

Amanda dropped her head, very close to tears.

"Listen to me," the Yankee said. "You're hardly more than a child, and I feel sorry for you. That's the God's truth. I've already told the lie for your sake. Are you going to help me carry it off?"

She looked up at him, but she didn't answer him. He was right. She had only three choices: the reverend, or Shanley, or him. But she didn't want him feeling sorry for her.

"Are you going to help me?" he repeated.

"No," she said. "I'm going to help *me*."

Chapter Two

Amanda sat with her back turned while the Yankee
bathed. In his condition, it was quite an undertaking—one
that seemed to give him great pleasure in spite of the injury
to his left side. She hadn't realized that the reverend had
wounded him. She had to help him off with his uniform coat
and his shirt—or what was left of a coat and shirt—and she
still had the stench of it in her nose.

She looked at the shuttered windows Shanley had barred
from the outside, then at the doors he'd locked before he
went to make arrangements for their leaving. He had been
very blunt about his reasons for locking them in; he had to
make sure the reverend hadn't raised the alarm. He didn't
want her and the Yankee on the loose until they had a
chance of not being caught. But she didn't like being shut in
like this. She didn't like it at all.

"Are you going to cry or what?" the Yankee said in the
middle of his scrubbing and splashing.

"No," she assured him, but she couldn't keep her mouth
from trembling when she said it.

"Look, there's nothing for you to cry about—"

"I'm not a complete fool!" she snapped at him. "Shanley's not going to take any chances trying to get us out of
here. He's better off with both of us dead and you know it!"

"Yes, but he wants the money. Men like him always want the money."

She tried to fight down the need to quarrel and lost. "This is all *your* fault! If you'd had the sense to get into the right house in the first place, I wouldn't be in this mess!"

"*My* fault! You try being on the run in enemy territory with every goddamn man in town out and see how clever *you* are. And your crazy father would have shot the both of us!"

"He's not my father!"

"Well, thank God for that. At least I don't have to worry about the insanity in your family. Come over here. I want you to help me."

She gave him an incredulous look, and she stayed where she was.

The Yankee grinned. "I wish you could see your face. I want you to come and cut my hair. That's all. Look around for a pair of scissors or something. Well, go on. I can't go on the street looking like I do—and I don't want to have to keep telling you everything twenty times!"

She exhaled sharply and began to halfheartedly look for a pair of scissors. She found a paring knife in a table drawer.

"That's good enough," he said. "Come over here."

"I'm not a barber," she said, trying not to look at his bare chest. Until the reverend had started dragging her to the military hospitals, she'd never seen a man's bare chest.

"Here," he said. "Suppose I do this." He took the blanket Shanley had warming by the stove and draped it over the tin tub. "Is that better?"

He was working hard at embarrassing her; she knew the lengths some soldiers would go to to make a woman blush and she wasn't about to let him get the best of her. She walked toward him with the knife.

"Just a minute," he said, taking up the reverend's revolver. He reached up and put one hand firmly on her waist, making her kneel down beside the tub on the wet floor. His other hand pushed the Colt firmly into her ribs. "Now," he said. "Barber. And don't bump my left side."

"I'm not anywhere near your left side."

"You're close enough to worry me. Go on. Cut."

She hesitated. She could feel the soapy water on the floor seeping through to her knees. She abruptly grabbed a handful of wet hair, making him jump. This man really thought she'd try to slit his throat.

She gave a small sigh and began to saw away at his hair, cutting away big chunks around his face so he could at least see and throwing the loose hair in a pile on the floor. She kept expecting him to protest her rough treatment. He didn't say anything. There was merely more pressure from the gun.

"Cut a little off the beard, too," he said.

She tried, fully aware of the fact that while she concentrated on his beard, he rudely inspected her face. She found it most disconcerting. Even Thayer had never looked at her with such obvious intent, and it was what that intent might be that disturbed her so.

"I wish you wouldn't frown like that," John said after a moment. Yes, he thought again, and regardless of the fact that he'd only just pronounced her "hardly more than a child," she was a pretty little piece.

She didn't answer him, and she didn't stop frowning. It occurred to him that he had no idea why he wanted to annoy her; he just did. "I *said* I wish you wouldn't frown like that. It makes me nervous."

"What have you got to be nervous about?" she snapped. "You've got the gun."

"That's true," he conceded. "Keep cutting."

She glanced at him. His mouth was smiling, but not his eyes. She tried to move around to cut some long strands of hair in the back, but he wouldn't let her behind him with a knife.

"So who's the dead man you've got on your conscience?" he asked, because he suddenly remembered the old man's comment.

She pressed her lips together and kept cutting.

"All right," he said when she didn't answer. "Then why did your old man try to shoot you?"

She could feel her face flush. "I've told you he isn't my father," she said.

"Why did he try to shoot you?" he persisted.

She kept cutting his hair.

"Did you hear me?"

"He wasn't going to shoot me. He was going to shoot you."

"The hell he was. Why would he do that? Answer me!" he suddenly barked, making her jump.

She leaned back so she could look into his eyes. "Because," she said evenly, "I look like my mother."

John stared back at her. There it was again, he thought. That look he'd seen when the old man hit her. She was stiff-necked, all right. He hated to think how hard the old man must have worked to take it out of her. His eyes went to her mouth. Her lower lip was bruised and swollen.

"What is he then?" he asked.

"What?"

"The old man. If he's not your father, what is he?"

"It doesn't matter," she said. "He's all the father I'll ever know."

He abruptly let go of her. He was feeling sorry for her again, and he couldn't afford to do that, not if he wanted to get out of here. She was expendable, and he'd already had a moment of weakness where she was concerned. There was a limit to how much responsibility a man was expected to feel toward an unsuspecting object of his lust.

"Is Shanley going to kill my—the reverend?" she asked quietly.

"I don't know," he answered. He laid the revolver aside and tried to wash what she'd left of his hair. "Shanley has no reason to if the old man doesn't know anything." He stopped soaping his hair. "Assuming I haven't saved him the trouble."

She had nothing to say to that, but she was thinking. He could feel that mind of hers working away.

"Stop staring at the gun," he said. "Even if you could get it and kill me, you're still locked in here and you'd have to deal with Shanley."

She gave him such a guilty look, he nearly laughed. Perhaps she had been planning his demise.

"Take the lamp and find us something to eat," he said, and for once she didn't hesitate. She picked up the oil lamp, an ornate thing with a warmer on the top for heating a cup of water.

"Verillia would love this," she said idly.

"Verillia?"

"My stepmother. She left the house before you..." Amanda glanced at him, then away. She couldn't find any polite words for their meeting. And she realized suddenly that he was looking at her breasts. Again. Why do men do that? she wondered. Surely there was nothing to *see*.

"Odd name," he said, going back to washing his hair.

"Is it? Yes, I suppose it is," she said. "It's a family name. Her clan is full of Verillias."

The Yankee abruptly stood up, leaving her to look or not, as she pleased. She went blindly into what she hoped was a pantry. The washing noises continued behind her.

John glanced at the pantry doorway. He couldn't hear her. "What are you doing?" he called after a moment.

She didn't answer him, and he still couldn't hear anything. He stepped out of the tub, wrapping the blanket around him as he went. He felt the panic rise. Surely to God he hadn't sent her into a way to get outside.

She was standing in the back of the pantry, and he thought for a moment she was about to cry again.

"What's the matter?"

She looked at him and swallowed.

"What, for God's sake!" It was obvious that she was upset, but damned if he could see anything that might have upset her. It would be just his luck to have taken up with somebody who screeched over every spider and cricket she came to—except that she never screeched, not even when he'd first grabbed her and held her down. It occurred to him that he was probably much more repulsive to her than any spider or cricket she'd ever encountered.

Amanda took a deep breath and tried to pretend that she wasn't behaving like a complete fool. "It's nothing." She looked over her shoulder at him. "It's—all this food. I didn't realize how much I missed it, real food." She gestured toward the wheel of cheese. There hadn't been any cheese for sale in this town for nearly two years. And Shanley had loaves of bread—real bread made with flour—and maple syrup, and eggs and butter. She nearly laughed, thinking of the pitiful sacks of cornmeal the reverend insisted be kept under lock and key.

"Don't you eat regularly?" the Yankee asked.

"Not very. And not *this*." She reached up to touch the wheel of cheese. It had been wrapped in a vinegar-soaked cloth and it was still fresh. "We eat cornmeal mostly. Potatoes sometimes. And cabbage. I was looking forward to this evening. We were having our last cabbage." She sighed.

"Well, don't start feeling nostalgic about that. *I* ate the cabbage."

She looked at him. "You ate it?"

"Damn right," he said, with no remorse whatsoever. "It scared the hell out of me when the other woman—Verillia—wanted you to go have some. There wasn't anything left by then but a couple of leaves. And I'd have eaten those, too, if I'd had the time.''

"You ate it," she repeated with enough indignation to make him smile.

"I was hungry," he assured her.

"Well, so was I!"

The smile broadened, and he turned away from those dark eyes of hers to do inventory. Shanley was indeed well stocked.

He lifted the cheese off the shelf and gave it to her to hold.

"What are you going to do?" she asked when he picked up the knife beside it.

He gave her an arch look.

"We can't. That's stealing," she protested. "We can't steal his food—can we?" she added, as the possibilities began to dawn. She abruptly held out the cheese so he could cut off big chunks of it.

"What are you doing?" she cried when he began pulling at her dress.

"Looking for pockets," he said mischievously. "I don't seem to have any. Well, stand still! I swear you wouldn't make a bummer."

"What's a bummer?" she asked nervously while he stuck a hunk of cheese into every pocket she had, including one smaller piece into her mouth. His fingertips were warm against her lips, and they smelled of lye soap. She didn't mean to look into his eyes, but there seemed to be nowhere else to look. He did have beautiful blue-gray eyes, except for the melancholy in them, and except for the fact that he was tired and unwell. Enemy or not, she'd never seen soap and water and a little hacking with a paring knife do so much for a man. Even wet, his hair was a much lighter color than she'd first thought. It would be light brown—perhaps dark blond—when it was dry, the kind of hair that got all sun-streaked in the summertime. The beard was hopeless. It needed to be shaved or trimmed by someone who knew the ins and outs of barbering and had a pair of scissors. But, even so, he was almost handsome.

"Bummers forage for the army," John said. "Food, horses...*women*." He raised and lowered his eyebrows once, enjoying her scandalized look immensely.

"Nothing your army does surprises me," she said around the cheese. Stolen or not, it was wonderful. She obediently opened her mouth when he offered her another piece.

It suddenly occurred to her that she ought not be in a pantry with a half-naked man.

"You're frowning again," he said.

"I have a lot to frown about."

"Now that's the damned truth—"

Amanda heard a key in the back door, and she panicked, shoving the cheese at him and nearly trampling him in the rush to get out of the pantry.

He wouldn't get out of the way. "It's too late now," he said. Clearly, he was feeling none of the apprehension that had seized her. He handed her a loaf of bread to take the place of the abandoned cheese. She had never stolen anything in her life and she was about to be caught red-handed.

"Get out of my way!"

"We might as well be shot for a sheep as a lamb," he said, picking up the bread she'd flung back on the shelf. "Let me give you a piece of advice. Never, *never*, act guilty until you're sure you're caught. After you," he added graciously. And he turned the cheese around so the places where he'd been hacking didn't show.

Shanley was already inside, his eyes cutting to the bread the Yankee carried boldly out of the pantry. He set a black and gray carpetbag on the kitchen table, and the Yankee calmly moved it aside so he would have room to slice the bread.

"You've been gone a long time," he said pleasantly, as if he'd been invited to help himself to Shanley's hoard.

"It took a while to find the right clothes," Shanley said. Amanda could almost feel him mentally tallying up the price of a few slices of bread so he could add it onto the Yankee's note. "And the Reverend Douglas," he said, glancing at her, "is still...indisposed. But he might as well have been running all over town shouting his head off. There were more escapees than you, Howe. The entire garrison is on alert."

Shanley opened the carpetbag and pulled out a Confederate cavalry officer's uniform that was not new enough to be conspicuous, a long gray coat and a pair of worn black boots. "There are two passes. One will get you as far as Gordonsville—if it hasn't changed hands again. The other will get you the rest of the way to Alexandria. Get rid of the uniform before you use the second pass—and for God's sake, don't get the passes muddled." He emptied the carpetbag to show him the civilian clothes—a white shirt and a pair of corduroy trousers.

"I need money," the Yankee said.

Shanley reached into his breast pocket. "I've got a few dollars. You shouldn't need any more than this."

"Most of this is Confederate."

"You're in the Reb army now, Captain. Reb soldiers don't carry hard money—even officers."

"But you want hard money in repayment."

Shanley smiled. "I see you understand the situation, Captain Howe. This is dangerous work. My family—what's left of it—must have recompense if things go awry. You'll purchase your tickets on the train."

"God, man! How do you expect us to get out of here on the train with the whole town alerted!"

"They won't be looking for a Reb officer traveling with a *lady*, now will they?" He looked at Amanda. "You keep a tight rein on her. Our people will be around the station, but don't expect much help if you get into trouble. If she gives it away—"

"She won't," John said, but he understood the threat just as he thought she did. He stood up and threw the blanket aside.

Amanda turned her head, going to stand at the stove with her back to the two men, as much because of the grin on Shanley's face as her offended sensibilities. Whatever the Yankee had told him about her, it was more than obvious he believed it.

"You don't have much time," Shanley said. "Sign the note."

"My hand's not steady," the Yankee said.

"Sign it! I won't take a chance without something that's legal and binding. Hurry, man."

"Your patriotism is overwhelming."

"Overwhelming or not, you'll live to see another day because of it."

Amanda turned around. The Yankee was signing the note.

"What about her?" he said.

"What about her?"

"It's cold out. She's not dressed for it."

Shanley hesitated, then went into another part of the house. When he returned, he brought a threadbare, gray wool shawl and a black silk bonnet that was stained and battered. "My wife was going to throw these out. She's a true Southerner, but she wouldn't begrudge anyone having them—even a Yankee officer's whore. Take them. And hurry."

Yankee officer's whore.

John could see on her face how much the words hurt. She stood it, but he expected her to cry when they were outside, and he plotted frantically how to get out of this hellhole of a town with a bawling woman on his arm.

Except that she wasn't a woman. She was hardly more than a little girl; he'd better remember that. But she didn't cry.

"You shouldn't have signed the note," was all she said.

"Is that so?"

"It is," she said. "Now he has nothing to lose."

"None of us does," he said, hurrying her away from the Shanley house. "And you'd do well to remember that."

Chapter Three

The Yankee kept her so close to him she could hardly move, his fingers clamped around her elbow under the shawl. He walked her into the shadows under the depot porch, away from the general milling around, and he kept watching the crowd, looking, she supposed, for Shanley's "people." The place was crowded, but she saw no one among the farmers, the traveling wounded and the relocating families that she knew. And certainly, she saw no one she would have suspected of aiding escaped prisoners.

There were not many women about. Decent women didn't come to the depot unless they were about to board a train or were engaged in some charity work for the wounded at the Wayside Hospital nearby. The loose women of the town were another matter. In spite of the cold, a number of them waited conspicuously on the platform for the military trade, accosting passing soldiers with their lewd suggestions and the heavy scent of their rose and violet perfume. Amanda had always liked the excitement of the depot, the wonderful conglomeration of smells—leather and burlap and cotton and cooking food. And she had liked best the fact that here was a place where people actually had the means to get *away*. They simply got on a train and escaped all their troubles—as she vehemently hoped to do.

She took a deep breath. Someone was frying onions in pork fat. Her stomach rumbled. She was still hungry, but she didn't dare go to her pockets for more cheese. She would have loved to find Verillia and show her what a delicacy she had. There was a chance that Verillia might even be here, if she were still helping the doctor with people who had been burned in the fire.

But the Yankee had Amanda by the arm, and she couldn't go looking for Verillia. Not now. Not ever. She glanced furtively at the people closest to her. The atmosphere at the depot was different tonight. There was more than just the excitement of arriving and departing trains or the worry about the fire. Everyone was afraid, military and civilian alike. She could sense the false bravado among the soldiers. Times were desperate, and no one could pretend otherwise.

She gave a soft sigh. She had troubles of her own. She had to make some kind of plans for herself—but she had to get out of here first. She looked up at the Yankee. He was afraid, too, and he'd freely admitted it. In that one thing, at least, she believed he'd been truthful. He didn't look afraid, however. He looked determined and wary.

"Are you cold?" he asked abruptly, and she nodded, trying not to lend credence to her misery by shivering.

"I'll warm you up, darlin'."

The offer came from a big artilleryman, who happened to overhear. He had a corncob pipe clenched between his teeth, and his uniform coat was full of holes he'd tried to patch with newspaper. He smiled broadly, giving Amanda a big wink so she'd know he was only teasing. The smile abruptly faded when he looked into the Yankee's eyes.

The artilleryman doffed his hat and withdrew with as much dignity as he could muster.

"You are going to be a damned lot of trouble, I can see that already," John said. She was pretty enough to make a man remember he was a man, no matter how beaten down he was, and one wrong word from her would see him back in the stockade. He had to be out of his mind for trying this. The garrison was alerted; the bloodhounds were out. At least two people in town knew him on sight. And here he was trying to sneak away in front of God and half the damned Confederacy, on a *train,* for God's sake, with a Reb girl he didn't trust any farther than he could throw her, when he was too sick to go in the first place. He had to keep his knees locked now even to stand up. He was scared to death of falling on his face.

"It's not *me,*" she said, clearly taking exception to his observation. "It's the war. Soldiers take...liberties."

He couldn't keep from grinning. It wasn't the war, and he was damned tempted to tell her so. It was those big, dark eyes of hers, and the sweet woman smell she had, and the promise of kisses and soft white arms and breasts to keep a man warm on a long winter night.

"Is that a fact?" he said, still grinning.

Amanda turned away from him. He was laughing at her, and she didn't like it. He looked down the platform, and the grin suddenly slid away.

"Oh, damn!" he said, abruptly hustling her along in the opposite direction.

"What's the matter?" she asked, trying to see.

"Just keep walking—"

"I can't walk as fast as you can!"

"Amanda!" someone called behind them. "Hey!"

She looked over her shoulder.

"Hey!" Charlie Wood yelled again.

"Wait!" Amanda whispered frantically, trying to stop. "I know him!"

"So do *I!*" the Yankee assured her. "Keep walking!"

"Amanda!" Charlie yelled, and he was running along after them now.

"It's me he's calling, not you! Let go of my arm!"

The Yankee didn't let go, and Charlie had nearly caught up with them. She had known Charlie Wood since they were children. If he had something to say to her, he was going to say it, if he had to keep yelling until he had everybody in this end of town staring. Again she tried to stop, digging in her heels to keep the Yankee from dragging her on.

"Amanda!" Charlie said, nearly running into her. "What are you doing here?"

There was no sense in running now. She braced herself and decided to keep it simple.

"I'm ... waiting for a train, Charlie."

Her heart was pounding; the Yankee's grip on her elbow intensified. Charlie, whose military uniform consisted of nothing that matched, looked at the Yankee with only mild interest.

"Didn't you hear about the train accident?" he asked.

"No," she said, near panic because she thought he was going to tell her the train wasn't coming. "Where was it?"

Charlie grinned and leaned closer. "Not *where,* honey. What. *What* was it?"

"Oh," Amanda said, trying to get out of his silly grin. His breath smelled like the whiskey jugs Verillia smuggled into the house every time she came back from visiting her brother James in the mountains. Charlie was too tangle-footed even to notice that she shouldn't be at the train depot in the first place, much less with a strange man.

But she was afraid not to humor him. "What was it?" she amended.

"Damn train came on time!" Charlie hooted, slapping his thigh in self-appreciation. Amanda glanced at the Yankee, who gave her a pained look and a token grin he managed to pull out from somewhere.

"Sorry about the language, 'Manda, honey," Charlie said. "It just ain't funny without it."

"It's not funny with it, Charlie."

"Is, too. You been over to see how they're doing with the fire?"

"No. Why aren't you helping?"

"Aw, it ain't much to do now but watch it burn the rest of the way out." He looked off in the direction of the fire. "I got to stand around down here so the folks don't think the Yankees is breaking out."

"Aren't they?" Amanda asked, trying to ignore the increased pain in her elbow.

"Oh, hell, no. They learned their lesson the last time— Charlie Wood," he abruptly announced, taking notice of the Yankee after all and thrusting out his hand.

"Howe," the Yankee said, shaking Charlie's hand. "John Howe."

"You going home?"

"Trying to," the Yankee said with just enough strain in his voice to make Amanda nervous. He put his right hand back into his coat pocket, the one she was sure held the reverend's Colt revolver.

"Got your pass?" Charlie asked.

The Yankee gave up the Colt rather than her elbow, rummaging through an inside pocket and giving Charlie the pass. Charlie hardly looked at it; he had other things on his mind.

"Amanda, honey, have you seen Anne Giffen tonight?"

"No, Charlie."

"Well, hell. I got to find that girl. She owes me a kiss."

"She does not," Amanda said, unable to let a statement that preposterous go without comment. Anne Giffen intended to marry a man of substance and reputation; Charlie Wood had neither. Anne wouldn't waste her time or her kisses on him.

"Yeah, she does—you ask her when you see her. She owes me a kiss, and I'm getting it, too." He looked down the platform. "Jimmy!" he yelled.

Amanda thought she would lose her arm entirely. All this social exchange was unnerving her Yankee companion, and she would have bruises to prove it. Another prison guard came running. He was redheaded, and likely as drunk as Charlie.

"Hey, Charlie," he said as he trotted up, but he was looking at Amanda. And he kept looking, finally poking Charlie in the ribs for an introduction. "I don't believe I know her," he said pointedly.

"No, and you don't want to, neither," Charlie assured him. "Her daddy'll kill you. Amanda, are you—what!" he said in exasperation, because Jimmy was poking him again. Jimmy subtly pointed with his eyes and his head toward the bouncing feathers and swinging hips that were coming down the platform.

Clearly, Charlie considered them worth the interruption.

"Well—Amanda, honey—I got to go," he said, backing away.

"Oh, don't rush off, Charlie," Amanda said, even if she lost an arm for it. "Where are you going?"

"Oh," Charlie said airily, "I got to check passes—me and Jimmy both. You tell Anne I'm wanting my kiss."

"Charlie?" Amanda persisted as he tried his best to get away. "You give your mother my regards."

"Yes, honey, I'll surely do that," he assured her from farther away.

"And tell her Verillia wants her to call. She was saying just the other day—"

"I *will*, Amanda!" he said in exasperation, all but running in the direction Jimmy and the woman with the feathers had gone.

Amanda threw back her head and laughed, delighted with Charlie's silliness. But she remembered herself almost immediately, suppressing the laughter into painful dimples around her mouth. She glanced upward into the Yankee's eyes. He was smiling.

"You ought to be ashamed of yourself," John said. She was a funny little thing. Given the opportunity, he might rather like her. In fact there were any number of things about her he might like—if he felt better.

"So the Reverend Douglas tells me," she answered, her amusement fading. She was cold and hungry. She wanted to be home with Verillia.

But she had no home anymore. She had only this man, who, among other things, had threatened to kill her. She looked up at him. His face was illuminated by the lantern hanging on a bent nail in the porch post. He needed a decent haircut and a shave; he needed rest and good food, and he wasn't likely to get any of those. She shivered suddenly. Verillia had told her once of hearing that a Yankee prisoner had been so hungry he'd chewed the flesh off his own arm.

"What is it?" John asked, because she was staring at him so.

"Nothing."

He abruptly looked down. "God Almighty! I swear I don't know who's watching the stockade tonight. They're all here."

Amanda tried to walk in the direction the Yankee was pushing her, but it was too late.

"Pass!" the guard said, catching up with them and sticking out his hand. It was clear that, unlike Charlie, this boy took his business seriously.

John reached into his coat, his fingers finding nothing where the pass should have been. His eyes cut to the girl. Surely he'd taken the pass back from Charlie Wood.

"It's just been checked," Amanda said, realizing that something was wrong.

"Pass!" the boy repeated, his hand still extended.

John continued to search through his pockets. He must have been addled enough by the encounter with Charlie to have put the pass in the wrong pocket. He finally brought out a piece of paper, but another piece came with it. The guard snatched away both of them, eyeing them closely from several angles. He looked up at John, then back at the passes again, and John could feel the cold sweat on the back of his neck. His heart pounded in his ears as the boy continued to study the pieces of paper. It was all he could do to follow his own advice. *Don't look guilty, damn it!*

Then the boy abruptly gave back the passes and walked away.

"I have to sit down," John said. His knees were shaking. He moved toward a stack of wooden crates, pulling the girl along with him. The crates were far enough out on the platform to catch the wind. It was much colder, but there was no other place for him to sit. She didn't join him on the crate. She stood as far away from him as he would allow, huddling in her ugly shawl.

"He didn't know me," he said after a moment.

Amanda looked at him, not knowing if he were talking to her or to himself.

"I have seen that boy nearly every day since last May, and he didn't know me. I even tried to bribe him once to write a letter to my parents. The little bastard wouldn't do it."

"I don't think he could," she said.

"The hell he couldn't. I just didn't have a big enough bribe."

"I don't think he can read. He wouldn't have wanted you to know that."

"He can't—you mean he just put me through that hell with the passes, and he can't *read!*"

"Or he can't see well enough. He had one of the passes upside down."

John gave a short laugh, one with no mirth in it, one so desperate sounding it was disturbing even to him. But he felt like crying, and he didn't know why. He hadn't been caught. Everything was all right. Or as all right as it could be at this point.

"Why didn't you give me away?" he asked suddenly.

"What?"

"You heard me. You had two good chances. Why didn't you give me away?"

"I have to get out of here, too. You heard what Shanley called me. Between him and the reverend, everybody here will think it's true."

She was looking at him, directly into his eyes in that straightforward way she had. He turned his head. He didn't want her staring at him like that. He had enough on his conscience as it was; he didn't want to add her tarnished reputation to the pile. He did concede her earlier point. If he'd gotten into the right house in the first place, she wouldn't be in this mess.

He searched the crowd for familiar faces. Others had gotten out of the stockade tonight. They had to have gone ahead of him, because the tunnel had collapsed when he went through. No one could have gotten out after he did. The others had gone ahead, and that was why the end of the tunnel had been filled in. They had wanted to hide it. And they had probably started the fire downtown, too—both good ideas as far as they went, but a hell of an aggravation for Johnny-come-latelies like himself.

He saw no one he recognized other than the two prison guards. A baby cried somewhere, and soldiers laughed and swore around him. He could hear the dialogue and prayers associated with a chuck-a-luck game on the other side of the crates, and every now and then one of the whores gave a high-pitched whoop of protest when some overencouraged soldier took a liberty.

"How old are you?" he abruptly asked the girl.

She looked at him a moment before she answered. "Close to eighteen."

"How close?"

Amanda shrugged. "Not . . . very."

He made a small noise of disapproval.

"Well, how old are you?" she asked.

"I'm a damn lot older than 'close to eighteen.'"

"How much older?" she persisted.

"Twenty-four," he said after a time.

"You look older than that."

"Oh, thank you," he said sarcastically. "If you'd been where I've been, you'd look old, too."

"I didn't say you looked old. I said you looked older. Than twenty-four."

He didn't say anything.

"At least you smell better," she said, because she thought he was annoyed. It made her uneasy to have him angry, even if she didn't know the reason. "That's probably why Charlie and the rest of them didn't recognize you."

She thought he was going to smile, but he didn't. He looked away toward a fiddler who had begun to wander through the crowd.

"What is that song he's playing?" he asked.

She listened for a moment. " 'Pretty Polly.' "

"I never knew what it was called. I used it in the prison and I never knew. . . ."

She waited for him to go on. "Used it?" she asked when he didn't.

He made an impatient gesture with his hand. "To keep sane. To keep alive. To—" He looked at her. "To keep warm. I used to walk so I wouldn't freeze to death. They wouldn't let us stay in the burrows in the daytime, so I walked. From one dead line to the other. And I used to listen to that song, in my head, so I wouldn't . . . see anything. Somebody used to play it all the time in camp and I remembered it." He looked back at the fiddler. "You think I'm crazy."

"No," she said.

"Why not? *I* think I am."

She thought he was going to say something else, but he didn't.

"What is a dead line?" she asked after a moment.

He pulled a splinter off one of the crates. "It's a boundary around the inside of the stockade walls. If you step over it, the guards shoot you. And sometimes . . . if you don't."

"Charlie Wood does that?"

"They *all* do that, my dear."

"And what's a burrow?"

"You know what a burrow is—it's a hole in the ground."

"You stayed in a hole in the ground?"

"Listen, I was damned lucky to have it. Tanner died, and I got there first!"

"I'm . . . sorry," she said lamely, and he laughed, that same mirthless laugh she'd heard before.

"You don't know how much better that makes me feel. You're *sorry.*"

"It's not *my* fault!"

"No? Well, somebody has to take the blame for it, and you'll do."

"I don't know what you mean."

He wasn't listening to her. He was looking at the two women who had wandered up, one of them the Feathers and Hips that had so impressed Charlie. The Yankee looked her over appreciatively, and she gave him a sly grin. Amanda looked as well, trying her best to see what there was about this woman that interested him and Charlie so. Whatever it was, she couldn't find it. Of course, the woman wasn't wearing enough petticoats. Her skirt outlined her behind when she walked. And she was big-breasted. Amanda had been around soldiers enough to know what an attraction *that* was. This woman would never have to sew ruffles in her bodice.

But the rest of her. She wasn't pretty. Her hair was a strange orange color. And some attempt had been made to pin it up, but it was coming down again. And it was all tangled—like a stump full of granddaddy spiders. The woman giggled a lot, speaking to her companion in some sort of affected baby talk.

Amanda rolled her eyes upward and shook her head in defeat.

"What's the matter?" the Yankee asked, grinning.

"You and Charlie," she answered.

"Me and Charlie what?"

"I don't know what. You and Charlie obviously like her. I was just trying to see *why*."

John laughed out loud. He shook his head. Now there was an intriguing problem. How to tell a little girl like her what a restful woman a whore could be. A man could have his fun with a whore—drink, smoke, do whatever he liked, say whatever he liked and not be held responsible for it— because they'd both know he didn't mean it. "I can't tell you *why*," he said, still laughing.

"Don't laugh at me!" Amanda said. But the train was coming in. The Yankee was on his feet, and this time she clutched *his* arm.

"Mr. Howe," she said. "Mr. Howe—please—" He was trying to walk away, and he was trying to take her with him. She couldn't get him to listen to her. "Mr. Howe! I want to tell you something!"

"Tell me," he said, because he thought she might cry if he didn't. People were swirling around him, already vying for a place on the train.

"I'm not—what the reverend said—what you told Shanley," she said in a rush. "It's not true. I'm not that kind of woman...."

He nearly laughed again. She wasn't a woman at all, much less the kind she was talking about. "Let's go!" he said impatiently.

"Please!" she said, her bottom lip quivering. "Please—"

He grabbed her by the wrist. She tried her best to get away from him. He jerked her around in front of him.

"Don't! You're a sweet little girl, and I don't want to hurt you. But I'll do whatever I have to do to get out of here. I'm not going back into that place. Now walk with me!"

"No, I can't! Please!"

"Walk with me, damn you!"

She stiffened and grabbed on to his arm again. "Wait—wait! I see him."

"Who?" he said sharply, his anxiety rising. If they didn't get on the train *now,* they stood a good chance of being left standing.

"My—the reverend!"

He believed her, but he didn't take the time to locate him. He shoved her forward, thrusting both of them into the middle of the crowd. "Stay close to me. Don't look for him. Keep your head down. Maybe he hasn't seen you. Just keep going."

He handed her up on the train, edging out a rather large woman who thought she should precede them, but the conductor immediately sent them back off.

"Damn it all, where is he!" John asked, his eyes frantically searching the crowd.

"I don't know, I don't know...."

He saw the reverend finally. So much for Shanley's clever arrangements. The old man had come out without his hat and coat, and he had the boy guard by his shirtfront. Apparently, the boy was still firmly entrenched in his own authority, because he seemed to be taking great exception to being manhandled. John didn't think the old man had seen them yet. The reverend looked as if he were trying to get information, not give it.

There was nothing to do but take his own advice again. He wasn't caught, not yet, and as guilty as he might be, he refused to show it. He looked down at the girl. She was so close to him the front of her bonnet scraped his chest. She was scared, as scared of that old man as he was of getting caught. And he wasn't much of an alternative for her. He pulled her against him. She was trembling.

"Are you sure it was him?" he asked, because he wanted to keep her attention.

"Yes! I'm sure!"

"Easy. Take it easy. It's going to be all right. I promise you. Here—get on the train."

Chapter Four

Amanda had no faith in any man's promises. She would do whatever she could to take care of herself. She was more in control now. She had fought down the panic, and she was seeing this predicament for what it really was—her only chance. She wasn't surprised that the reverend had come to spread the alarm. She remembered all the times people had tried to compliment him on his well-mannered daughter, and how he'd stood and listened with that long-suffering and condescending look he always wore, as if only he knew what a moral disappointment she really was. He had waited a long time for the proof that she was like her mother, even if he had to deliberately misunderstand the situation to get it, and now he could have the sympathy of an entire town as well. She had no doubt that he would tell them that his dutiful daughter had become a garrison whore.

She kept her head down. The train windows were dirty, but she thought that the reverend would have no trouble seeing her in the lighted car. Her only hope was that if he couldn't see her face, he wasn't apt to recognize Mrs. Shanley's shawl and bonnet. And, unless someone had recognized her or the Yankee, he wasn't apt to suspect that she was on the train in the first place.

"Wait!" she heard the Yankee whisper, but she kept pushing her way to the back of the car. If the Yankee was at all recognizable to the reverend, she didn't want to be close by him.

She got caught in the press of people trying to find a place to sit. The regular seats had been pulled out to make room for the stretchers when the train made its Wayside Hospital runs. The only places to sit were long wooden benches along the sides of the car or on the dirty floor. From the shoving going on around her, no one intended to stand.

She finally found a space near the rear, but there was no room on the bench for the Yankee.

"I told you to wait!" he whispered when he caught up with her.

She ignored him. She had no practice at not looking guilty the way he had. Her only weapon against the reverend had been her willingness to endure—but she couldn't even do that, if the Yankee wouldn't leave her alone. She had to worry about what to do if the reverend came on the train; she couldn't be bothered with his annoyance at her not following his instructions.

The Yankee dropped the carpetbag at her feet and sat on that, leaning back against her knees. A very unsubtle maneuver, she thought, to keep up with her whereabouts. His hand reached under her skirts and squeezed her ankle hard when she tried to move her legs away.

She was so cold, even in these close quarters. They were sitting too far away from the small potbellied stove for it to do any good. Her nose was beginning to run, and she didn't have a handkerchief. She didn't have anything but some pockets full of cheese.

"Stop fidgeting!" he snapped at her. But it was he who was fidgeting, trying to find some space for his long legs.

"I'm not—"

John gave her a threatening look, and she didn't say anything else. Six more soldiers pushed their way into the car. The damned infantry, he thought. There was no love lost between the horse soldiers and the walkers, no matter which army they were in. These particular foot soldiers were drunk, and they all looked at him warily—he hoped because he was in a cavalry uniform. He had to draw up his legs for yet another of them to get in, their lieutenant, he supposed, an overly handsome sort with a flowing blond mustache. The lieutenant was quick and mischievous-looking, the kind who was the very devil with the women and knew it. He took the liberty of sitting down on some-one's bushel basket of clothes, and it didn't take him ten seconds to notice the Reb girl. He kept staring at her, until John felt the need to clear his throat in warning.

The lieutenant ignored him. He kept staring at the girl, obviously pleased with his good fortune and trying to decide what he was going to do about it. John had been in college with any number of these Southern lady-killers, and half of him waited with interest to see what modus operandi the lieutenant would use to turn the little Reb's head. The other half of him wanted to punch him in the nose. He did *not* feel up to playing chaperon.

"Your pardon, miss," the lieutenant said finally. "I believe you have soot on you."

"Have I?" she said, looking down the front of her shawl.

"No, there on your face, honey," the lieutenant said. "May I?" He didn't wait for her to say, leaning forward and brushing at the corner of her mouth with his fingertips, making her wince as he tried to wipe away the bruise.

John reached up and grabbed him by his jacket front. "If there's soot or anything else on her, *I'll* take care of it."

The lieutenant gave him an arrogant grin, then he yielded, leaning back in his basket. But his capitulation lasted only a moment. He kept staring at the bruise on the girl's face, and John recognized the very instant the lieutenant realized what it was. He frowned suddenly, and he seemed about to say something, but he folded his arms over his chest instead, giving John the kind of accusatory look he must reserve for recalcitrant privates. John knew perfectly well what the man thought, but he returned the narrow-eyed glare with equal fervor. Hell, he wasn't the one who had hit her. The lieutenant might consider himself the Great Protector of Southern Womanhood, but he was going to have to go intimidate someone else.

There was no room anywhere, but people kept filing into the car—fragmented families, many of the women in heavy mourning. Amanda watched the hostility between the Yankee and the lieutenant escalate until she could have screamed. She sat with her head down and her fists clenched, praying for the train to start.

"Hey, look at Dolan," one of the soldiers said. "What's the matter, Dolan? Weddings make you cry?"

"It ain't the *wedding*," the soldier named Dolan said morosely. "It's the goddamn honeymoon. God, I wish I was in that Alford's shoes—lucky son of a bitch."

"Aw, who'd go on a honeymoon with you, you ugly bastard?" the soldier said.

"Your sister would," Dolan suggested, and the fight was on.

The aisle was suddenly filled with flying arms and legs and curses. Amanda was shoved and jostled but still able to note that some of the best of the curses were coming from her traveling companion, who seemed to be on the bottom of the pile. He and the lieutenant both were trying their best to intervene, but clearly, rank meant nothing when the honor of one's sister was at stake.

The conductor was just coming in from the other car, still directing passengers—these particular ones, several of the fast women who had been hanging around the depot. Feathers and Hips was among them, taking loud exception to being moved from the other car.

"All right!" the conductor bellowed over the commotion, and several of the women in the front of the car screamed. He plunged forward, leaving Feathers and Hips still talking, and he grabbed up two of the brawlers by the backs of their collars. "Gentlemen!" he yelled. "I am as patriotic as the next man—but I am *not* having this on my train! Now, if you want to walk, you keep it up! And that goes for all of you! You stay quiet and you stay put!" He lowered his voice and spoke directly to Dolan. "And you. You leave those whores back there alone. Now, I mean it!"

The conductor was a big man, and apparently they all believed him. They began to settle down with only a few more token shoves and insults. Amanda could see that the Yankee was out of sorts, glaring at her as if all this were somehow her fault.

"My apologies, miss," the lieutenant said to her. "They've had a bit too much wedding frivolity. It's getting so I can't take them anywhere in decent society." He smiled too familiarly, and she looked away, right into Dolan's hungry eyes.

John could see it coming. The conductor had told Dolan to leave the whores alone—but he hadn't said anything about *her*.

Dolan rubbed the side of his nose with one finger. "Damn cold in here," he suddenly noticed. Then he was all over John as he tried to offer her a sip from a whiskey bottle he pulled out from somewhere. "Take a swig, darlin'," he said to her. "It'll warm you up. Yes, it certainly will."

"Sit down, Dolan!" the lieutenant said.

He didn't sit down, and the bottle hovered under Amanda's nose. The Yankee was trying to get up, and she put her hand on his shoulder and bore down hard.

"You're very kind, Private Dolan," she said sweetly. "But I've promised my dead mother." She didn't say what she'd promised, so it wasn't precisely a lie. She gave Dolan a long, regretful gaze, hoping that he could accept the way mothers were without losing face.

"Oh," he said, a bit crestfallen.

"Why don't you share it with the others," she suggested—to Dolan's horror. "I'm sure they're cold, too."

"That's right, Dolan," one of his comrades said, snatching the bottle out of his hand. "Why don't you share it with the others."

Dolan watched the bottle go down the line, pausing at every man, clearly puzzled as to how this magnanimous gesture of his had come about.

"How about you, horse soldier?" the lieutenant said when it was his turn.

"Oh, no!" somebody protested in an affected falsetto voice. "The cavalry don't *drink,* do they?"

John took the offered bottle. It was a long time since he'd had whiskey, and the taste of it was already in his mouth. "Only on cold winter nights," he said, pulling deeply, feeling the whiskey burn all the way down. With the reverend running around outside, this could be his last draft, and he was damn well going to savor it.

"Sitting on the floor," somebody else continued.

"On a goddamned train," another one added.

"That ain't moving!" they yelled in unison.

"By God, I'll drink to that," John said, and he did, ignoring the knees that protested in the middle of his back.

The train lurched forward, and Amanda's heart sank. She was actually doing it, actually sitting quietly by and letting the train pull out with an escaped prisoner on it. The Yankee abruptly turned around to look at her, his hand going inside his coat pocket, as if he knew what she was thinking. She tried to avoid his eyes, but the nervous glance she gave him somehow caught and held. She could see so many things in his steady look: fear, bravado, gratitude—and distrust. In that one thing they were equal. She had learned the hard way that the only person she could rely on was herself, and perhaps Verillia. It occurred to her suddenly that Verillia might never know what had happened to her. What would the Yankee do when he didn't have to worry anymore about her giving him away?

The train picked up speed, and she abruptly avoided the Yankee's eyes. He was only one man, she reasoned, and in his present condition, not worth much to himself or his cause. She knew he was ill, no matter how hard he tried to hide it, and perhaps he wouldn't be able to make his escape alone. It might be easier to get away from him than she had thought. She had to formulate some kind of plan for herself, but what? She had no one in this world who would feel even the slightest inclination to help her. Except . . .

Thayer had once told her to come to him if she ever needed anything, but she was in such dire straits now she didn't even know what she needed. Money? Protection? She knew what could happen to women alone with undisciplined soldiers and deserters and bushwhackers about, what might happen to her anyway, if she continued to travel with the Yankee. He had assured the reverend that he didn't feel well enough for any kind of misbehavior. She had no way of knowing if he'd been telling the truth, and she had no way of finding Thayer, even if her pride would allow her to look. She almost smiled. She could imagine the look on Thayer's face if she went to him and tried to explain *this*.

Her amusement abruptly faded.

"Are you all right, my dear?" the lieutenant asked.

Amanda looked up at him. "A touch of homesickness," she said, because she felt very close to tears, and any denial that something was amiss would likely only prompt more questions.

"Are you traveling far?" the lieutenant persisted.

"Not far," she said obscurely.

"To visit?"

Her mind worked frantically for a plausible story, but nothing came. "Yes," she said, hoping that simplicity would satisfy him.

"Relatives?"

She smiled her answer, *yes,* or perhaps *no.*

The lieutenant leaned forward. "You are about the prettiest thing I ever saw," he said, his voice intimate and low. "What do you think of that?"

"I think it's a pity your experience in such matters is so limited," she answered.

John laughed. He couldn't help it. The little Reb wasn't any more impressed by the lieutenant's bold compliments than she had been by Dolan's whiskey, and she made sure he knew it. She had followed the rules of decorum and remained properly modest and demure while she did it—but she still took the would-be Lothario off at the knees.

The lieutenant gave a little half smile, knowing he'd been bested.

John wanted to talk to her. He wanted to tell her how well she was doing. But the infantrymen were watching, listening, apparently finding this little drama between him and their lieutenant most intriguing. He would have to wait them out; they were all too drunk to stay awake long. He was beginning to wish he'd exercised a little temperance himself. The first warm flush from Dolan's whiskey had worn off now, leaving John chilled and close to shivering. It was all he could do to keep from shaking like a wet dog. His head ached; he wanted desperately to sleep, but he didn't dare close his eyes. The lieutenant obviously considered himself in competition for the Reb girl's attention, and he was nothing if not determined. Of course, John was determined, himself. Determined to get out of this wretched place, determined to stay out of any more brawls so he could do it. He considered the conductor to be the sort of man who would have made an excellent sergeant. He meant what he said, and John was in no condition to hike it up the railroad tracks to northern Virginia.

His mind went to the prison suddenly. How many had gotten out? He hadn't known anything about another escape attempt. The fiasco in November had taught them all a lesson about informers. No one was to be trusted.

But someone had trusted Max Woodard. Max had known where and how and when. God! Poor, honorable Max. He had been trusted enough to be privy to the plan, yet he had been left behind by them all.

He closed his eyes, trying to get the vision of Max's anguished face out of his mind. He had seen that expression only once before, in a minor skirmish in the woods of Virginia. A fellow officer he'd been talking to took a sniper's minié ball in the head midsentence. For one brief second, the man had looked so... dismayed.

The pain of the memory made him give a sudden intake of breath. He opened his eyes, ignoring the curious stares. He hated being jammed up with so many people like this. It was too much like the prison. It was suffocating with no chance of air—like the tunnel. He willed himself to relax and not to remember, and he prayed for daylight.

John came awake with a start, not knowing where he was. The train was slowing. He couldn't see anything out the dirty windows, only that this was no regular stop. There were no lanterns lit anywhere outside, no buildings.

What now? he thought, attempting to get up. One foot was asleep. He had no idea how far they'd come. He remembered Greensboro, but not much after that. The moon was still visible, but it had to be nearly dawn. He looked at the Reb girl. She was asleep.

The train stopped.

The conductor was picking his way among the sprawled passengers, obviously looking for someone. John's heart began to pound. He didn't think the conductor could have gotten word that there was an escaped prisoner on the train, but he was scared anyway. He put his hand inside his coat for the revolver. If worse came to worst, he'd make a run for it—except that just sitting upright was hard enough. It was going to take a damn lot of willpower to run.

The conductor stopped right in front of him, reaching down and putting his hand on his shoulder.

"Yankee cavalry raid," he whispered. "You're the ranking officer."

The relief that flooded John was only momentary. He knew from experience what a lark harassing a train could be, and he didn't begrudge any fellow cavalryman his fun, but for God's sake, did it have to be now?

Of course, it does, he thought miserably. *Let's get into a damn cavalry skirmish with me in the wrong damn uniform.* That should top off the evening just about right. And if he lived through it, what a story it would make at his mother's Washington society dinner parties.

"Where?" he asked quietly.

"Up along the line. The track's torn up. That may be enough to satisfy them—or they may be after the train. I don't want the women upset if you can help it."

"How many guards have you got?"

"Not enough, but they're at their posts. I'm not a military man. You decide how to handle it."

Damn!

Amanda heard every word, but a raid on the train was the least of her worries. She had been sitting in the dark for hours trying to ignore the call of nature, and she couldn't stand it anymore. She abruptly stood up and moved toward the end of the car, stepping on a sleeping soldier along the way, who returned a great string of epithets for his pains.

"Where are you going!" the Yankee whispered fiercely after her, but she didn't stop. She knew he was coming behind her, but she managed to stay ahead of him until she reached the end of the car. He grabbed her roughly by the arm.

"Where the hell are you going!"

"I have to get off the train!" she said sharply.

"Are you crazy! The cavalry is out there. You can't get off the train!"

"I *have* to! I can't wait any longer!" That was all the explanation he was going to get, and she jerked her arm free, expecting him to grab her again. She managed to get away from him, but he was still following behind her. She abruptly turned on him, ready to do battle if she had to. This was not a matter to be negotiated.

John stared at her in the darkness. She had both fists clenched and ready to fend him off.

"Come on, then," he said.

"You're not going with me!" she said in alarm.

"Yes, I am. Now come on."

They met the conductor at the exit door.

"Apparently she needs some privacy," John told him.

"I wouldn't go out there, son—"

"Neither would I, but there seems to be no help for it. Kindly ask the guards not to shoot her." He shoved her out onto the platform, helping her to the ground whether she wanted his help or not.

"I don't want you to come with me," she said, marching ahead of him.

"That's too bad," he said sarcastically.

"How far do I have to go with you, anyway?"

"Until we find a big enough clump of bushes?" he suggested, deliberately misunderstanding.

She stopped walking. "Is there no topic too indelicate for your comment?"

"Nothing comes to mind," he assured her.

She was off marching again.

"Oh, you mean this trip?" he called after her, hurrying to catch up. "Washington, I should think." He was trying his best to annoy her. He was beginning to admire her control—enough to want to make it come undone.

"Washington!" she said, as if he'd suggested Sodom or Gomorrah.

"What's the matter with Washington? You'd like Washington. You might even get to see the real president."

"I don't want to see the president," she said over her shoulder. "Real or otherwise."

"He'd want to see you, though. I believe he'd find this whole matter most entertaining."

"You don't say."

"Oh, surely. The dashingly handsome John Howe, nearly trapped into a shotgun wedding, when for once he hadn't done anything—"

"That's not funny!"

"Not at the time," he agreed. "Now it's taking on a different light. Do you mind if I ask what is the matter with the sanitation facilities on the train? Is there any particular reason why you've waited until it's literally a matter of life and death?"

Amanda stopped walking and looked around at him, appalled by his uncouthness. He wanted to be vulgar, she realized. He wanted to send her into some kind of fit by trampling her delicate sensibilities. She took a deep breath. "The soldiers have bored peepholes in all the walls. Like the conductor, my patriotism has its limitations."

"I didn't think you had any patriotism. I mean you're here with me, and you haven't said anything to that lieutenant."

"How do you know I haven't said anything to the lieutenant?"

"Because the son of a bitch hasn't killed me, that's how. He'd love an excuse to shoot me—so he could sit on my corpse and entertain you."

She took off walking again, and he went with her.

"Stop following me!"

"Why?" John asked. "Is this it?" He gestured toward any number of low pines along the track.

She made a noise of exasperation and disappeared into the nearest clump. John stood listening; he couldn't hear anything in the woods around them—no horses, no clanking canteens or rattling sabers—and sound should carry on a night as cold as this one. God, he was cold! His feet were getting numb. He felt a little better since he'd slept. Not much. But a little. He kept listening for cavalry, until he realized he'd lost track of the little Reb.

"Hey!" he whispered, peering into the dark pines for some sign of movement. "Hey!" He was beginning to panic. If she'd bolted, or if she'd run into a cavalry scout—

He heard a scramble of noise off to the opposite side.

"Amanda!" he yelled, just as she came into view.

"What?" she answered testily. "You're going to have the whole Yankee cavalry—"

She didn't get to say the rest of it. The reason for the noise burst from the woods near the railroad bank. Union cavalry, riding hard—and yes, by God, he was in the wrong uniform.

The first shots whizzed by his ear. "Get down!" he yelled at the girl as she tried to run past him. He sidestepped to intercept her, blocking her rush back to the train as he drew his revolver. She crashed into him and went sprawling in the dirt along the tracks. "Stay down, goddamn you!" he yelled, shoving her hard when she was about to get up again. He had no time to worry about her, no time to explain to the cavalryman who was about to ride him down that they really should talk about this first. And he no longer cared who was who. His only concern was that this horse soldier intended to kill him—when he'd come too far and at too great a price to stand for it.

There were shouts from the train, breaking windows; his revolver misfired. He had no time to try again, but dived into the dirt as the cavalryman charged past. He caught a glimpse of the Reb lieutenant as he tumbled away from the horse's hooves. The lieutenant was firing from the platform, as calmly as if he were shooting fish in a barrel.

Damned fool, John thought, but not without a certain admiration. A man was only as worthy as his enemies, and this lieutenant was nothing if not bold.

The cavalry made only one pass. John sat up as the sound of their hoofbeats receded. His side, where the reverend's shot had grazed him, was killing him. He looked around. The girl was still lying facedown where he'd pushed her, her bonnet tied but lying off to one side.

He scrambled over to her. "Get up," he said, putting his hand on her shoulder.

She didn't move. He turned her over.

"Are you hurt?" he asked, running his hands over her, looking for wounds. "Are you hurt!"

"If I'm not, it's no thanks to you," she said, sitting up. She had dirt in her mouth, and she tried to spit it out. He pulled the bonnet around and plopped it on her head.

"You aren't going to cry, are you?"

"I never cry," she said. "Never!"

"Don't you have any more sense than to stand up in a cross fire?" He tried to help her up, but she slapped at his hands.

"How would I know—that!" she said, still spitting. "No one ever shot at me until I met you!"

"Get up."

He stood, and she slapped his hands away again. Hard. It made him angry. He caught her arm, dragging her to her feet.

"When we get back to the train, I don't want you talking to that son of a bitch lieutenant again."

"Why?"

"Because I said so! Damned Reb. They are all alike. They think they can say anything to a woman they please as long as they hang 'honey' or 'darlin'' on the end of it. And you encourage him—"

"I do not!"

"Yes, you do!"

Amanda closed her eyes and drew a long breath. Dear Lord, how much he sounded like the reverend! She walked faster to get ahead of him, but there was no one around when she reached the train car, and she couldn't climb up on the step.

"Want some help?" he asked mildly.

She backed away from him. "Not from you."

"Not from me? Look, girl! I've saved your life tonight. Twice!"

"And I don't necessarily thank you for it."

He stared at her in the darkness. "Here. Let me help you—"

"Go help somebody you haven't threatened to murder!"

He lifted her onto the bottom step anyway, and then he let the hand he had on her waist slide upward in a deliberate exploration of her breast. She swung at him as hard as she could with her fist, but he was too quick for her, catching her hand before she hit him.

"Don't you ever do that again!" she cried.

"Never?" he asked innocently, and she took another swing. She had more luck that time, grazing his ear, but he caught her to him, chuckling in a way that made her furious enough to attempt a third swing.

He held her fast. "Don't try to hit me anymore, Amanda," he whispered, his breath warm against her ear. "I'm sorry. Truly—"

She pushed herself out of his arms and made her way into the car. Someone had lit a lantern at the far end. Her stomach heaved at the smell of rank bodies and babies that needed changing. Several of the windows were broken out, and a woman wept quietly in the semidarkness. There were no casualties that Amanda could see.

She put her hand to her nose in an effort to adjust to the smells, grateful for the cold air that came in through a broken window. The lieutenant reached out to take her arm, but she ignored him. She sat down on the hard bench, keeping her mouth clamped tight so she wouldn't cry. She could still feel the Yankee's hand on her breast. She had done nothing to make him treat her like that!

She gave a wavering sigh. She didn't have to do anything. She was the enemy; he'd threatened to kill her. He owed her no respect. She gave him a furtive glance as he sat back down on the floor.

There was more room on the bench than there should have been. One of the whores was missing. She tried to slide down so that the Yankee couldn't lean on her knees, but Dolan was coming in from outside with Feathers and Hips in tow.

"How much did *that* cost you?" the lieutenant asked him when he took his place on the floor.

"Oh . . ." Dolan said airily, "not much. So what was all the shooting about?"

Everyone within earshot laughed. Amanda moved uneasily on the bench. She could feel the lieutenant's eyes on her, and she thought for a moment he was going to lean forward again to speak to her.

"If you have anything to say to her," the Yankee said loudly, "say it to me. I'll pass it on."

Amanda could feel her face flush, and she bowed her head, grateful for the semidarkness. Everyone was looking at her—even the whore who had so reasonably accommodated Dolan. The train suddenly lurched, then began to move slowly backward in the direction they'd come from. The lantern began to sway, causing the shadows in the car to circle wildly. She was so tired. Her palms burned from the fall on the frozen ground, and her body ached to lie down somewhere and sleep. The last thing in the world she wanted to do was backtrack.

The lantern burned out, and the woman still wept in the darkness. Amanda could hear the soft murmur of voices trying to soothe her. She closed her eyes and willed the woman to stop crying, shivering in the cold air that poured in through the broken windows as the train picked up speed. If the woman didn't stop soon, Amanda would join her, only she wouldn't be so quiet about it. She'd howl, like some lost, abandoned child. She tried to move out of the draft and couldn't.

"Sit still!" the Yankee whispered, but then, he stood abruptly and made his way over the sprawled infantrymen to the exit door. He was gone long enough for her to worry, long enough for her to have to fend off another solicitous overture from the lieutenant, and to get a whispered piece of advice from Feathers and Hips, who had made a point of moving closer.

"Listen, honey," she said in Amanda's ear. "If you want to keep that blue-eyed devil of yours in hand, you'd better learn to be a good ride."

Amanda had no time to be offended, no time to assess the woman's comment to even decide if she should be offended. The blue-eyed devil was back and he was *not* happy.

"Don't you have any more sense than to talk to a whore?" he whispered angrily, and if the rest of the car couldn't hear him, it wasn't for lack of trying.

"Don't you know there's not a whore in the world I shouldn't talk to—thanks to you!" Amanda countered. She had no home, no reputation, because of his bumbling escape, and she had no intention of being put on the defensive for it.

"You don't talk to whores—and you don't talk to *him*, either," he said, jerking his head in the lieutenant's direction. Amanda tried to move her legs away so he couldn't lean on them, but there was still no place to move. She had to sit there and let him sprawl all over her.

Except that he wasn't exactly sprawling. He was leaning against her, but he was holding himself rigid, as if he were trying to keep from falling. Then, he suddenly put his head down on her lap.

She waited. He didn't move. Tentatively she touched his neck and brow. He was burning with fever. She took her hand away, but he caught it and brought it to rest on his forehead, as if it gave him some kind of relief. He became very quiet; she couldn't tell if he was asleep or awake.

The train was slowing, finally jolting to a rough stop at a railroad crossing that seemed to be in the middle of nowhere. The Yankee moaned.

"Everybody off," the conductor said. "There's an omnibus coming that will take the ones of you who don't want to walk the rest of the way to the spur. Should be another train there by the time you get there."

A cry of protest went up from the passengers, but it did no good. Yankee cavalry or no Yankee cavalry, they were getting off the train.

Amanda leaned down to whisper in the Yankee's ear. "We have to go. Get up."

"Where's Max?" he said with a start.

"We have to go," she said again.

"They'll catch us!"

"Shh!" she whispered, their faces close. "The omnibus is coming. Stand up!"

He managed to stand, but not without worrying about the passes and the man named Max.

"It's all right," she kept telling him, trying to soothe him the way he'd once soothed her. "Come on, hurry!"

The ride to the spur was a nightmare. She couldn't keep him quiet. He was nearly too sick to sit up, but some part of him kept trying to monitor their escape. He asked her again and again if she had the passes, if she had the money and the clothes, if she saw Max.

The small Virginia town they eventually came to had wooden fences with gates across the streets, each one a checkpoint for travelers. The infantrymen suspiciously disappeared from the omnibus before they reached the first gate.

"What's wrong with him?" the guard at the fence asked, because she was having to hold up the Yankee now. "Is he drunk?"

"No, he's ill. I'm taking him home."

"Where's home?"

She launched into a detailed description of a farm, the only one she was familiar with—Verillia's brother James's in the North Carolina mountains. Apparently, farms were all alike, because he let them go on through. She rummaged through the Yankee's pockets for his money, and she half dragged him toward the only hotel, a dismal place with one small room left. The room had nothing in it but a washstand, a slop jar and a narrow bed pushed against the wall. There was no lamp that she could locate; she could hear rats gnawing somewhere. She kept fumbling around in the dark looking for candles, trying to get the Yankee to sit down on the bed and stay there. He wouldn't sit down. He kept trying to take her bonnet off instead.

"What are you doing?"

He didn't answer her; he kept pulling at her bonnet until it came off. He gave it a sling behind him.

"What are you doing!" she said again, trying to get away from him.

"I'm cold," he said. "I have to lie down. I don't want you running off anywhere. I'm cold—"

She tried to tell him that she could have run off long before now if she'd wanted, but he wasn't listening to her. He pulled down the quilts on the bed and pushed her bodily onto it until he had her shoved against the wall.

"Come this way," he said, lying down beside her on the narrow bed and pulling up the quilts. "Come close—" He grabbed her wrist and pulled until she was lying against him.

"Be still, damn it! I'm not going to hurt you!"

He pulled her arm over his chest. She tried to take it away, but he grabbed it back again, holding it tightly. She couldn't move.

"Keep me warm," he said, his voice tight and strained. "I'm so cold. Keep me warm."

She stopped struggling, folding her other arm and resting her head on it to keep from having to lie on the sweaty-smelling pillow. He was on his back, his face turned toward her so that he was breathing into her neck. She tried to shift her position again, but she couldn't move. He had her pinned against the cold wall. She couldn't keep from shivering.

"What's my name?" he asked abruptly.

"What?" she asked in alarm, certain now that she was caught here with a man who was completely out of his mind.

"My name, damn you! Do you know my name!"

"Yes," she answered, her voice wavering.

"Say it."

"What?"

"Say it! My God, is plain English beyond you!"

"Howe," she whispered.

"Yes! Howe—John David Howe. Do you understand? John David—"

"Yes," she lied.

"Don't forget it. And don't let them put me in a hole without a marker. I want my name. And I want my face covered. Don't let them shovel dirt in my face. At least do that."

She lay beside him, too frightened to move.

"Answer me, damn it!"

"Yes . . . all right. . . ."

"And watch for me. So I can sleep. Watch for me."

"Yes," she said again.

He put his arms around her. "Please," he murmured. "I have to sleep. Watch for me. . . ."

"I will," she promised.

But he didn't sleep long. He came violently awake, thinking she was the soldier named Max, having no idea where he was. He cried out so loudly the hotel clerk banged on the door in warning.

"Shh," she kept whispering in his ear. "It's all right." She tried to reason with him, but he was beyond reasoning. She wrapped her arms around him, pleading with him to be quiet, holding him tightly, forgetting that if she herself were to survive this ordeal, she had to make some kind of plan.

But she couldn't force herself to think. Her mind was filled with but two directives. *Watch for me. Keep me warm.*

Chapter Five

"**W**here are we?"

The question startled her so she nearly dropped the revolver. It had been a long time since he'd said anything at all, much less anything sensible. Most of the time he thought he was in the prison.

"What the hell are you doing with that revolver?"

"Shh!" Amanda said. "He'll hear you!"

John looked around. Where the hell was this? It looked like some kind of barn. How could he have gone to sleep in a hotel and awoken in a barn? He was cold, but not unbearably so. His coat was thrown over him and he was lying in a huge pile of unbaled cotton. "Who will—where are we?"

"Will you be quiet!" Amanda said. "He's right outside. I think he's a deserter."

"Where is he?" he asked, even though she had just told him.

"Outside," she repeated.

John tried to sit up. Everything swirled around him, and he sank back down again. He turned his head to look at her, willing the dizziness to subside. She was sitting cross-legged on the rough plank floor. She wasn't wearing her bonnet, and her dark hair was coming undone. She had the ugly gray shawl Shanley had given her thrown over her lap. Incrediply, she held the revolver ready with both hands, and she never took her eyes off the only door.

"I think I hurt him," she whispered.

"What makes you think that?" he asked cautiously.

"He was trying to get in—I shot through the door."

Odd, he thought, that he'd never heard a gunshot. She glanced at him, and he could see how frightened she was. She was scared to death. He closed his eyes and tried harder to get his bearings. He was thankful he wasn't dead yet, and he was thankful that the man outside wasn't the reverend. But all he needed was another damned problem. "I swear I can't let you out of my sight for a minute. Is he still out there?"

"I don't know! I didn't go look. I've only got one shot left. I haven't heard anything for a long time."

He tried sitting up again. This time he made it. After a moment, the dizziness abated somewhat. "What is this place?" he asked, thinking she'd left out some really pertinent details here.

"We're in Mr. Herndon Riggs's cotton storage shed."

"Does Mr. Herndon Riggs know it?"

She gave a small sigh. "I doubt it."

"How do you know his name—how do you know it wasn't Mr. Riggs you tried to put a hole through?"

"I know because he keeps his ledger book on the shelf there. The man outside was hiding in the woods. I guess he was waiting for somebody to rob. The conductor wouldn't let me bring you on the train, so I—"

"Why not?" he interrupted.

"Why not? Because you weren't going to be able to stand up much longer and I couldn't carry you. He said I had to wait for one of the trains to make a hospital run, because you were too sick for the regular passenger one."

"How did we get here?"

"We walked. I was looking for a church where they let soldiers stay while they're waiting for the trains. This was as far as you could make it. It was raining—the door wasn't locked very well— Well, I had to take you somewhere!" Amanda said in exasperation. She was hungry, exhausted—she hadn't slept in days—and she didn't like the disapproving expression he was wearing one bit.

He raised both eyebrows. "Am I complaining?"

"Yes! You're complaining and you've got no room to do it—considering."

"Well, I made it this far," he said. "Wherever 'this far' is."

"Almost Gordonsville," she said.

"*Almost* Gordonsville."

"Yes, thanks to you."

His temper flared. This girl couldn't do anything but find fault. "Look! I'm sorry you were inconvenienced! I profoundly beg your pardon! What do you want me to do—shoot myself?"

"No," she said pointedly. "We've only got one shot and we're likely going to need—"

"Hey, gal!" a voice called from the outside. "I'm getting tired of this! You get yourself out here! You hear me!"

"Dare I hope the gentleman isn't referring to you?" John asked sarcastically. He had known she would be a damned lot of trouble, and trouble she was. The leer in the deserter's voice suggested that he had a lot more on his mind than robbery.

"You can hope all you want," she said, leveling the revolver at the door. It was too heavy for her; it was all she could do to keep it steady.

"Give me the revolver," he said.

"I don't think that's a good idea."

"Give it to me! Half-dead or not, I'm bound to be a better shot than you are. You can't even lift the damned thing."

"Maybe you can't, either."

"Give me the revolver!"

Amanda looked at him doubtfully. She'd had two long days of watching over him, and now that she could relinquish the responsibility, she was hesitant to do it. He was sitting up at least. And he seemed to be in his right mind.

She handed over the revolver.

"Anything left to eat?" John asked as he checked the gun. She was right. One shot in the chamber.

"Hardtack," she said, hunting in her pockets for the two crackers she'd saved for him.

"I can't eat damned hardtack."

"If you just hold it in your mouth until it gets soft, it's all right."

"I see. You're an expert on army rations now, too, I take it."

"I have enough sense to make do when I don't have a choice," she said angrily. "Thayer told me once he was so hungry he had to take some hardtack from a dead soldier and cut the blood off it so he—"

"Please! Spare me the Reb war story. I have enough stories of my own."

But he took the crackers she'd offered him. He realized that he'd hurt her feelings, but he made no apology. She sat quietly for a time, then handed him a canteen.

"Where did you get this?" he asked in surprise.

"At the Wayside Hospital. They have a lot of things there people don't need anymore."

"I can well imagine. Is that where you got the hardtack, too? Did you steal it off some dead body like what's-his-name?" He put a piece of the hard cracker into his mouth and held it the way she'd told him.

"I bought it. I didn't have enough money for anything else."

He tried to swallow the cracker. "You went through my pockets and took my money?"

"Yes, I did!"

He took a drink of water from the canteen before he choked. "In that case, I'm very much surprised you're still here."

Amanda stared at him, and he held her gaze. The blue-gray eyes were no longer fever-bright, and they bored into hers. She refused to look away, refused to be intimidated by his return to lucidity. She hadn't expected his undying gratitude, but she had thought he would at least be civil when and if his right mind returned.

"I wouldn't be if it weren't for the man outside," she said. That wasn't the truth. She had wrestled only briefly with the temptation to go off and leave him. She had taken the very best care of him she could under the circumstances. Clearly, it wasn't enough for him. She felt like crying.

"Well, you're honest. I'll give you that—"

The rest of what he said was lost as the door to the shed burst open. The man from outside rushed forward with a loud bellow, expecting her to have the revolver and intending to get to her before she could use it. Amanda toppled over on her side and flattened herself on the plank floor, jumping violently as John Howe fired his last shot. The man staggered from the impact of the ball going into his skull, his knees buckled, and he fell face forward onto the floor.

Amanda sat up slowly. The echo of the revolver faded inside her head; she was amazed by the sudden quiet. She couldn't hear anything but the rain falling, a soft pattering of raindrops in the puddles outside the open door. A cold wind blew the door open wider, bringing the rain inside, and the hinge squeaked loudly in the silence. She took a quiet breath.

"Is he dead?" she asked John Howe for the second time in their short acquaintance. She watched him turn the man over, careful of the blood that was beginning to pool. She was afraid to look, and she was afraid to turn away.

"He's dead. Are you . . . all right?" John looked over his shoulder at her. She was very pale.

"Yes," she said. "I knew what to do."

"What?" he asked, puzzled.

"Never stand up in a cross fire."

He almost smiled. My God, the things she was learning from him—damned military tactics and murder. He looked down at the dead man, then back at her. "I had no choice about this. You understand that."

She was looking at him gravely. "I can't blame you for what I would have done myself if my aim had been better."

"I think he was a ruthless man and he would have hurt you—"

"Yes," she interrupted. She didn't want to talk about the man lying dead on the floor. It was done; it couldn't be undone. And she realized fully that the only thing that worried her about it was that she was *not* worrying. She had listened to the man's threats for a long time before John Howe woke. She had no doubt about his intent. But shouldn't she be more upset by having seen a man killed?

"Are you all right?" John asked again.

"Are you?" she countered.

Incredibly, she helped him dispose of the body. The simple truth was that he couldn't have managed it alone. He wasn't feverish anymore, but he still felt like hell. He supposed, however, that hell without fever was better than hell with it. He expected her to want to do something crazy like reporting the man's death to the authorities, but she didn't. He watched her for some signs of hysteria. She was so damned quiet. She helped him dig the shallow hole and drag the body out into the rain, but she balked at going through the man's pockets. He did that himself with no remorse whatsoever.

"What army do you think he ran away from?" was the only thing she said.

"I don't know," he said. He agreed with her that the man was probably a deserter and a thief. He was carrying too many rings and watches to be anything else. But he wore nothing at all that would tell them his politics or his name. He had a whole pocketful of money, Reb mostly, but still useful. John kept the money, because he was still a long way from Washington. And he did for the man what he would have wanted done for himself insofar as he could. He tore out the back of the man's shirt and used the piece of cloth to cover his face. That the bastard had to lie in an unmarked grave was his own fault.

When they were done and back inside the shed, the girl sat down wearily on the rough floor. She was wet through and shivering.

"What's the matter, Reb?" he asked, surprising himself at how kindly the question came out.

"Nothing," she answered.

Nothing. She was homeless. Wet. Shivering. Starved. She'd been stuck with him when he was more than half-crazy, and now she was an accomplice to murder. But it was still *nothing.*

She began to take the pins out of her hair and rake through it with her fingers. Her hair was thick and heavy, and quite beautiful, particularly when it was undone. He let his eyes travel over her face and drop to her breasts. She was still pretty, even ragged and travel-stained the way she was now.

Sweet, pretty little thing.

Damn, he thought at the sudden, urgent stirring in his groin. She still had the power to affect him, and he was feeling better than he had thought. A lot better.

Amanda knew he was watching her. She raised her eyes to meet his, letting them linger as she tried to decide just what she thought about him. There was no denying that he was a complex man, never the same from one minute to the next. She wondered if he were like that all the time, or if this mercurial nature of his was simply the result of his past circumstances. Living as close to death as he surely must have done had to affect one's disposition.

I like the way he looks, she thought with some dismay. He was too thin and hollow-eyed, he was in dire need of expert barbering, but she still liked the way he looked. He truly had beautiful eyes. The melancholy she saw there only seemed to enhance them. Unfortunately, they gazed at her much too boldly at the moment. She continued to look back at him, but she couldn't begin to tell what was on his mind.

Yes, she could. His was the kind of staring that went with having an uninvited hand all over the front of one's dress. She should be insulted by the way his eyes moved over her with the same hungry look he'd used on a train station whore.

She wasn't insulted. She was afraid. What was happening to her that she took anything where he was concerned completely in stride? Two days of delirium. Murder. Lust. None of it mattered. She still wanted to crawl over to him and put her arms around him the way she had in the hotel room.

He was the first to look away. "You're going to have to get out of those wet clothes," he said.

She heard him perfectly. She looked down, fiddling with the hairpins she'd just taken from her hair.

"Look," he said. "I have a change of clothes in the carpet bag. You don't. You can put on my coat until yours get dry. You'll get sick if you don't—"

"No," she said.

"For God's sake! I'm not going to do anything to you! You're nothing but a child to me. You don't have to be afraid of me."

Amanda looked up at him. Is that what he thought? That she was afraid of *him?* It was herself she was afraid of.

"You don't—" she began, then broke off.

"I don't what?"

She didn't say anything.

"I don't what!" he demanded.

"You don't look at me as if I were a child!"

He laughed. "And what would you know about things like that? I've said you're nothing but a child, and that's what you are. I've done without a *woman* for a long time, but I'm not that desperate yet. You're just not up to my usual high standards. I'm not interested. I promise you. You are safe with me."

Now she was insulted.

"Take off your wet clothes and put on my coat," he said quietly. "If you don't, I'll do it for you."

She didn't think he had the strength, but she didn't want to challenge him. She stood up and turned her back to him, grabbing up the heavy wool coat from the pile of cotton. She took it with her into the farthest corner of the shed, huddling under it as she began to strip off her wet dress and petticoats. The chemise and drawers, he noticed, she kept on.

"No crinoline?" he asked mildly.

"I gave my hoops to Robert E. Lee to make a cannon," she said sarcastically. She glanced at him in time to see him grin.

John was finding her hiding in his coat most provocative. The way the sleeves kept falling down over her hands. The way she clutched the front of it shut as if it were a matter of life and death.

She doesn't look like a child.

Where the thought came from, he couldn't say. But there it was. She hadn't looked like a child back last August when he'd been on that work detail. The lustful thoughts he'd had then were considerably magnified now. Now he knew more about her. Now he knew the way her skin smelled—like rose water and sunshine. He almost knew the softness of her breasts. He wondered how informed she was about what happened between a man and woman. Of course, she'd had somewhat of an education on the train, thanks to Dolan; she was worried now about his seeing what he ought not see. But he didn't think she knew the precise details, and God, at that particular moment he wanted to teach her. He almost smiled. Better he taught her that than military tactics.

He gave a sharp sigh and dumped out the carpet bag, taking off the wet Reb uniform quickly and putting on the civilian clothes Shanley had given—sold—him. There was something in the shirt pocket. Half a withered apple.

"I put it there to save it for you," Amanda said, because he was looking at it as if he were trying to remember how he came by it.

"I don't want your apple, Reb."

"But I saved it for you—"

"I don't want your goddamned apple!" He glanced at her. Her eyes were big and afraid and very nearly his undoing. He wished she wouldn't look at him like that! It made him want to take her on his lap and hold her and tell her everything would be all right, and he knew exactly where *that* would lead. Didn't she have any idea what she did to a man when she looked at him like that?

He was cold, damn it! He told himself that he regretted giving her his coat. He tried not to look at her, but the more he couldn't see, the more he wanted to. It was all he could do to keep his hands off her; they both would have been better off if he'd let her stay soaking wet.

There was no place for him to go for warmth but the cotton pile. After a few moments he found that it was better than a burrow in the ground had ever been. The girl stood awkwardly in the corner, then came and joined him—

wrapped tightly in his coat and sitting as far away from him as she could and still be on the pile.

He ate the apple after all, because he was hungry and because he wanted to take his mind off her. But he wanted her. It was as simple as that, and he was plagued by the notion that there was no reason why he couldn't have her. He'd told Shanley that he was taking her with him as recompense for his suffering in the prison, and he'd all but said what that recompense would be. What better vengeance than that? No one was around. He could even believe himself capable of taking her—as long as he didn't look into her eyes.

He drew a deep breath. By God, he'd sunk low. He was a lot of things, but he was not a man who did rape. He'd never had to. He was like the lieutenant on the train—the very devil with the women. Except that Amanda wasn't a woman. She was an innocent young girl and perhaps he owed her his life.

He finished the apple, leaving nothing but the seeds.

"Why didn't you want me to kill him?" he asked abruptly. "The reverend."

"Verillia loves him," she said simply.

"I don't imagine he was very easy to love."

She shook her head. "But I would have been a good daughter—if he'd let me."

"But he didn't, did he?"

She looked into his eyes again. "No."

"Because you look like your mother."

Amanda regretted telling him that. She had hoped he wouldn't remember. "Yes."

"And you love Verillia," he said, as if he were trying to sort out the facts of how all this had come about.

"You can't help loving Verillia. She's good. I don't mean she *acts* as if she were good. She—"

"Go on," John prompted when she abruptly stopped. Conversation was better than lying here with his thoughts, particularly the kind he was having.

"I—I think she's the only truly good person I've ever met."

"Then why did she marry the reverend?"

Amanda smiled, remembering. "She said one time it was because she was arrogant. 'Prideful' was how she put it. She said the reverend never learned to laugh, and she was prideful enough to think she could teach him."

"Well, so much for that."

"Yes," she said sadly. "So much for that."

"Don't you have any other relatives?"

"No." There was Verillia's brother James, but he wasn't precisely *her* relative.

"Got a sweetheart?" John asked, surprising himself.

"Not—" Amanda stopped. *Not anymore,* was what she was about to say, but she certainly didn't want to get into that. She really didn't understand why John Howe persisted in calling her a child. She had been both betrothed and jilted. Surely that counted to give her some kind of adult status.

"Do you or don't you?" he asked. "You're wearing CSA buttons on your dress for somebody."

"That is none of your business," she said quietly.

She was so weary suddenly. She pulled the coat tighter around her, wishing he hadn't reminded her of Thayer. It only made her realize how truly alone she was. Where was he now? Dead? Alive? Off to see his wife?

The conversation lagged. John lay in the cotton with his eyes firmly shut. It didn't help. He was too aware of her. He wondered idly if the sweetheart she didn't want to talk about had taught her anything about kissing, and the notion that he might have gave him a pang very akin to jealousy.

"Where are you from?" he asked abruptly, forcing himself to give conversation another try. *Maybe the son of a bitch is dead,* he thought with a certain amount of satisfaction.

"From?"

"Yes, *from,*" he said testily. "Were you born in Salisbury—you know, that nice, quiet little North Carolina town with the hellhole of a Confederate prison in it—or did you move there from someplace else?"

"I was born there," she said, her mouth trembling. Her eyes stung with tears. She couldn't bear any more of his sarcasm.

The rain fell, and John rambled on. "I'm from Philadelphia. I was in the Sixth Pennsylvania Cavalry—Rush's Lancers. Ever hear of us?"

"No," she whispered because her throat ached so.

"Well, thank God for that. I was afraid our reputation had spread all the way down here. You should have seen us. Nothing but nerve bred of ignorance and Philadelphia's best tailors. What did we know about going to war? Not a goddamn thing. And we just *had* to carry lances—like King Arthur and his Knights of the Round Table or somebody like that. The other units called us 'turkey stickers.' That's about all we were good for—the damned things got hung up in every tree and bush you came to. You ever charged cannon or two rows of bayonets with a stick? Damned hard for a sane man, I can tell you.

"I was captured at Yellow Tavern. If you think my prison escape was bungled, you should have seen the capture. My damned horse surrendered me—can you believe that? Well, it wasn't actually *my* horse—it was shot out from under me. I'd picked this one up on the battlefield—had a mouth like stone—I couldn't do a damn thing with it. It took me right over the Reb entrenchment and into their lines. Of course, those Reb bastards saw the whole thing. I don't know when I ever gave anybody such a good laugh—"

He glanced at her. Tears were running down her cheeks. He sat up.

"Don't," he said quietly. "You never cry. Remember?" He reached out a hand to touch her, but didn't.

She gave him a little half smile. The smile promptly faded. She suddenly bowed her head. She was trembling.

"Well, then," he said. "If that's the way it is, I guess you'd better...come here."

Again, he held out his hand to her, expecting her to slap it away the way she had the other time he'd offered it to her. She didn't, and she didn't hesitate, scrambling to him and hiding her face in the front of his shirt, clinging to him like the child he still tried to convince himself she was. He put his arms around her, closing his eyes against the rush of feeling her body against his elicited. She was wrapped up tight in that damned coat, but she might as well have been naked. He didn't say anything, and neither did she. He simply held her, listening to her try not to cry, feeling himself tremble, until she fell asleep.

Then he lay down with her, burrowed deep into Mr. Herndon Riggs's cotton pile. When he awoke in the morning, she was gone.

John looked for the girl all morning. He kept asking himself why he was even bothering. He had enough money to last until he reached his own lines, he felt better than he had in days, and he had been miraculously relieved of his responsibility for her. What more could he want out of an endeavor that had done nothing but go awry from the very start?

Nothing, he kept telling himself. Good riddance. She was a damned nuisance to him. He had enough to worry about. She could get along on her own; she was clever enough;

hadn't she taken care of herself *and* him when he had a raging fever? Of course, unlike him, she didn't have any money. The appropriateness of pilfering cash from a man's pockets was clearly determined by whether the man was dead or alive. And what a quandary that must have been for someone as practical as she seemed to be—when the man with the pockets was alive, but the money in them had come from the dead.

But he was certain she was resourceful enough to think of something to alter her penniless state. Of course, God only knew what that might be. She had nothing with her but the clothes on her back, and he knew perfectly well that her cleverness was severely limited by her inexperience. If she'd go off with an escaped prisoner, she was liable to go off with anyone, and that thought troubled him enough to keep him looking, that and the terrible empty feeling he'd had ever since he awakened and found her gone.

The settlement around Mr. Herndon Riggs's cotton shed wasn't big enough to be called a town. It was a whistle-stop for farmers and not much else. The girl had to be around somewhere. He bought fried cornmeal from a vendor at the railroad shed, and he kept looking for her, stopping everyone he met on the road and waiting for a while outside the church she'd mentioned. Finally, a farmer concluded that he might have seen her—riding on the tailgate of a wagon headed for Gordonsville.

John decided immediately that the girl was likely Amanda. He could well imagine her innocently lowering those long eyelashes of hers and making some hayseed farmer fall all over himself offering her a ride. He was certain, too, that Gordonsville was his best chance of finding her—if he could get there quickly enough. He didn't want to waste the time waiting on the road for another obliging farmer with a wagon. If he were to get to Gordonsville with all possible speed, he'd have to take the train. With any luck at all, he'd arrive ahead of her.

But luck didn't seem to know his name. For all his determination, he missed the northbound train. He ran all the way to the railroad shed, using up what little stamina he might have acquired from his days of oblivion, only to get there in time to see the back end of the train well down the tracks. The weather had turned colder, and he put on parts of the still-damp Confederate uniform, until he looked like damned Charlie Wood, the piecemeal prison guard. It took him hours to get another train, hours more to get to Gordonsville, and another whole day of looking.

As a last resort, he went to the town's only army hospital, yet another "wayside" facility that was part of the military hospital network set up along the railroad line. He spotted her behind one of the outer buildings of the hospital complex, standing over a washtub that had been set on a tree stump, scrubbing bloody sheets for all she was worth. A weak sun was shining, but the ground was still muddy from the recent rain. She stood ankle-deep in the mud. The wind was sharp, but she'd done away with the shawl and the bonnet, her sleeves rolled high to keep them out of the filthy water. As he approached her, he thought he'd never seen so dejected a figure in his whole life.

"Do you have any idea what army laundresses do after the laundry is finished?" he asked much more calmly than he felt.

She looked up sharply, and of all things she smiled. It was most disarming. She was very careful with her smiles, and he could only conclude that she was actually glad to see him. He realized suddenly that he hadn't been thinking of her as a person at all, but as a piece of property he'd inadvertently misplaced. His property. His reparation for his imprisonment, even if he hadn't taken advantage of her when he'd had the chance. But no. He'd been a perfect gentleman. He'd held her all night while she slept, and he'd endured one of the worst nights of sexual frustration any man ought to have to suffer. She didn't appreciate what he'd done for her, of course. She'd run off.

Amanda's smile faltered at the look on his face. She pressed her lips together and tried to recover as much dignity as she could muster. She'd come within a breath of throwing herself at him, wet hands, dirty sheet and all, when it was obvious that he hadn't come here for that.

"I imagine," she said without looking at him, "they fall flat on their faces in exhaustion."

"Wrong. It's not their faces they fall on."

She looked up at him. He was in that mood, the sarcastic, superior one with the innuendos about what men and women did together she almost but not quite understood. She let her eyes meet his by sheer force of will, surprised by what she saw there. There was anger, of course, but there was something else. Worry? If he were worried about anything, it had to be himself, she thought. He was still in enemy territory, and she knew where the bodies were buried.

Body.

She went back to scrubbing the dirty sheet on the washboard, trying not to think about the man in the shallow grave at the cotton shed. The sheet was nearly thin enough to read through; it kept coming apart in her hands. Her back hurt from bending over the tub, and she still had a huge black washpot full of dirty bed linens. She was so hungry she could hardly think straight. "How did you find me?"

"Well, it wasn't easy, if that's what you're thinking."

She stared at him for a moment. He had been more than kind to her when she'd cried so in the cotton shed, but he didn't appear now to be inclined toward anything that even faintly resembled kindness.

"Let's go," he said.

"No. This is where we part company—"

"The hell you say," he interrupted, taking her by the arm.

"I'm not going with you!" she cried. She tried to jerk her arm free, stepping backward to get away from him, bumping into the washtub and causing it to topple off the uneven stump and onto the ground. The filthy water sloshed all over the both of them. "Let me go!"

He didn't, and she suddenly leaned down to grab the washboard she'd been using, taking a swing at him with that. He threw up his arm to block the blow, knocking it out of her hand. She tried to run, but he still had her by the arm. She took another swing at him with her fist. He jerked her around in front of him and lifted her bodily off the ground, hauling her along with him.

"You are traveling with me!"

"I'm not going with you!" she cried, trying to get her arms free.

"Yes, by God, you are!"

He set her down on the ground. Hard. And when she would have tried to run again, he grabbed her to him, holding her tightly against his chest until she stopped struggling. They were both out of breath, and she looked wildly around, hoping they had drawn a crowd of onlookers. There was no one in sight. He shook her hard and made her look at him.

"A laundress—what the hell were you thinking?"

"I'm going to buy a train ticket to Richmond—"

"Well, being a laundress isn't the way to get the money for it—unless some rutting army surgeon takes a fancy to you. And then you'll get a lot more than a damned train ticket!"

"This is none of your business! I don't want to go with you!"

"I told you, you're safe with me! I'm not going to hurt you! I'm not going to hurt you," he whispered urgently, his face close to hers. "Look. It's as much a surprise to me as anybody, but it seems I need to keep my word. I said I'd see you situated, and I will. But I can't do it here. I'm in the wrong uniform, damn it! I have to get to my own people—"

"Why would you want to keep your word to *me!*"

"Because I can't stand anything else on my conscience! Or aren't you old enough to know about guilt? It's for sure you're a damned pain, but I'm getting used to you."

"And suffering is good for the soul," she suggested, glancing up at him. "Especially one as black as yours."

"Exactly. I told you I'd take care—"

"I have to know," she interrupted. "I have to know what you're planning to do with me."

"I'm not going to *do* anything with you! I just want you to go with me to my lines, that's all. So I can find something a little more respectable for you than being a damned camp follower!"

"I'm not a—" she started to say, but didn't. Perhaps she wasn't a camp follower yet, but she was well on her way to becoming one. She knew perfectly well why the women who supposedly washed sheets with her disappeared at regular intervals. Several of them had gone to great lengths to explain to her exactly what was in store for her, what was in store for any woman who found herself abandoned and destitute. But she was cautioned not to despair. Not to worry, they assured her. She was sitting on a virtual gold mine—unless of course she was hampered by her virginity. In which case she should find some man she liked—really liked—to get rid of it for her, then she wouldn't mind so much the paying ones who followed.

"It's not entirely unselfish," John said. "I'm...not sure I can make it alone. I trust you to help me if I need it. To bury me if I can't."

She looked at him, her eyes searching his. He meant it.

"Do you understand?" he said.

"I understand."

"Yes, but will you do it?"

She took a deep breath and looked at the muddy ground. She was in no hurry to begin a life of ill-repute, no matter how suited the reverend thought her. The life of a traitor would do for now, and as unlikely as it might be, she trusted John Howe as well, regardless of his threats and his inquisitive hands. "All right," she said, looking up at him.

"You swear?"

"You're not the only one who can keep his word!"

"Is that a fact?"

"It is."

"Imagine that," he said, taking her by the arm again, but more gently this time. "A Southerner bound by an oath."

"What is *that* supposed to mean?" she asked as he walked her along with him.

"It means your part of the country seceded from the Union, not mine—when one would have thought the Constitution was as binding a contract as one could get."

She stopped walking. "I've changed my mind. I don't want to go with you."

"Sure you do," he said mischievously. "I've got fried apple pies in my pockets."

Chapter Six

John Howe really did have fried apple pies in his pockets. They were cold and greasy and not very sweet, and they were wonderful. Amanda ate two of them, one more than he would have given her if he'd felt better. He was no longer feverish, and for that she was thankful, but he had no appetite and no stamina. He was weak and trembly, and she thought that he was more right than he realized; perhaps he couldn't make it without her.

The train was slow but steady the last miles to Alexandria. John stared out the dirty windows, saying nothing. She sat quietly by him on yet another bench, feeling his anxiety because he was almost there. Free. He was too sensitive to the cold to discard the Confederate uniform; he took a chance and still wore it—under the corduroy pants and the now dirty shirt Shanley had given him. Both those garments were hardly fit for anything but the rag bin, and she was as bedraggled and dirty as he. They were a sorry-looking pair, both of them.

When they finally entered the town, Amanda thought that it looked more like a Yankee army camp. She expected John Howe to contact the military authorities straightaway, but he didn't. With the second pass Shanley had provided, he made arrangements for yet another train trip, this time to Washington itself. She would have protested—if she hadn't looked into his eyes. That desperate, haunted look was back, the one she'd seen the first night, when he'd gotten into the wrong house. He was barely able to stand without using her to lean on, and if he thought he had to get to Washington, then she'd go with him. She'd already sold her loyalty, even before the two fried apple pies; a few more miles wouldn't matter.

The day was dreary and cold, the sky a heavy gray. She supposed that the first sight of Washington must have made her feel the same way John Howe felt when he arrived in Salisbury—overwhelmed by the realization that one is among the enemy. There were blue-coated soldiers everywhere. The muddy streets were packed with vehicles, and the smell of the canals seemed to permeate everything. She wondered if cities had characteristic smells like people. She had been to Wilmington once when her mother was still alive. It had smelled of saltwater and dead fish. If she lived to be a hundred, she thought, Washington would be to her the rank stench of a cesspool.

And she'd never seen so many painted, fancy women. They were an army in themselves, parading back and forth in their hiked-up dresses, calling to the many soldiers who passed their way. From the street near the train station, she could see directly into one of the brothel windows, where a man and woman writhed together on an unmade bed—a fascinating sight—if John Howe hadn't caught her looking at it.

But for once he made no pointed comment, not about the man and woman or about the loose women walking up and down the street. And he gave none of his bold, appreciative glances in return for the blown kisses and taps on the arm he encountered along the way. Amanda thought it was all he could do to put one foot in front of the other, but he was determined now to find an army officer—or rather he was determined that *she* should find one—who could direct them to the nearest provost marshal's guard. He insisted that she approach one soldier after another on his behalf, while he held on to the nearest lamppost or iron fencing. The officers were all willing to help her—with anything except what she asked.

It began to rain, cold, icy, pelting. Wet and shivering, she finally found an ambitious second lieutenant who was not only willing to speak to John, but who immediately enlisted the services of two armed soldiers from the Veterans Reserve Corps and insisted that John be taken immediately to the Forrest Hall Military Prison in Georgetown.

"Are you new at this, Lieutenant?" John asked, staring down the lieutenant. "That's a long way out to find a provost marshal. What's wrong with Old Capitol?"

The lieutenant wore a plume of black feathers in his hat and they drooped heavily in the pouring rain. His cheeks flushed at John's remark, but, if anything, he became even more self-important.

"*You* are in no position to make suggestions," he said, deliberately omitting John's rank. "I happen to know the Sixth Pennsylvania Cavalry's old commanding officer is making inspection at Forrest Hall today. I'm sure he'll want to take a look at you."

"It's been a long time since I've seen Colonel Rush—"

"Brigadier General Rush," the lieutenant corrected. "If you're who you say you are, he'll settle this matter quickly. If not, we won't have the aggravation of finding a prison for you, will we?" He glanced at Amanda. "The woman can stay here."

"She stays with me," John said quietly.

"That is quite impossible."

"She stays with me, Lieutenant!"

Amanda could feel the lieutenant wavering. Whether John Howe was who he said he was or not, he certainly sounded authentic—to them both.

The lieutenant abruptly turned on his heel, waving down a passing wagon.

"You're making a trip to Forrest Hall," he told the soldier driving.

"Sir, I can't do that. I'm—the general—"

"You heard me!" the lieutenant bellowed, and the soldier-driver shrugged his compliance.

"Damn fool thinks he's caught a ring of Rebel spies," John said to her as they climbed onto the back of the wagon.

Amanda wiped the rain out of her eyes and looked at him for a moment, then down at herself. "Some ring," she said, and he smiled.

"I'm sorry. Maybe that frying pan is looking better to you all the time."

"I didn't have anything better to do," she said tiredly. The wagon jerked forward before she could sit down, and she grabbed his arm, holding on tightly until she could reach a wooden box to sit on. He smiled at her again, and she suddenly wanted to weep. They must be in terrible trouble if he was being this kind to her.

"Is General Rush going to know who you are?" she quietly asked him, turning her head so the two guards who rode on the back of the wagon with them wouldn't hear.

"Hell, my own mother wouldn't know me."

They had to cross a bridge to get to Georgetown. The rain had changed to sleet, and the bridge was already icy. She closed her eyes as both the horses and the wagon slid treacherously along. A fitting end to a traitor to the Confederacy, she thought. Drowned in the Potomac, or whatever body of water they were going over. It wasn't until they reached solid ground again that she realized she'd been holding her breath.

She turned her head to read a nearby street sign. Wisconsin Avenue.

"It's not far now," John told her, and she nodded.

She sat on the box with her hands clenched, feeling the interest of the guards, trying to endure. They passed a candy store. P. May's Bakery and Confectionery, the sign said. She couldn't remember the last time she'd had cake or candy. The store was next to Forrest Hall Prison, and the prison looked exactly like what it was. A prison. Cold. Gray. Foreboding.

The wagon stopped, but she made no attempt to get out until one of the guards took her arm. John Howe already stood in the muddy street, but he was looking at the candy store.

"Do you see that?" he asked her as she got down from the wagon. "A damned candy store next to a prison. Peppermint sticks in the window—do you know what that does to a man? To be in prison and to know that normal things like that are just out of his reach?"

He was wearing that bitter expression she hated and he was clearly waiting for her response. She was soaked to the skin; it was all she could do to keep her teeth from chattering. "I . . . can imagine," she offered, but it only made him angry.

"No, by God, you can't!"

He turned away from her, his face grim.

"This way, sir," one of the guards said, moving him along.

She didn't know what to say to him. She never knew what to say to him. "I'm sorry," she finally managed—because she was. Sorry for all the bad things that had happened to him, sorry for the things that had left him the way he was now. But the words came out in a whisper he didn't hear.

The inside of the prison was even more dismal—dimly lit and drafty and hollow sounding.

"This way, sir," the guard said again, and John walked off with him, leaving her to stand or follow, as she chose.

She followed, but only a short distance before another guard blocked her way.

"In there, miss," he said, pointing out an empty room on the right of the entrance corridor. "It's better if you stay in there."

She had no choice but to do as he said, but she stared after John Howe as long as the guard would let her. He never once looked back.

The room had a fire in the fireplace, and several straight chairs. She dragged one closer to the heat and sat down, surprised at how weak her legs had suddenly gone. There was a single window she couldn't see out unless she got up again, and she didn't think she had the strength to move. Now and then the wind drove the sleet and rain against the glass. She looked down at the front of her shawl and dress. She was filthy. It was so long since she'd had a bath. She looked awful; she *felt* awful. Her head hurt from the lack of food and sleep. She was shivering from the cold, in spite of the fire.

She closed her eyes for a moment, listening intently to the sounds around her. She felt so uneasy in this place of echoing footsteps, and banging doors, and voices of men she couldn't see. What if John Howe disappeared altogether and left her here? Soldiers passed the door from time to time; they all carried stacks of papers and walked fast. None approached her or even looked in. Apparently, the men in this place were accustomed to bedraggled women hanging about.

She could smell coffee brewing somewhere—real coffee, not some inferior substitute a desperate Southerner might make out of roasted sweet potato skins or acorns or peanuts. The aroma made her so homesick suddenly that she let out a wavering sigh. Verillia. Those prewar Sunday mornings when the reverend had already gone off someplace and she woke to the smell of hot coffee and frying bacon and

Verillia humming one of her sad mountain songs. She'd never have any of that again.

She was so tired! Her exhaustion was so great that her hunger didn't seem to matter anymore.

"Here," John said behind her, making her jump. She was so relieved to see him, she nearly knocked the cup he was holding out of his hands.

"Easy! Well, take it," he said, offering her the cup.

She took it. It smelled wonderful!

"Wait a minute," he said when she was about to take a sip. He rummaged into his pocket and brought out a brown paper packet with the ends twisted shut. "How much do you want?" he asked.

"What is it?"

"Sugar."

"*Real* sugar? It's real?"

"Absolutely. How much do you want?"

"All of it," she said, and he laughed. "Please, John Howe!" she said, motioning him closer and holding up the cup. She was prepared to wrestle him to the ground for it if she had to, and in his present condition she had little doubt that she could do it.

"You really know how to ruin a good cup of coffee," he said, but he tore open the pack.

"All of it," she insisted, taking the packet herself to make sure he'd dumped it completely. She rotated the cup briefly and attempted a sip. The coffee was too hot to really drink, but the little bit she managed tasted heavenly. She gave a contented sigh.

He sat down in the nearest chair and reached to take back the cup, making a face when he tasted the sweetness. "It doesn't take much to make you happy, does it?"

"Not much," she agreed, impatiently waiting to get the cup back again. She'd seen soldiers waiting for the train sometimes share whatever they had from a common cup. She didn't mind sharing with John Howe in the least.

He sat bent forward with his arms resting on his thighs, holding on to the cup as if to warm his hands. He was in a better mood now, she thought, hoping it was a good sign. It was so hard to tell with him. His moods seemed to have nothing to do with whatever was going on around him. Here was a man who could make jokes when he was running for his life; she never knew what to make of him.

She stared at his profile. Even as starved and tattered and ill as he was, he was still a handsome man. Beautiful blue-gray eyes and thick, long eyelashes. The bold cavalryman. She could easily imagine how dashing he must have been in better times and how the Yankee women must have whispered about him behind their fans and sighed.

"Do you have a sweetheart?" she asked abruptly, surprising them both. But the question was out now, and there was no point in pretending she didn't want to know. "Do you?"

He gave her a mischievous smile. "I've got a hundred of them. Why?"

"I was just thinking she'd—they'd—be glad you're home again."

He didn't reply to that, and their eyes met and held. A long time. Too long. She wanted to shift in her chair, to look away, but she didn't. She stared back at him, feeling a different kind of weakness in her knees now, feeling her belly grow warm. It was as if she were hungry, but not for food. It was all she could do not to reach for him. Suddenly, she desperately needed his nearness, his comfort. She'd had a small sampling of that in the cotton shed, and she wanted it again. She hadn't felt this terrible need for Thayer. Her breath seemed to slip away from her, and yet it was all . . . pleasurable somehow. She wanted him to look at her. She wanted him to touch her, even if it were in that rude way he'd done helping her onto the train. She didn't care that he was the enemy or that he called her "girl" or "Reb" or worse. She didn't care that she'd shamelessly followed him all the way to Washington or that they were in the middle of a Yankee prison. The sudden realization that nothing mattered to her but him, not reputation, not politics, not herself, was overwhelming, nearly as overwhelming as the realization that, one way or the other, their journey was nearly done. She forced herself to look away.

"Here," he said, handing her the cup again. Their fingers brushed as she took it from him. Hers were trembling. She had to hold on to the cup with both hands.

"What . . . happens now?" she asked after a moment.

"Rush is checking a few things."

"What kind of things?"

"Ah, hell, I don't know," he said, tiredly rubbing a spot between his eyes. "He doesn't remember me exactly. He remembers Max Woodard more than he remembers me. I guess he's trying to satisfy himself we aren't spies."

"We?" she repeated, and her tone of voice made John smile. She had a way of doing that for him—among other things. His smile broadened, and yet he had never in his life felt more like weeping. He took a deep breath to fight off the urge to put his head in her lap.

"Lie down with dogs, get up with fleas," he said philosophically to annoy her. He had to do something if he was going to keep from making a fool of himself. He reached again for the coffee cup.

"I *hate* it when you do that," she whispered.

"Do what? Take back *my* coffee?"

"You know what! You know I'm scared to death and you do everything you can to make it worse."

"Can't help it. It's been my vocation for the past four years to annoy Johnny Rebs whenever I can."

"Don't say that here!" she cried, and he laughed out loud.

"I don't suppose Rush could ask this Max Woodard to identify you."

John's amusement immediately faded. "No," he said, taking another drink of coffee. "He couldn't."

Amanda was fully aware that she'd said the wrong thing. Again. They sat in silence for what seemed to her a long time. She could feel his annoyance. In fact, in their time together, she'd become quite accomplished at recognizing it.

"I'll...need money," she said finally. She was going to need a lot of it if she wasn't going to end up parading and blowing kisses like the rest of Washington's "other" army.

She waited until he looked at her. "This is where we part ways, isn't it?" He might think she was too childlike to anticipate the next logical step—if they weren't both shot for spying—but she wasn't. She was old enough to understand that her usefulness was at an end, even if she had somehow developed an attachment to him, and to know that, for her own good, she had to go.

He didn't answer her.

"John Howe?" she prompted.

He made an impatient gesture with his free hand. "I can't turn a baby like you loose on the streets. I have to make some arrangements for you. I need to talk to my father and—"

"Why?" she interrupted.

"Because he may need to pull some strings."

She didn't want to have anything to do with John Howe's father. She didn't want *anyone* to know how she happened to get here. She just wanted what he had promised her. She wanted to be "situated"—before she said or did anything any more stupid than she already had. He'd told her plainly that she had no appeal, and here she was sitting and pining after him like a schoolgirl with her first crush. He didn't know how she felt, and if he did, he'd laugh. She'd laugh herself. What a joke she would make for his fellow officers.

"What kind of strings?" she persisted.

"How the hell should I know? I've been the guest of the Confederacy for the past eight months."

"Who is your father that he can—pull strings?" she asked, refusing to be put off.

"He's a lesser government official," he said, and she stood so abruptly he nearly dropped the coffee cup.

"I see," she said. "A lesser government official. I would like money for a hotel, John Howe. Or a respectable boardinghouse."

He looked up at her. "Amanda, I don't have any money. We spent it all. You know that. You're going to have to go home with me—"

"I'm not going with you!"

"Do we have to have this same damned conversation *again?*"

"I can't go home with you!"

"Why not? If you can ride on a train with me for six days, lie in the same bed—"

"And what choice did I have about that!"

"—sleep in the same pile of cotton—"

"I didn't *sleep!* I was too afraid you'd die!" It wasn't quite true. She *had* slept. That last night in the cotton shed, she'd slept in his arms, after she'd cried until she couldn't cry anymore, and they both remembered it.

"All the more reason to let me take care of you now," he said. "My family already knows you're coming. I just sent them a message."

"What kind of message!" she cried. She'd just love to know how he explained her in a message.

John reached out and grabbed her by the hand. Her fingers clung to his, frightened and trusting like a child's. She did trust him, he thought, and he'd do well to remember that.

"Sit," he said. "Sit, *sit!*"

She sat back down in the straight chair, and he let his eyes travel over her face. God, she was a pretty little thing, he thought yet another time—if she just wouldn't frown so. She suddenly dropped her head.

"Amanda, look up here at me. Look at me." He cupped his fingers under her chin to lift her head. "You have nothing to be ashamed of. Nothing."

Her eyes searched his; her bottom lip trembled. She pursed her mouth as if she were about to say something, but she didn't say it. *Ah, God,* he thought, forcing himself to remember that she was too young.

"Amanda—"

"I feel ashamed," she said. "I feel—"

"Captain Howe," an orderly interrupted. "We've found a buggy for you. The general says you and your wife can go now."

"You told them I was your *wife?*" Amanda cried, hardly waiting until the orderly had gone.

"Will you hush! Actually, I said you were my lady. It seemed better to let them think I was robbing the cradle than to—well, what the devil did you want me to tell them! You're the biggest Reb since Jeff Davis?"

"I don't want you to tell them anything. I just want—"

"Yes, I know. You just want me to finance your train ticket to Richmond. Well, I can't do that here. Let's go."

"John Howe!"

"Now don't you start with me!" he said, pointing a finger in her face. "I am almost home, when I thought I'd never see home again, and I am *not* in the mood."

"I can't go to your house!" she wailed as he all but dragged her along with him into the corridor and out the front entrance of the building. He was a lot stronger than she would have guessed, and she couldn't get away from him. It was still sleeting hard, and he had no compunction whatsoever about hiking her up on his hip to thrust her into the waiting buggy, with any number of soldiers looking. "I can't!" she kept telling him.

"You can," he answered. "And you will."

He kept one hand on her while he climbed inside, as if he thought she'd make a run for it. And she might have, if she'd thought of it sooner. He picked up the reins and sent the horse forward, the wheels of the buggy for a moment sinking deeper into the mud.

"Please," she said, her voice quavering.

"Now, don't you cry! I hate bawling women and in the mood I'm in I'm apt to shoot you for it."

"You don't have any ammunition."

"Then I'll strangle you with my bare hands!"

"I'm not crying!"

"Good! Keep it that way!"

The horse shied and the buggy lurched crazily, but he didn't slow down. She found immediately that a horse and buggy on an icy bridge was worse than a horse and wagon. As soon as they were off it, he whipped the horse into an even faster gait, sending out a spray of mud behind them. They abruptly turned a corner, changing direction and causing the wind to blow the sleet directly into the buggy. Her face stung from it; she was certain his did, too, but he didn't slacken the pace. And he certainly seemed to know where he was going, turning down street after street until they reached one lined with great houses and high stone walls and stands of bare trees. In front of the last house on the street, he brought the buggy to a stop.

"Come on," he said as he got out.

"Can't I just wait here or on the back steps or somewhere?"

"No," he said, pulling her out after him.

"John Howe—"

"What!"

"I—"

"What?" he said in a somewhat kindlier tone.

"I wish *you* looked a little happier about this."

"I'm happy," he assured her.

"If this is 'happy,' John Howe, you are in for a miserable life. Do we have to go in the *front* door!" she cried as he dragged her directly toward it.

"I live here, Amanda. I always go in the front door."

"Oh, my Lord," she whispered, because he was determined to do it and because there was nothing she could do to delay it, nothing to cling to, no railing or handy bush or tree. "Oh, my Lord!" she said again as he was about to knock, but the door opened ahead of him.

An elderly servant stood quietly in the open doorway, and if he found it the least bit curious that John Howe should be tussling with a strange girl on the doorstep, it didn't show.

"Smith!" John said, stepping inside. He jerked her along with him over the threshold. "How are you!"

For a moment, Amanda thought the old man would smile, but he didn't. "Quite fine, sir. A touch of the gout as always. Shall I have the horse stabled, sir?" he asked gravely.

"What? Oh—yes. It needs to be returned to Forrest Hall, but that can be done tomorrow. Where's my mother?"

"In the drawing room, sir," the servant said, attempting to help John off with his coat. It took a bit of doing, because John didn't let go of her wrist. Amanda supposed that this lack of curiosity must be the mark of well-trained help. The servant, Smith, simply waited politely until John had changed hands.

"There are guests tonight, sir," Smith went on when he had the coat. "Your mother wishes you to join them the moment you arrive."

"Damn! Guests, you say—how many?"

"About fifty come for refreshments and bridge, sir."

"Damn!" John said again, and Amanda could very well have joined him. The servant hardly looked at her, and she stood there wishing she were half as invisible as he was trying to make her feel. She glanced furtively around her, trying to be nonchalant, trying not to gawk.

But she had never seen such a house. The entry hall was black and white marble with a great, gas-lit chandelier hanging from an ornate plaster medallion in the ceiling. It was breathtaking, and she made a soft "oh" sound as she looked up at it. The draft from the open front door had set the prisms into motion and they still tinkled lightly.

Lord, if Verillia could see this, she thought. If everyone she *knew* could see this—Anne Giffen and Charlie Thayer. Even the reverend. It was torture to behold such a splendid place and not have anyone to share it with who would be as awestruck as she.

On her left, two chairs with gold brocade seats had been placed on either side of a huge gilt mirror with Cupids on the top. She wanted to walk over and touch it, but even though John Howe no longer had her by the wrist, she refrained. There was a table beneath the mirror, with a blue-and-white porcelain bowl filled with fresh flowers, marguerites and red roses—in winter! The wallpaper had stylized engravings of bouquets of flowers on a yellow background, and each of the bouquets was surrounded by scrollwork and more Cupids.

She had never seen such elegance—or such a lack of warmth. There was nothing to suggest that people lived here; there were only these perfectly arranged and stylish *things*.

A door on the left of the entry hall suddenly opened, and a woman came rapidly forward, giving a small cry and flinging herself into John Howe's arms. Her hair was streaked with gray and it had been elaborately done up with strings of pearls. She was quite stunning, and she was wearing the most beautiful dress Amanda had ever seen, a rich, dark blue silk.

The woman leaned back to look into John's face, then clung to him again. "I can't believe you're here!" she kept saying.

"You know what they say about bad pennies, Mother," he said in an attempt to tease, but she wouldn't have it.

"Don't!" she said, pressing her fingertips against his lips. "Let me look at you, you're so thin and shaggy— Oh, but you must come speak to the others. You must let them *see* how you've suffered for this great nation—"

"Mother, wait," John said. "There is someone I would like you to meet."

"What?" she said, still smiling as he turned her around. Her smile faded as her eyes riveted on Amanda.

Amanda stood where she was, because she couldn't do otherwise, and she realized immediately that whatever John Howe had told his family about her in that message, it had left his mother ill prepared. Amanda was suddenly acutely aware of her shabbiness, of how badly she needed a change of clothes and a bath. With great effort, she kept her head up, all the while wanting desperately to die or to disappear—whichever came first—but she'd had too many sessions with the reverend to know that such things never occurred when one needed them.

"Mother," John said, bringing Mrs. Howe forward as if this meeting were the most natural thing in the world. "May I present Miss Amanda..." He suddenly faltered. "Miss...ah..."

Well, fine, Amanda thought. Here she'd been agonizing because she was convinced she was completely smitten where he was concerned, and he had forgotten her last name. And she wasn't about to help him remember, either, though in fairness, it occurred to her that he might never have known it.

He looked at her hard and raised an inquisitive eyebrow; she ignored him.

Fairness, be damned! She had *told* him not to bring her here. In his hardheadedness, he had already made a bad situation absolutely intolerable—and she was barely inside the door.

"Amanda, you could tell my mother your entire name," he said in a tone of voice that suggested that he was working hard to leave the swear words out.

"I could," she agreed. But she let him flounder a moment longer before she did.

"Amanda Lee Douglas," she said to the woman finally, to John Howe's clear relief.

"Miss Douglas," John's mother said politely. "You are...visiting in Washington?" Her eyes traveled up and down the front of Amanda's clothes.

"Amanda came with me from North Carolina, Mother," John said.

His mother looked from one of them to the other. "Well!" she said brightly. "How interesting!" But her expression looked as if she'd just realized that she'd allowed her stays to be laced too tightly, and it was a *long* time before the end of the bridge party. "You must come into the drawing room—both of you," she added, clearly trying to make the best of a bewildering situation. "I'm sure everyone will forgive your—" her eyes traveled up and down again "—attire."

"I doubt it," Amanda said under her breath. She had Thayer Giffen's CSA buttons on the front of her dress. She could be *shot* for this attire.

"Amanda is very tired, Mother," John said to Amanda's great relief. "Smith—see to her."

Smith was already giving hand signals to a maid who hovered in the background.

"Take her upstairs, Alice," John said as the maid came closer. "Make sure she has everything she needs."

"Welcome home, sir," the maid said timidly.

"Thank you, Alice. And bring Miss Douglas plenty to eat, will you?" he added, still giving orders.

"John—" his mother said pointedly.

But he ignored her. He reached out to take Amanda by the hand. "Go with Alice," he said, squeezing her fingers and thrusting her in the maid's direction. "She and Smith will take good care of you. And stop frowning."

She looked up at him and all the anger went out of her. He was so pale.

"Are you all right?"

He managed a smile that might have fooled someone else. "Quite fine, thank you, Miss Douglas."

She ignored his attempt at levity. "You haven't been well. Shouldn't you—"

"Ah, but we must keep up appearances," he interrupted. "You wouldn't want the senators' wives to know there's a war going on, would you?"

"There are senators' wives here?"

"I imagine so. Just on the other side of those doors."

"Oh, my Lord," she murmured.

"I know exactly how you feel," he said, smiling again, a mischievous but painful little smile that left her even more uneasy. "You don't have to look after me now," he said. "Go on with Alice."

The doors he had just indicated suddenly burst open and people poured into the entrance hall—women in flowered and striped satins and dark velvets and silk, men in their evening dress.

"Got the sons of bitches on the run, eh, boy?" a man boomed, slapping John heartily on the back as people surged around him. Mrs. Howe stepped in front of Amanda as if to block her from view, but she needn't have worried. Amanda had no desire to be seen by these people. She quickly turned and followed Alice, feeling the eyes of the guests on her regardless of Mrs. Howe's maneuvering, and fighting down a tremendous urge to run. Poor Mrs. Howe, she thought, wondering what excuse she'd give for her son's unseemly choice of traveling companions. Alice led the way up the staircase—another ornate wonder to Amanda's eyes. It was amazing to her the architecture that enough money could accomplish. These stairs looked as if they led to heaven.

She looked back once when she reached the landing. John was still surrounded by well-wishers. Someone stuck a cigar in his mouth, and he laughed. Even as unkempt as he was, it was evident that he belonged in this place and with these people.

She willed him to look in her direction, but he didn't. She wanted to call out to him. She wanted to tell him: *Don't send me away. Let me stay with you. And let's get out of here!*

"Miss?" Alice prompted.

"Yes, I'm coming."

"Mr. Smith says to put you in the green room. Have you any baggage, miss?" Alice asked as she opened the door to a lovely firelit room on the second floor. There was a huge canopy bed draped in two shades of green moiré silk with gold fringes, and bare wood floors tastefully strewn with thick Oriental rugs. Mahogany tables stood on both sides of the bed, one holding an ivory washstand, and the other, a cobalt-blue glazed pitcher and drinking glass. A lady's desk and a straight chair with the same green silk on the seat had been placed at the foot of the bed, and there was a small upholstered couch in front of the fireplace. The fire in the coal grate burned brightly, and Amanda wanted desperately to cry.

"Any baggage, miss?" Alice said again.

"I *am* the baggage," Amanda murmured, sighing heavily and fighting down the burning in her throat. She glanced up in time to see Alice suppressing a grin.

"Sit down, miss, do," she said. "By the fire. Oh, you're all wet and rained on, aren't you? I'll get you some night things and bring you your bath. And then you can have a nice supper—is there anything in particular you'd like?"

Amanda stared at her. The girl asked that as if it were really possible to just choose. "No, nothing in particular," she answered. She never wanted to eat cornmeal again as long as she lived, but she was too polite to say so. She was her mother's daughter, after all—and Verillia's. She knew how to behave. She smiled a bit, remembering when she was younger, Verillia's familiar admonishment whenever they went places: Now act like you are *somebody*.

Alice left the room, and Amanda stood forlornly in front of the fire. She was going to have her work cut out for her if she were going to behave as if she were somebody here. She supposed that John Howe must be explaining her presence to those people downstairs—if he could remember her name.

"Oh, Lord, what am I doing here!"

She put her hands up to her face. She had never felt so abandoned in her life. She had been with John Howe night and day for nearly a week and, whether he knew her name or not, she didn't want to be without him now.

From time to time, Amanda heard rustlings in the hallway outside, but no one came near the door. She didn't know if John would come see about her or not. She took off Mrs. Shanley's shawl and bonnet, making a small noise of dismay at how battered and dirty they were. No wonder Mrs. Howe had been so obviously appalled.

Someone rapped sharply on the door, making her jump. She crossed the room quickly and took a deep breath before she opened it. A young boy, about eight years old, stood in the hallway in his nightshirt. He was solemn-faced and handsome, and he had very familiar eyes. She waited for him to say something, but he was busily inspecting her from head to toe.

"Are you her?" he asked finally, and Amanda smiled.

"I'm afraid so."

"How do you do?" he said in very correct, very adult tones.

"How do you do?" she responded. "Won't you come in?" she asked, because he was peering behind her.

"Are you alone?" he whispered.

She nodded and stood out of the way, smiling again because he took very long strides as he entered the room, she supposed, in an effort at bigness. When he reached the fireplace, he turned to look at her, staring at her gravely as if he were still making his assessment—and Lord, he had John Howe's eyes, she realized.

"My name is Harry," he said. "I don't know yours."

"Amanda."

"Amanda," he repeated thoughtfully. "Do you know what it means? I have a book that tells if you don't. I would be happy to look it up for you."

"Yes, thank you. That would be interesting."

"Do you really think so?" he asked earnestly. "I find it interesting myself but there are those who don't." He sighed, and Amanda had the sudden mental picture of him offering his name service to others in the household and being rather rudely rejected.

"They're having a terrible row," he said after a moment, wandering about the room, curiously touching whatever came to hand, as if he had never been allowed in before. "Mother says she won't have it. She says John has ruined his political career. John said being dead would have ruined it, too. He's behaving badly again, I'm afraid."

"Is he?"

"Oh, yes. He cursed something awful. Have you done something bad?" the boy asked.

"Why do you ask?"

"Well..." he began, and with the fascination all small boys had with things they ought not to play with, he took the poker out of the stand and began to push some of the coals in the fire. "Mr. Beale is coming. He always comes when somebody does something bad—John," he specified, looking up at her. "John is a hell-raiser, you know. Mother was hoping the war would take it out of him. Now she says he's worse than ever."

There was no doubt in Amanda's mind *why* he was worse than ever.

"I have to go now," the boy said. "I'm supposed to be asleep. *Have* you done something bad?" he asked again.

"If I have, I didn't do it on purpose," Amanda said, and he nodded.

"That happens to me sometimes," he said sympathetically. "I hear Alice coming!" he added abruptly, dropping the poker. He ran for the door, turning to give her a quick wave on the way out.

Alice was indeed coming, with everything Amanda needed for a hot bath. She even helped Amanda wash her hair—once Amanda grew accustomed to the fact that Alice was going to be in attendance no matter what. Alice reported firmly that Captain Howe had said she was to be taken care of, and that was that.

But, Amanda had to admit, it was wonderful to be clean again, albeit somewhat publicly. Finally left alone, she sat in front of the fire to eat her supper and to dry her hair. The food Alice brought on a silver tray was incredible: cold ham, cheese, cooked apples, bread and butter and strawberry jam. And a real pot of China tea with all the cream and sugar Amanda wanted. She ate heartily, trying not to think of Verillia and the kind of meal she must be having tonight.

She could hear laughter and music downstairs, Yankee songs mostly—"The Battle Cry of Freedom" and "The Faded Coat of Blue." A celebration of their soldier's return. She wondered if John Howe, a week out of the prison pen, was singing with them. She couldn't imagine that he was; he'd seemed too tired and too sad for singing.

She gave another heavy sigh. She was so lonesome up here, fed and washed though she might be.

When her hair was dry enough, she climbed into the turned-down bed, stretching out between the crisp lavender-scented sheets, thinking that she'd never fall asleep in this strange house for all her notions of exhaustion earlier. Her body was weary, but her mind labored on, worrying the problem for which there was no solution the way a hunting dog worried after some quarry that had disappeared into a hole.

John David Howe.

She had no difficulty remembering *his* name. She had lost everything because of him. Her family. Her honor. She had no home and no prospect of one, and yet she had put her trust completely in him simply because he'd asked her to— when she knew better than to trust *any* man. A woman's trust became a shackle, an embarrassing encumbrance a man had to be rid of at the earliest possible moment, because it demanded honorable behavior. John himself had taught her not to stand up in a cross fire, but she'd certainly let him place her firmly in the no-man's-land between him and his family.

Mother says she won't have it, the boy Harry had said, and Amanda didn't blame her. What mother would want her son to drag home penniless, misbegotten contraband?

She closed her eyes tightly and prayed for sleep to come. She did trust John Howe, God help her; she had to, at least for now. And she was very much afraid she'd let him know it. She was aware, too, that for the first time since she was twelve years old, her every waking thought had nothing to do with Thayer Giffen.

Chapter Seven

She stood alone in the darkness along the railroad tracks in the wilderness of Virginia. She was lost and cold. The train was where it was supposed to be, but it was completely abandoned. She was afraid in this place and yet she didn't dare leave it... but someone was calling her, someone out in the mists where she was afraid to go. She could hear the voice, over and over—

"Amanda!"

She jolted awake, the sound of her name echoing in her head. She was completely disoriented by her surroundings and by that agonized cry.

"Amanda!"

She abruptly sat up in the huge, green silk canopy bed, realizing where she was and that the voice was here, now, and coming from somewhere downstairs.

She slid out of bed. She had no slippers, and she couldn't find her shoes or clothes. She reached for the too-big, dark blue wool quilted wrapper Alice had left for her and tip-toed barefoot into the corridor. She saw no one about, but she could hear an undertone of voices coming from downstairs. Not music and laughter as before, but hushed voices that reminded her of the conversations of the people who had come to call after her mother had died.

She stopped at the head of the staircase and leaned over the banister as far as she dared, but she couldn't see anything.

Something crashed loudly and broke behind the double doors where the senators' wives had been.

"Amanda!" John yelled again, his voice coming from inside that room. She could hear him quite plainly. "You people don't believe me—then you listen to someone who can tell you! Smith! Get her down here!"

She stood there in a panic, not knowing what to do. She couldn't go downstairs dressed like this!

"Amanda!"

She stood for a moment longer, then grabbed up the long tail of the dressing gown and hurried down the stairs. She moved quickly across the entry hall to the double doors. One door was slightly ajar. She could see John through the narrow opening. He was standing, holding on to a long mahogany table for support. Two men approached him from either side, trying to take his arms, but he shoved them away, nearly falling.

"What do you know about it?" he cried. "Nothing! You people know nothing! There is no war *here!* I won't be shuffled off like some mad relation because I tell you the truth...."

Amanda slipped into the room, ignoring the people nearest the door, who turned and stared. She worked her way through them, pushing when she had to get past.

Mrs. Howe was near tears, trying to make him hush, whispering urgently to him, pulling at his sleeve to get him to let the men help him leave. She had wanted John to let everyone see how he had suffered, and clearly she had gotten more than she bargained for.

"Amanda," John said again, but he was no longer yelling. Now, he didn't have the strength for it.

"I'm here, John Howe," Amanda said, stepping forward. He reached out toward her, nearly falling. His hands were trembling. He was completely exhausted, both physically and emotionally. She thought perhaps he'd been drinking as well.

"Look at this!" he said, gesturing wildly at the silver platters laden with breads and fruit and roasted meat Mrs. Howe had arranged for her guests. "I went hungry all the time in that place! Tell them, Amanda! Tell them what it's like to go hungry!"

Amanda caught his hand; she had to make him stop this. "John," she said, reaching up to touch his face. "Don't. Don't—they don't know. How can they when they live like this? You can't explain it to them."

He looked at her, and he suddenly smiled. "How are you fixed for pockets, Amanda? Have I made a bummer out of you? Shall we put a little away for hard times—" His voice broke and the smile left him. He struggled hard for control. "Ah, God, look at me. I'm going to cry. The Howes never cry, did you know that? Never! It's just not *done!*" He glared at the guests, who stood in silence around the room, then suddenly bowed his head as great sobs racked his body.

"John," Amanda whispered, putting both arms around his shoulders. Tears streamed down his face. He tried to say something, but couldn't manage it, shaking his head in despair.

"Come with me," she said, still whispering, trying to support him enough to lead him out. His mother came forward to take his other arm.

"No," he said, holding her off. "You have—guests, Mother. Give them my—apologies. Say I had—too much— brandy. Say—whatever you like. Amanda will take care of me."

"I expect your father home any minute," Mrs. Howe said urgently, as if that would make a difference. "John, you've imposed on this young woman quite enough—"

"I said she'll help me!"

"I swear you never change!"

"No—Mother," he managed with great effort. "I never do. Let me lean on you," he said to Amanda. "Hurry."

They left his mother standing. Amanda could feel how badly he was shaking. She tried to hurry, but he was leaning on her too heavily for speed. She tried not to look at any of Mrs. Howe's guests. For herself, she didn't care what they thought; she kept going as best she could. It wasn't the first time she'd had to drag him around like this. No one else tried to interfere, and she struggled hard to get John across the entry hall and to the stairs.

"Do you need to rest?" she asked halfway up the staircase. He shook his head and renewed his effort to get to the second floor.

"That way," he said when they finally reached the top step. She took him toward the door he wanted, but the doorknob was more ornate than functional and she had to fumble at it for a moment to get it open.

"Shut the door. Lock it," he said as they went inside.

"There's no key."

He swore under his breath, and she led him to a leather chair by the fireplace. He sat down heavily, leaning back with his hand over his eyes. She couldn't tell if he were crying again or not.

She moved to punch up the fire, adding more coal until she had it burning brightly. This room was definitely masculine. There was a chess table and bookshelves filled with books. The large bed was made of carved and turned wood and had no canopy or ruffles, and there were no skirts on any of the tables. The walls were paneled in dark wood, and there were a few brass instruments sitting about—ships' in-

struments, she thought. Had John once been interested in
ships and sailing the high seas?

"I'm so tired," he said, and she knelt in front of him to
take off his boots.

"You'll be all right, John Howe," she said with a good
deal more assurance than she felt. "But you have to sleep.
The longer the better."

"I can't—the dreams—or is it real? I can't tell anymore—what in the name of God are you wearing?" he
abruptly asked.

She looked down at the wrapper. At first glance, it looked
more as if it were wearing her. "Beggars can't be choosers.
You should know that. And you've got your nerve men-
tioning it with what you have on. Does your mother know
you're Confederate under your farmer clothes?"

She had his boots off, and he managed a sad smile.

"She can only take so much."

"Yes, I can imagine."

He closed his eyes. "I need laudanum—"

"No!" Amanda said, taking him by both hands to make
him look at her. "Please, John. Don't do that. Don't take
laudanum."

"I need to sleep—"

"My mother was addicted to laudanum, John. Verillia—
Verillia says the mind has to know it is suffering and get used
to it. If it doesn't, it will try to hide in the opium forever. It's
not very pleasant, the craving for laudanum. If I had
Verillia's herb boxes I could make you something that
would—"

"You think my mind is . . . suffering?" he interrupted.

She looked into his eyes. "I know it is."

He was about to say something else, but there was a quiet
knock and Smith came into the room.

"Your father asks if you will see him, sir."

John took a long time to answer; Amanda could feel him bracing himself to deal with his father's visit. "Tell him to come in," he said finally.

Amanda stood up from her kneeling position as Mr. Howe entered. He was tall, like John, but there the resemblance stopped. He gave her only the briefest of glances, and she turned to leave.

"Where are you going!" John said sharply, his voice commanding in a way she hadn't heard since the night they met.

"I'll leave you with your father—"

"You'll leave when I say you do!"

"John, I'm sure the girl is tired," Mr. Howe said.

"The *girl*," John said sarcastically, "is determined to drive me crazy. I swear you'll do it, too! You are always trying to get away from me! You think I don't know that! I get no—rest—from it. I'm going to look around again and you'll be gone, won't you!"

"I won't argue with you when you're like this, John Howe."

"Like this? What is *like this*? You heard me, damn it! You are not to go anywhere!" He was trying to stand up, and both Smith and his father were trying to keep him down.

"All right!" she said to pacify him. "Whatever you say."

"Liar!" he cried, and she thought he was about to cry again.

"I don't lie, John Howe." She came closer to him. She wasn't afraid of him. She had seen him worse than this. "You need to rest."

"Is that going to ease my suffering mind?"

"More than what you're doing now, I think."

"Your bath is waiting, sir," Smith said quietly. "Perhaps you would find that helpful."

"Helpful? If not helpful to me, then to the rest of the household, I suppose. I smell like a bloody mule." He began unbuttoning the shirt he had on over the short Confederate cavalry jacket. "Want to help me with my bath, Amanda?"

"John!" his father said sharply, glancing at Amanda. "I don't care where you've been, I won't have this. There is no need to be so vulgar. You will apologize for that remark and for your swearing."

"Amanda has heard worse from me."

"And that is not to your credit or to mine."

John looked at her, then gave a sharp sigh. "I... apologize, Miss Douglas. My father is quite right. I am not fit for decent society."

Smith stood waiting to take his arm.

"Smith," John said, letting the man help him. "Good old Smith. This is like old times, isn't it? Like when I used to come home in my cups and you used to sneak me by the family."

"Not precisely the same," Smith said kindly. "We are all glad to have you home."

"Are you? I always thought I was a damned lot of trouble."

"Not at all, sir. You were merely high-spirited."

"Father," John said when he reached the dressing room door, "I won't be long. Don't let her leave. I want her here when I come back."

"I'm not going anywhere, John," Amanda insisted.

He stared at her across the room for a moment before he went into the dressing room. Even with Smith's help, it was all he could do to stand.

Amanda sat down in relief in the nearest chair. She could worry herself sick about him—he could *know* she was worried—and he still had nothing to offer her but obnoxious behavior.

A clock ticked quietly on the mantel; she could hear muffled voices and washing noises from the dressing room. She glanced up to find Mr. Howe watching her.

"I should go speak to my wife," he said, "but I'm rather... afraid to leave. John is so excitable."

She nodded and looked away from him into the fire. She didn't want John's father to feel that he had to make conversation. *She* certainly didn't require it, and she had no explanations she wanted to give as to how she happened to get here. She wondered how much information he'd gotten from Mrs. Howe before he came upstairs.

"Have you known my son long?" he asked.

She looked up at him to answer. "No."

He seemed waiting for her to continue, but she had nothing else to say. What could she tell him? They'd been on the run for nearly a week? She'd slept with John Howe in a hotel bed and in a cotton pile and now she was as bad as he, because she could hardly bear to have him out of her sight either?

"Do you know I wouldn't have recognized him if I'd met him on the street?" Mr. Howe said. "My own son."

"He's been ill. He needs something to eat," she offered.

Mr. Howe purposefully crossed the room to pull the bell rope, as if he were grateful to have something to do.

"What would you suggest?" he asked, and she looked at him in surprise. She simply was not used to being given all these choices about food.

"Some meat broth? Toasted bread?" she said after a moment.

Alice came quickly in response to the bell, and Mr. Howe repeated Amanda's suggestions.

"I understand he participated in too many toasts to the Union downstairs," Mr. Howe said when Alice had gone. He walked closer to the dressing room door and listened. "I don't—"

The door suddenly opened, and John came back into the room. His hair was wet, and he was wearing a nightshirt. Smith hurried to place a flannel blanket around him as he walked, as if John had been too impatient to wait for it before. He let Smith help him to bed, motioning all the while for Amanda to come closer.

She didn't. Both Smith and Mr. Howe were in the room, and after that invitation to help him with his bath, she was afraid that he'd want her to lie down with him and keep him warm the way he had in that terrible hotel.

"Get that chair for her, Smith. Sit down, Amanda. Talk to me."

She looked at him warily, trying to decide which would be worse—to defy him and send him into another rage or to make herself handy for more of his offensive remarks.

"Please," he said quietly, and she finally sat down. Immediately he made her get up and move the chair closer, as close to the bed as she could get. "Talk to me," he said again.

She pulled her bare feet up into the chair and covered them with the bottom of the borrowed wrapper. "You talk, John," she said, because she thought he was beyond listening and because she had nothing she wanted to say. "My experiences are of no significance compared to yours."

He was staring at her so intently, his sad eyes traveling over her face. She could remember how miserable he'd seemed the night they met. But he was home and safe now. Why was the misery still there?

What is it? she thought. *Why aren't you glad to be home?*

He looked away and closed his eyes. "What is it the Bible says?"

"About…what?" she asked cautiously, worried now that he'd bring up that passage in Deuteronomy the reverend had made her read.

He glanced at her. "It says, 'Thou shalt not kill.' It doesn't say 'except in time of war,' does it?"

He wasn't making any sense to her, and she was too tired to try to humor him. "Oh, please, John. When I asked you to talk, I didn't mean I wanted to hear your religious philosophy."

"I have no religious philosophy. No religion. No honor. I lost honor somewhere. *You* know that. And Max. Poor old bastard, Max. *He's* none the better for knowing me." He looked at his father. "You think I'm his friend, don't you, Father? Oh, I'm not his friend—I'm a spineless son of a bitch—"

"John," Mr. Howe protested, coming to sit down on the side of the bed.

"His mother is downstairs, did you know that? She kept asking me and asking me, 'Where's Max? Why isn't he with you?' I'm the one who killed him, Father."

"Son, you don't mean that—"

"I mean it!"

Alice came in with the broth and the toasted bread. Amanda took the cup from her and offered him a sip, but he turned his head away. "Please, John. You need it."

Smith brought more pillows so he could sit up. Reluctantly, he took a few swallows and a few bites of the bread she pressed on him.

"Max had the bloody flux," he said abruptly, pushing the cup of broth away, the words tumbling out as if he couldn't stop himself. "He was in some kind of secret group—only six men. They were afraid to have any more know what they were doing after that godforsaken uprising in November— because of the informers. They dug a tunnel, but he was too weak to get out when the tunnel was done—too sick. He begged me. He said if I'd get him out, he'd show me where it was. He cried like a baby and I . . . promised him. I promised. My word of honor.

"But I couldn't carry him. He was my friend, and I lied to him to get the information. I couldn't carry him and I knew it when I made the promise. They'd get us both, don't you see?" He suddenly leaned forward as if he were about to get out of bed, but his father placed both hands on his shoulders.

"Son, we don't have to talk about this now—"

John clutched his father's shirtfront, his fingers making scratching noises on the starched material. But he looked at Amanda, his eyes pleading. "Don't you see? Tell me!"

"John Howe, you—"

"Tell me!" he cried.

"I...see that you had no choice," she said, choosing her words carefully. "And I see that if you had it to do all over again, you'd do the same. I *know* you had no choice, John Howe. I was with you."

But he wasn't satisfied. "Ah, God! I'm not insane, am I? I keep thinking about him—dreaming about him. He must have been terrified when he knew I'd gone without him. I should have killed him! Better that than leaving him to die in that *place!*"

"Lie down, son," Mr. Howe said, trying to make him lie back.

"You don't know what it's like! Nobody here knows! You want me to tell you? There was a red-haired boy, Father. He stood on the dead line for a day. A whole damn day! Nobody would go get him. *I* didn't go. I should have—just the way I should have taken Max. I should have dragged him! I should have. There was a place in the trees the sun would shine through just as it went down. The boy waited until the sun was there, in that break in the tress, until he was in a burst of sunlight—and then he stepped over the line. He knew the Rebs would shoot him for it. He did it anyway. He was a handsome boy, Father—no, he was pretty. Pretty like a girl. He'd been raped—"

"John, don't!"

"No, I want you to know this so you'll see why those people downstairs can't begin to understand. I didn't help him. I didn't help anybody! I just kept that song in my head—I listened to it in my head so I wouldn't see anything, anybody. You know the song, Amanda. Ah, God, I left Maxwell in that!" He was crying again. "I'm so... cold!"

He was shivering. Smith was there immediately with the blanket he had warming by the fire. John lay back on the pillows as Smith and Mr. Howe put it over him.

"Amanda," John said, the tears running out of the corners of his eyes.

"What?" she whispered, because she didn't trust her voice. "I'm here." She leaned forward and took his hand, not knowing if he would allow it or not. His fingers closed tightly around hers, hurting.

His mouth trembled. "I should be ashamed for you to see me like this, but I—"

He couldn't say anything more; he could feel the tears, hot and wet, running down into his ears. He forced himself to stay quiet for as long as he could, his hand still clutching hers. But then he suddenly let go of her hand and took a deep, wavering breath.

Ah, God, I can't stand this!

He closed his eyes tightly, afraid he would say it out loud. Max Woodard was with him all the time. Asleep. Awake. It didn't matter. And he deserved the anguish. He deserved the nightmares and always thinking he'd open his eyes in the dark and see Max Woodard's face.

I left him to die! Why didn't they understand? There was no excuse for what he'd done. He deliberately left Max Woodard to die!

His throat ached and he could feel the tears welling again. He had to get himself together; he had to stop crying—he hadn't cried since he was sixteen, even in the worst of battles when his comrades were dying around him, even in the prison he hadn't cried. He had to be strong. He was a Howe.

Go on! You can do it!

He licked his lips and stared at the ceiling.

Amanda!

He wanted to take her hand again. He wanted her to put her arms around him. He wanted her to lie down beside him and hold him until he went to sleep. No. He didn't want to sleep. He wanted to uncover her soft body and touch her breasts. He wanted to lie belly to belly with her. He wanted to feel her pressed against him. He wanted her to say his name while he lost himself inside her.

Innocent, he thought. So innocent. She was as innocent as he was guilty. She didn't even *know* what she could do for him, what pleasure she could give him, what . . . oblivion.

I need you.

He needed her to *be* with him. He needed her to give him comfort, to give him ease, if only for a little while. Ah, God, he had sunk low. Was she a child? Sometimes he thought not. Sometimes he thought she looked at him the way a woman should look at a man. Now he could feel her quietly waiting. Why was she still here? Why hadn't she run from the room? She had seen him at his worst now, by God.

He took another deep breath, but he looked at no one. He was afraid of what he would see in their eyes. "I'm—forgive my outburst, Father. Please. Go back to your guests. Tell my mother I'm quite—all right now."

"John, I think—"

"Please. I'm sure it was the brandy. I've made as big a fool of myself as I'm going to. I don't want Mother to worry that it's worse than it is."

He sounded very much in control now, even to himself, but his father hesitated.

"I don't want to go if you need . . . anything."

"I need nothing," John said. "I'll send for you if I do."

"Yes. Do that—send for me." He stood for a moment, then quietly left the room.

"Smith," John said, his voice still firm. "You have duties downstairs."

"Are you certain there is nothing you need, sir? Cook has asked me to say that if you want anything from the kitchen at any hour, you have only to—"

"No. Nothing now. If you would thank Cook for me."

"Yes, sir."

"Good night, Smith."

"Good night, sir."

Amanda sat quietly by the bed. John's eyes were closed. She could see no outward indication of his inner turmoil—until another tear slid down his cheek, then another. She didn't know what to say to him. She swallowed again and again to keep from crying with him.

He opened his eyes, but he still didn't look at her. "You can go, too. The freak show is over."

Amanda opened her mouth to protest. He'd only just insisted—and none too graciously—that she stay.

"Go on!" he said sharply. "Go...wherever you were before the entertainment started!"

"North Carolina?" she said sarcastically, wounded by his abrupt dismissal. Some part of her understood that he wanted to fight his demons alone now, but her feelings were hurt anyway. She stood and would have shoved the chair aside, but he reached out and pulled her around to him, gripping her by both arms, his face inches from hers.

"I don't want you feeling sorry for me!"

"And how am I supposed to manage that! Look at you! Look at you, John Howe," she said more gently, her eyes searching his. The anger she saw in them slid away, leaving the tortured, haunted look she remembered from the first night they'd met.

"My God, what am I going to do with you?" he said, his arms sliding around her, holding her tight. "You won't go and you won't stay. We're always at odds, aren't we?"

"Always," she said, clinging to him, trying not to cry because he hated bawling women. The truth was she felt sorry for them both. She closed her eyes tightly against the rush of feeling. She wanted never to let him go. She loved the feel and the smell of him. She loved *him*, and if there was anyone who should be pitied at this moment, it was she.

There was a sharp, authoritative rap at the door, and she moved away from him. The door opened without his leave, and Mrs. Howe came in.

"John, I'm glad you have yourself in hand now," she said, but she was looking at Amanda, her eyes sharp and searching.

For what? Amanda wondered. For some more covert sign of misbehavior on her part? The Rebel baggage was alone in Captain Howe's bedroom, and both of them were in their nightclothes. That should be misbehavior enough to satisfy Mrs. Howe without closer inspection. It had certainly taken less for condemnation from the reverend.

Amanda glanced at John. "Good night, John Howe."

"Amanda—"

"John, I must speak to you," Mrs. Howe interrupted, and she said it as if she expected her wishes to take precedence over whatever other concerns he might have. "It's Harry," she added when he was about to protest.

"What's wrong with him?" John asked immediately.

"You have to speak to him. He's terribly upset," Amanda heard Mrs. Howe say as she quietly slipped out the door. "He thinks you've died."

She closed the door behind her. She felt dazed, exhausted. Patriotic music once again drifted up from downstairs; the scene John had made must have been adequately explained. She looked down the hallway to get her bear-ngs, her attention immediately taken by a rustling noise to her left. Harry stood in the dimmest part of the hallway, close to the wall, as if he didn't want to be seen. He hurried toward her, his small face anxious and worried.

"Is John dead?" he asked abruptly, his voice shaky and strained. "I've been waiting and waiting. No one came to tell me."

"Harry, no," Amanda said quietly, bending down so he could hear. "John isn't dead. He's very tired. That's all."

"Are you sure, Amanda? Are you sure? William Monihan's brother died—he came home from the war and then he got all wild and everything and he *died!*" He sniffed loudly.

"I'm sure. John is—"

"Harry!" Mrs. Howe said sharply behind them. "Please don't bother Miss Douglas. Your brother wants to see you now. He's very tired, so try to behave."

"I will, Mother!" he said, flashing Amanda a quick grin of relief as he ran toward the bedroom door.

"*Walk*, Harry! How many times must you be told? No running indoors!"

"Yes, Mother," he said dutifully, but he was already inside. And he didn't stop running—until he had flung himself into John Howe's arms.

"Miss Douglas, can you find your way?" Mrs. Howe asked Amanda, stepping between her and the open door.

"Yes, I—"

"Good. Then, good night." She turned abruptly and closed the door.

Chapter Eight

Amanda lay quietly in the darkness, once again listening to the noises of the house, doors opening and closing, muffled voices and music from downstairs. Whatever else she might not understand about this place, she understood Mrs. Howe. Hers was a difficult position, but her message was quite clear. *Stay away from my sons—both of them.* It must not be easy for a woman like Mrs. Howe to be indebted to someone she considered a threat to her son's political career, and Amanda wanted desperately to be able to put the woman's mind at ease, but there was nothing she could say. There was only the something she could *do* to alleviate Mrs. Howe's worries—leave the house as soon as possible and never see John Howe again.

It took her a long time to fall asleep, and it seemed as if she'd only closed her eyes. She could smell something was burning. Cigar smoke, she thought groggily. She abruptly raised her head. John Howe was up and dressed and sitting by the window on the other side of the room, one booted leg propped up on the footstool. It was barely daylight, and he sat staring at whatever might be visible through the frosty glass and calmly smoking a cigar.

"What are you doing here!" she whispered, pulling the cover up to her chin, half expecting Mrs. Howe to be hot on his heels and bursting into the room after him at any moment. She glanced at the mantel clock. It was a quarter past seven. She'd been asleep all of three hours.

"Waiting for you to wake up," he said with maddening logic. He blew another cloud of cigar smoke into the air.

"Why?" she asked pointedly, keeping an eye on the door.

He looked at her then. "I couldn't sleep."

He certainly wasn't lying about that, she thought. He looked terrible. "John Howe—"

"Get dressed. We'll go down to the kitchen and have some breakfast."

She looked around the room. Her clothes were still missing. "I can't."

"Why not?"

"I don't have anything to get dressed *in*. And I've done enough parading in public in my nightclothes."

"Yes," John said, smiling in spite of his melancholy mood. His mother had been furious, not so much at Amanda, but at him—because he hadn't been appalled enough at the "Douglas girl's brazenness." The truth was he hadn't been appalled at all. Quite the contrary. No woman had ever paid him such a compliment. He'd been desperately in need of her and she'd come to him, barefoot and in her nightgown, decorum and the prestigious onlookers be damned. "*That* is going to be a popular topic in Washington for quite some time."

"Really," Amanda said lightly, because she recognized immediately that he was trying to annoy her. Again.

"Really," he assured her, and she could feel him trying to assess whether or not he'd been successful.

"What do *I* care what a bunch of Yankee senators and their wives think?" she said. She cared a great deal what his mother thought, but she didn't say so. Mrs. Howe was of the opinion that John had ruined his political career *before* Amanda appeared shoeless in the drawing room. She truly didn't want to ruin anything for him, but she didn't say that, either.

"We'd better get you dressed," he said abruptly, getting up and crossing to pull the bell rope.

"Don't pull that!" she cried, but he pulled it anyway.

"Why not?"

"Alice will come in here!"

"I know that, Amanda. That's what the thing's for."

"*You're* here," she said, every bit as undone now as he'd wanted her to be. But, clearly, her meaning escaped him.

"She isn't going to mind."

Your mother will, she almost said. Word would surely get to Mrs. Howe; Amanda didn't want to offend her any more than she already had. And he was *not* helping.

"John Howe, has it ever occurred to you that *I* might like to sleep?"

"Certainly. I didn't wake you up, if you recall. You did that by yourself. So as long as you *are* awake, you might as well— Come in!" he yelled at the soft knock at the door, and Amanda groaned.

"Alice!" John said cheerfully. "Can you find Miss Douglas something to wear?"

"Wear, sir?" Alice said blankly, her eyes cutting to where Amanda still cowered behind the covers on the big green-canopied bed.

"She seems to have lost her clothes."

"Oh, no, sir. They were taken to be washed—but they couldn't be done yet— Oh, I see what you mean, sir!" Alice thought for a moment. "Well, there are the maids' uniforms in the locked cupboard in servants' hall downstairs."

"Excellent! Are there underclothes as well?"

"Yes, sir," Alice said, blushing hotly. "Madam doesn't want us ragged anywhere, sir."

"Good. Then bring Miss Douglas everything but the apron and the cap, will you? As fast as you can."

"Oh, yes, sir...but Mr. Smith has the key—"

"Just tell him what you want. Tell him I said so. Go on now. Quickly!"

Alice walked a few steps toward the door. "Should I say 'underclothes' to Mr. Smith?" she asked, blushing still.

"You can use whatever word you like, Alice," John said, trying not to smile. "Just bring what Miss Douglas needs. Everything you can find."

But the clothes were brought by Mr. Smith himself—with Amanda still cowering. All she needed was Mrs. Howe to find *two* men in her room. Smith arrived clearly believing some grave mistake had been made, but John reassured him, taking the garments out of his hands. And John had no reticence whatsoever about looking through the stack to see what Smith had brought.

"Very appropriate color for a Reb," he said, holding up the plain, gray poplin dress. He inspected a petticoat and a pair of drawers. "What happened to Alice?" he asked Smith.

"There are a number of unexpected guests for breakfast in the dining room this morning, sir," Smith said gravely. "She is assisting Cook."

"Well, don't include us. Tell Cook we'll be coming down to the kitchen to eat as soon as Miss Douglas is ready. I don't want to get tangled up with any more visitors."

"To the kitchen," Smith repeated, as if he couldn't possibly have heard correctly.

"Yes, Smith, the kitchen. You remember. Where I used to eat all the time when I was Harry's age—when I could get away with it. I'm hungry this morning, and I don't want to wait. My tolerance for overfed civilians is practically nil, and I most certainly don't want to have a repeat of last night."

"Yes, sir," Smith said. He glanced at Amanda. "Cook will be delighted."

"Will she?" Amanda asked from the safety of the bed covers as soon as Smith left.

"Will she what?" John said, looking through the stack of clothes again. Amanda found it most disconcerting that he should know whether or not everything a woman needed in the way of undergarments was there in the stack, though she had a good idea of where and how he might have learned. That was disconcerting as well. That and the pang of jealousy she couldn't help but feel at the other women he'd known. She remembered only too well his assessment of *her* appeal.

You are safe with me, he'd told her, and he apparently had meant it.

She watched him now. Perhaps she didn't want to be safe with him. Perhaps she—

"Will she what?" he asked again.

"Be delighted. He said that the same way he might have said she'd slit her wrists."

John looked up at her as if it had never occurred to him to wonder. "I...don't know. Do you need any help with these?"

Immediately indignant, Amanda pursed her lips to tell him what she thought of his offer, but for once he wasn't trying to insult or scandalize her. He was simply...asking.

"I can manage."

He smiled. "Then do so, Miss Douglas. I'll wait outside."

She did manage. Servants' clothes were clearly made for persons who had no one to help with laces or hooks or buttons. Both the corset and the dress fastened in the front. It was a long time since she'd been laced into a corset, and she had to loosen it almost immediately. In fact, nothing of the outfit was comfortable. Mrs. Howe might not want her staff in ragged undergarments, but she had no objections to how unyielding they were. The chemise, the drawers, the petticoats, were of the coarsest linen—warm, Amanda supposed, but as rough and chafing as burlap. Even the white cotton stockings felt as if they'd been heavily starched. Someone—Alice certainly—had included a hairnet, a snood made of yellow silk braid and chenille. Amanda smiled as she stuffed her hair into it. A dove-gray dress and a yellow snood. In this place it was a comfort to be wearing the Confederate colors.

She jumped nervously when someone knocked at the door—Alice instead of John Howe—bringing her shoes, cleaned and blackened now, and looking better than they had in years. Amanda hastily put them on, not missing Alice's scrutiny of the room.

"He's not in here, Alice," Amanda said bluntly.

"Miss?"

"Captain Howe. He said he'd wait outside. If he isn't there, I don't know where he is."

"Well, I'm sure he's not gone far, miss," Alice assured her on the way out.

Amanda stood staring at herself in the mirror. She was passable, but she would never make *Godey's Lady's Book*. She pinched her cheeks and bit her lips to give them some color, and John Howe nearly caught her doing it.

"Very... demure," he pronounced her, grasping her by the hand as if she were a little girl he had to take charge of and leading her out the door. She supposed that *demure* was a better adjective than some she'd heard him use in their short acquaintance, and she'd rather be holding his hand than not holding it, even if the act were so... neutral. To him. To her, the feel of his warm fingers was terribly unsatisfying. She wanted to fling herself on him and tell him how worried she was about him. He still wasn't sleeping and he was hiding his feelings again, pretending that the anguish he'd felt about leaving his friend Max was no longer there.

She kept looking up at him as they walked along the corridor.

"What's the matter?" he asked.

"Nothing."

"Then why are you looking at me?"

"I think you're in sore need of a barber," she answered. Not the truth, but not precisely a lie, either.

"Truthful to a fault, aren't you?"

"The truth is never a fault, John Howe," she said piously.

"Who in the world ever told you a ridiculous thing like that?"

"The reverend," she answered, and he laughed.

Cook was indeed delighted at John's arrival downstairs. She was a rotund, cheerful little woman of indeterminate age, who wept at the sight of him and hugged him to her big bosom until he pleaded for mercy. Then she laughed and swatted the air at him, and promised him not just a breakfast, but good, delicate food that would cause him no indigestion and would bring him back to his old self in no time.

"I'm so thankful you're home, sir," she kept saying.

"Well, here's the person to thank," John said, bringing Amanda forward.

"Yes, miss," Cook said when Amanda would have protested, taking her by the hand. "So we've heard belowstairs. And look at you both—half-starved you are. Well, I'll fix that, you can be sure."

She was as good as her word, pressing first soft-boiled eggs on them, and then something she called Boston Cream Toast. Both were delicious, and Amanda watched John carefully as he ate. He'd told the truth when he'd said he was hungry, and more important, he seemed to feel like eating.

"You're staring at me again," he said in the middle of the toast.

"Have you always been this conceited?" Amanda countered.

"Yes, miss, he has," Cook assured her, and they both laughed.

Amanda turned her attention to her surroundings. No wonder John had wanted to eat down here when he was a boy. This was the part of the house that was lived in. There were three large rooms. A sitting room with a settle and several rocking chairs and low stools and a warm fire. A dining hall with a table long enough for all the servants to eat at once and perhaps their guests, too. A huge kitchen with copper pots of every size imaginable hanging overhead and a bustle of activity as breakfast for the unexpected guests upstairs was being prepared—by women servants mostly, whose voices lifted now and again in snatches of songs and laughter. All three rooms were separated by glass-paned doors, which gave the place an open, airy feel in spite of the fact that this part of the house must be at least halfway below the street. Amanda sensed that the servants watched her through the glass as they passed to and fro, but when she looked up at them, she saw no reproach in their faces, merely curiosity about the girl Captain Howe had brought home.

She glanced at John again.

"You can stop worrying," he said quietly. "There isn't going to be a repeat of last night."

"I wasn't—"

"Yes, you were. And I don't blame you. I'm...all right." His eyes searched hers, as if he needed to see if she believed it, because if she did, then it just might be so.

Smith came into the room, carrying a small envelope on a silver tray. "This just came around for you, sir."

John frowned and took the envelope, carelessly tearing it open. His frown deepened as he read; it was all Amanda could do not to ask him why.

He looked up at her, his face grim.

"It's from Max Woodard's mother. She wants to see me."

Amanda waited anxiously in her room the rest of the morning, sitting in the same chair she'd found John in so she could watch out the window for his return. But her eyes ached from lack of sleep, and she kept dozing off. She was able to glean a few tidbits of information from Alice when she came to tidy the room—that Captain Howe had left to see Mrs. Woodard almost immediately, and that Mr. Beale, the family lawyer, was one of the unexpected breakfast guests, and that two other men had come with him, neither of whom Alice knew.

"Ruffians," she said, "from the looks of them."

Amanda doubted that Mrs. Howe would entertain ruffians in her dining room, but she knew from personal experience that sometimes Mrs. Howe had no choice.

"What about Max Woodard?" Amanda ventured to take advantage of Alice's somewhat talkative mood.

"What about him, miss?" she asked.

"He was a friend of Captain Howe's?"

"Oh, yes, miss. Since they was boys, I understand. They went to the same private schools—or they got throwed out of the same private schools is more the truth of it. Of course, Captain Howe was from Philadelphia and Mr. Max lived here in Washington, so it wasn't until the Howe family moved to Washington, too, that they really got to know each other. Hell-raisers, both of them," Alice said, lowering her voice and looking over her shoulder, "but different."

"Different?"

"Well, Mr. Max, he went at the gambling and the drinking and the fancy women—you know, like it was his life's calling. And Captain Howe—well, it was just something to pass the time, to my way of thinking, on account of he had too much money and nothing else to do with himself. But they were in each other's shadow all the time all right. Even went to war that way. Oh, miss, you should have seen them in their uniforms and carrying them lances. *So* handsome—like knights looking for a princess to rescue from a dragon. I was kind of surprised that the captain and Mr. Max stayed friends at all, after that thing with Mr. Max's sister.''

''What thing?''

''Oh, Lord, miss. I've let my mouth run away with me again. You won't tell Mr. Smith I said anything about that—please say you won't!''

Alice didn't wait long enough to extract a promise, all but bolting out of the room, and she didn't come back again.

Shortly before noon, Amanda ventured out into the corridor. She simply couldn't stand not knowing whether John had come back, and if she had to eavesdrop to find out, then she would. She encountered Mr. Smith almost immediately.

''May I help you, miss?'' he asked behind her in his same grave way, nearly startling her out of her wits. No wonder Alice looked over her shoulder all the time.

''I was just—that is, I was wondering—'' She sighed heavily. She couldn't bring herself to tell him that she was worried about John. John Howe's state of health or his whereabouts were none of her business.

They stared at each other, Mr. Smith *seeming* to wait patiently for her to reveal herself, whether he was or not.

''Captain Howe—'' she began.

''The captain has been back for some time, miss. I believe he is with his mother and father. Mrs. Howe has asked that they not be disturbed. For any reason,'' he added, Amanda supposed, in the event that she was completely dense.

"Thank you, Mr. Smith," she murmured. Of course John would want to be with his family. He'd only just escaped from a Confederate prison.

"Miss?" Mr. Smith said as she walked away. "Master Harry has made several inquiries about you this morning—something about looking your name up in his name book. Perhaps, if you have the time, you might go up to see him in the children's quarters."

"Yes, I'd like that very much," she answered quickly. "Would it be all right if I went now?"

She followed Smith down the corridor, glancing over the banister as they passed the second floor landing. A portly man in an overdone Yankee officer's uniform paced impatiently in the entry hall.

"This way, miss," Smith said when she would have lingered. Surely John wasn't in some kind of trouble with the military authorities, after all. She had thought all that had been settled at that place, Forrest Hall.

"Miss," he said again, and she followed him to a smaller staircase that led up to the third floor. Smith was the consummate servant, Amanda thought as she climbed the stairs behind him. If Mrs. Howe had said she was not to be disturbed, then he would see to it that the person most apt to disturb her was well occupied.

"Miss Douglas," he announced to Harry before he ushered her in.

"Amanda!" Harry cried, clearly delighted. "You came to find out about your name!"

"Yes," she said, smiling at him as he took her by the hand. He pulled out a chair for her at a large round table in the middle of the room. The room was big enough to be a combination classroom, library and nursery. There was a very large fan window in one wall and shelves around the other three, two of them containing numerous books and the third a collection of toys suitable for boys of various ages. The sun shone in brightly through the fan window, and where the sunlight hit the thickly carpeted floor, Harry had been playing with an array of small blue and gray lead soldiers.

"Shall I tell Cook there will be a meal tray for two, Master Harry?" Smith asked kindly. There was nothing condescending about the question, and the boy swelled with pride.

"Can you stay, Amanda?" he asked earnestly.

"I would be delighted."

"Yes, please, Smith," Harry advised him. "Two of everything."

When Smith had gone, Harry wanted Amanda to see everything, and he was an eager guide through his world of books and pictures and toys.

"There it is," he said, showing her *Amanda* in his special name book. "'Worthy to be loved,' it says." He looked up at her with John's eyes. "I believe you are very well named."

He showed her his collections of string and marbles, and which school desk was his. At his invitation, she sat down in it, seeing immediately the initials carved in the top near the inkwell. JDH. She ran her fingers over the letters and tried to imagine John as a boy, as anything but the saddened man he was now.

Harry took down a carved wooden box from one of the shelves and brought it to her, carefully removing a small key on a piece of red ribbon from his pocket and unlocking it.

"This is my new, special box," he said, lifting the lid. "I only keep my important things in here. See here? No one else has a picture like this—it was taken especially for me—John said he'd rather scare the Rebels than shoot them." He handed her a *carte de visite* of a stern-looking John in Yankee military garb with a Colt revolver in each hand. She smiled at his posturing, imagining him working hard to affect a pose that would impress his little brother—and the Rebels.

There were other *cartes de visite* in the box: military friends of John's, cavalrymen all, whose names Harry told her one after the other and whether they'd been killed and in which battle. What a terrible world it was, she thought, when little boys needed to commit things like that to memory. There was one photograph of Max Woodard. He was indeed handsome in his military dress, and he had his likeness taken with not one but two women.

"This is Kate," Harry said of the beautifully dressed one on the left.

"Kate?"

"Kate Woodard," he said, as if he were surprised she didn't know. "She brought me this box with the key and everything. It came all the way from Paris. It's very special—because *I'm* special, she said. She said I was to keep my very best things in it. She's beautiful, don't you think? Everyone calls her the Belle of Washington." He looked up at Amanda. "But I don't know what that means. She's a person, not a *bell.*"

"Well, there are bells and there are belles," Amanda said. She explained the difference, all the while staring at Kate Woodard's face. Kate looked directly into the camera, elegant, self-assured and yes, quite beautiful.

Aura Lee, Amanda thought. *Maid of golden hair.*

How drab she had always felt in the company of girls like Kate Woodard, rich girls with fathers who adored them. How drab she felt just looking at her photograph now.

She realized that Kate must be the girl Alice had mentioned, the one who had nearly cost John his friendship with Max Woodard. She wanted desperately to ask Harry about it, but she didn't. She wasn't above prying information out of Alice, but Harry was a child, and a very endearing one at that.

DOUBLE YOUR ACTION PLAY...

"ROLL A DOUBLE!"

Peel off label & place inside

**CLAIM UP TO 4 BOOKS
PLUS A LOVELY
"KEY TO YOUR HEART"
PENDANT NECKLACE**

ABSOLUTELY FREE!

SEE INSIDE..

NO RISK, NO OBLIGATION TO BUY…NOW OR EVER!

GUARANTEED

PLAY "ROLL A DOUBLE" AND GET AS MANY AS FIVE GIFTS!

HERE'S HOW TO PLAY:

1. Peel off label from front cover. Place it in space provided at right. With a coin, carefully scratch off the silver dice. This makes you eligible to receive two or more free books, and possibly another gift, depending on what is revealed beneath the scratch-off area.

2. You'll receive brand-new Harlequin Historical™ novels. When you return this card, we'll rush you the books and gift you qualify for ABSOLUTELY FREE!

3. Then, if we don't hear from you, every month, we'll send you 4 additional novels to read and enjoy. You can return them and owe nothing, but if you decide to keep them, you'll pay only $3.19 per book—a saving of 80¢ each off the cover price.

4. When you subscribe to the Harlequin Reader Service®, you'll also get our newsletter, as well as additional free gifts from time to time.

5. You must be completely satisfied. You may cancel at any time simply by sending us a note or a shipping statement marked ''cancel'' or by returning any shipment to us at our expense.

The Austrian crystal sparkles like a diamond! And it's carefully set in a romantic "Key to Your Heart" pendant on a generous 18″ chain. The entire necklace is yours free as added thanks for giving our Reader Service a try!

"ROLL A DOUBLE!"

PLACE LABEL HERE

SCRATCH HERE

SEE CLAIM CHART BELOW

247 CIH AEK9
(U-H-H-04/92)

YES! I have placed my label from the front cover into the space provided above and scratched off the silver dice. Please rush me the free books and gift that I am entitled to. I understand that I am under no obligation to purchase any books, as explained on the opposite page.

NAME _____

ADDRESS _____ APT. _____

CITY _____ STATE _____ ZIP CODE _____

CLAIM CHART

🎲 🎲	**4 FREE BOOKS PLUS FREE "KEY TO YOUR HEART" NECKLACE**
🎲 🎲	**3 FREE BOOKS**
🎲 🎲	**2 FREE BOOKS**

CLAIM NO.37-829

HARLEQUIN "NO RISK" GUARANTEE

- You're not required to buy a single book—ever!
- You must be completely satisfied or you may cancel at any time simply by sending us a note or shipping statement marked "cancel" or by returning any shipment to us at our cost. Either way, you will receive no more books; you'll have no obligation to buy.
- The free books and gift you claimed on this "Roll A Double" offer remain yours to keep no matter what you decide.

If offer card is missing, please write to: Harlequin Reader Service, 3010 Walden Ave., P.O. Box 1867, Buffalo, NY 14269-1867

Smith intruded with the "tray for two" before Harry's guided tour could continue. Again, the food was amazing to Amanda—clear soup, numerous small pieces of roasted chicken, buttered potatoes, bread and more strawberry jam, slices of raw apple and milk. They moved the table into the patch of sunlight where it was warmer, Harry chatting constantly while they ate, as if his having someone to talk to was a rare occasion for him and he intended to make the most of it. He didn't mention John. Neither of them did. Seemingly, they couldn't voice even the mildest of comments regarding the one person they worried about most.

When the tray had been taken away, Amanda read Harry the program for the "Union Minstrel's Show" in the *New York Times*. The newspaper was nearly three years old, but he didn't seem to mind.

"Comic song," she read while he sprawled on the floor with his soldiers.

"What comic song?"

"It doesn't say," she said, moving down onto the floor with him. "It just says Gideon's Band will do it—and then there's the Essence of Old Virginia."

"What is that?"

"That's the other—"

She looked up at a noise in the doorway. John stood there watching.

Oh, she thought immediately. How tired he looked. And how she wished she'd stayed sitting demurely in a chair instead of sprawling on the floor with Harry like the child John already thought she was.

"So this is where everybody got to," he said. He smiled, but the smile was forced and strained. He crossed the room and sat down on the floor with them.

"I had Smith bring up a tray for *two,*" Harry advised him mischievously.

"What!" John said with mock indignation. "Dining with *my* lady? We'll have none of that!" He made a grab for Harry, engaging him in a token display of wrestling that precipitated more giggling than aggression. "Bring me that cushion over there, will you?" he said after a moment. "Your old brother is nearly done in."

Harry ran to the window seat and snatched up the cushion, then ran the short distance back to give it to John. Unlike Mrs. Howe, John made no comment about Harry's running indoors.

"Do you know what the Essence of Old Virginia is?" Harry asked as John put the cushion under his head and lay down.

"Yes, but it's not something I'd want to hear a song about. So how is the war coming?" John asked, gesturing toward the toy soldiers.

"Fine!" Harry assured him. "We're making Georgia *howl!*"

John smiled, and Harry went back to playing, showing John particular soldiers, the ones he'd named, from time to time.

Amanda watched John closely, and when she couldn't stand it any longer, she simply asked. "John Howe, are you in trouble with the Yankee army?"

He looked at her in surprise. "No, why?"

"There was an officer here. He wasn't very happy."

"Probably something to do with the ladies' petitions. The wives of Washington's Most Powerful gang up on various and sundry members of generals' staffs to get favors granted. It's quite the pastime. One really has to know the ins and outs of Washington to play, and the petitions aren't for themselves usually, so nobody need feel guilty."

"What kind of petitions?"

"Oh, hardship cases mostly, I imagine. And men are still being drafted into the army. There is a certain number who take great exception to being volunteered—or their wives do.''

"And the staff members give in to them?"

"Usually. Most of the generals' staffs are politicians. They want to run for office later. They don't want the newspapers printing that they were asked to send poor Georgie home to his dying mother for a week or two and they were too hard-hearted to do it. Of course, it goes both ways. If you give a favor, that gives you the right to get one.''

Amanda frowned. "Doesn't seem a very efficient way to run an army."

He folded his arms under his head and closed his eyes. "Unfortunately, the only two people who know that are you and me."

"Your mother is a petitioner?"

"Knowing my mother, she's *the* petitioner. Why?" he asked, looking at her.

"I was just wondering." There were a lot of things she was wondering, and it was clear to her she was going to have to ask. She tried to look into his eyes, but he turned his head away.

"John Howe—"

"I meant to tell you about the lieutenant," he interrupted, as if he wanted to avoid whatever she was about to say.

She sighed. "What lieutenant?"

"The pompous jackass who took us to Forrest Hall—the one with the feathers. He didn't know General Rush is a stickler for the regulation uniform or he wouldn't have been wearing them. I didn't tell him until Rush yelled for us to come into his office." He looked at her and smiled. "I thought Rush was going to make him eat the damn things."

She smiled in return. "I'm sure the lieutenant didn't thank you for that."

In the background, Harry supplied the noise of cannon and rifles for his lead army, and John's smile faded. He abruptly looked at the ceiling, and the silence between them lengthened.

"It . . . didn't go well with Max's mother," he said finally. "She would like to see me dead. As dead as the son I left behind."

"She said that?"

"Quite distinctly."

"I'm sorry. Maybe later, when she's had time to—"

"No. She wouldn't let me tell her how it was. That I'd left Max in that hellhole of a prison was all she needed to know."

"You got out. Perhaps he—"

"He didn't get out!"

The battle noises stopped. "What's wrong?" Harry said, looking from one of them to the other.

"Nothing, Harry," John said. "I'm . . . just feeling a little low."

"Aren't you glad to be home?"

"Glad! Little brother, if I got up early for a week, I couldn't be any more glad than I am right now."

"You don't look very glad."

"What!" John cried again, flinging his arms wide and making another lunge for his little brother. There was more wrestling and giggling, with Amanda getting the worst of the flying arms and legs. Her eyes met John's over the top of Harry's head, and her heart nearly broke.

Oh, John, she thought. He was trying so hard. She said nothing, smiling as the roughhousing escalated, then ended. Both Harry and John sprawled on their backs with their heads on the horsehair cushion, though only a moment for Harry, before he was back to his soldiers. The patch of sunlight had moved to their spot on the floor. It was warm and quiet. Amanda sat with her head bowed, looking at her hands. She wasn't in the cheeriest of moods herself. She could feel John's eyes on her, but she didn't look up. She was so self-conscious suddenly, aware of her breathing and the rise and fall of her breasts, aware of the drag of the rough linen across her nipples each time she breathed and that his eyes wandered boldly where no gentleman ought to look. But she hadn't asked him what she really wanted to know.

What's going to happen when I leave here, John Howe? Will I never see you again?

"You have beautiful hair," he said quietly, his voice husky and strange to her. He reached out his hand to stroke the top of her head, loosening the snood as he did so, and the touch of his warm hand was nearly more than she could bear.

She looked up at him. "Don't," she whispered, her eyes welling. He was used to girls like Kate Woodard, beautiful girls with beautiful clothes, who knew just what to say, just what to *feel*. Didn't he know that she wasn't like that? She couldn't hear him call her "his lady," even if it was in jest to Harry, or have him admire any part of her without taking it to heart. She knew, she *knew* he didn't mean it, and knowing made her want to sit and cry, as if she were no older than Harry, as if she were exactly the child he'd accused her of being. She was nearly overcome by the longing she had for him. She wanted to lie down with him right now, on the floor, and put her arms around him and be as close to him as she could get. She had never felt like this with Thayer Giffen. Never.

"Amanda," he said, trying to take her hand.

"I can't stay here," she said, forcing herself to look at him without wavering. "Have you lied to me or will you keep your promise? I need your help, John Howe. I have to find someplace to go."

When he made no response, she tried to move away from him, but he caught her arm to keep her from standing. "Amanda, I didn't—don't run off from me. Damn it all, I owe you my life—"

She stood up in spite of his efforts, but there was no place for her to run. Mrs. Howe was coming up the stairs.

"Here you are," she said in the doorway with her same false brightness, her eyes in one sweep taking in the fact that John was in the room. "Miss Douglas, I've been looking for you. I'm afraid I've neglected you today. As John has pointed out, we must take care of you— John, are you all right?"

Amanda glanced at him; with Harry's help, he was wearily getting up from the floor.

"Mother, if you and I are going to get along, you're going to have to stop asking me that. I've seen the doctor. Cook is making sure I'm eating or drinking something every two hours just as he said. He says I'm fine—considering. I say I'm fine. All right?"

Mrs. Howe smiled at Amanda. "Grown sons never understand that there is no end to a mother's love and concern, regardless of how *grown* they are. Will you come with me now, Miss Douglas?"

"Yes, of course," Amanda said. "Harry, thank you for looking up my name for me, and for inviting me to visit for a while."

"The pleasure was mine," Harry said, giving a proper bow.

"Well done," she heard John whisper to him. "Amanda, we'll talk later," he said to her.

"There's no need—"

"Miss Douglas?" Mrs. Howe interrupted, leading the way out the door. "John," she called over her shoulder, "dinner will be at eight. Harry, I shall be back later to hear your prayers and tuck you in."

There was only one "yes, Mother" in her wake—Harry's.

"I didn't realize you'd brought clothes with you," Mrs. Howe said as they walked down the stairs. Amanda could just catch a whiff of the rosewater scent Mrs. Howe wore, and once again she was struck by what an attractive and youthful-looking woman she was.

"I didn't," Amanda said. "These don't belong to me."

"Oh? To whom do they belong?"

"To you, Mrs. Howe. The dress—everything—is from the clothing you keep for the maids."

"Is it?" she said incredulously, then laughed. "Well, so it is. How... did you come by these things?"

Amanda hadn't lived with the reverend all that time without recognizing a double-edged question when she heard one.

"Captain Howe arranged it," she said, because it was the truth, and because she thought he could hold his own with his mother better than Alice and Smith could. And she certainly didn't want Mrs. Howe to think she'd been pilfering locked cupboards.

"I see," Mrs. Howe said, still cheerful. "Four years of war have made my son so... enterprising. Tell me, Miss Douglas. How do you think he is?"

Amanda looked at her. The false cheerfulness had slid away, and there was only concern in Mrs. Howe's eyes.

"He doesn't sleep, Mrs. Howe."

"Our doctor has offered him laudanum, but I believe *you* were the one who talked him out of taking it."

Amanda stopped walking. "Yes. I was afraid for him to take it, Mrs. Howe. My... mother had the laudanum addiction. It's a terrible craving. I think it must be very hard to let go of the peace it gives when one needs so badly to escape."

"My son is not a coward who needs to escape, Miss Douglas."

"He blames himself for Max Woodard—"

"We don't know what has become of Maxwell. And until we do, *I* believe it is best not to assume the worst. Come along," she said, smiling again. "I have something for you."

The "something" was a brown silk dress with a maroon and black velvet bodice and the same velvet trim on the long sleeves and on the pockets in the skirt. No, it wasn't simply brown, Amanda thought. It was *tan d'or,* a color she had read so much about in *Godey's Lady's Book* just before the war. And it was just as rich-looking as the fashion book had described.

"I'm afraid it's somewhat out of style," Mrs. Howe said.

"It's beautiful, Mrs. Howe—but I couldn't take it."

"Of course you can," Mrs. Howe insisted. "I don't wear it any longer. I would much prefer that you had some use out of it. Alice will be along shortly to see what alterations are needed. As I said, dinner is at eight."

"Dinner?"

"Yes," Mrs. Howe said, smiling. "We want to get to know you, Miss Douglas. We want to express our gratitude for getting John back to us."

"You don't have to do that, Mrs. Howe—"

"Well, of course, we do, my dear. Now, Alice is a clever girl. She'll have you and the dress all ready by dinnertime."

Alice isn't that clever, Amanda thought. If she had a hundred years to prepare, Amanda wouldn't be ready to go to dinner in the Howe dining room dressed in one of Mrs. Howe's dresses—even if it was *tan d'or.* She felt as if she'd just been advised of the time of her execution.

She kept pacing around the dress after Mrs. Howe left— it was so *beautiful*—and wringing her hands. She was still pacing when Alice arrived with everything else Amanda needed. Hairbrushes, combs, hairpins. A real crinoline with steel bands, one that no one here even realized was a worthwhile donation to men who wanted to make cannons. And another set of petticoats and undergarments, these of a soft cambric. And there was another corset and finely knit stockings. And shiny black leather shoes—that fit.

Amanda made a small noise of dismay.

"Miss?" Alice said, but Amanda only shook her head.

The dress had to be taken in at the waist and hemmed. Amanda helped with the latter over Alice's protests. She had to do something to keep herself occupied—or throw herself out the second-story window.

She had a bath she hardly remembered taking, using whatever soaps and oils Alice handed her. Then Alice did her hair in a chignon with braids until she hardly recognized herself. Then she was firmly laced into the second corset, no matter how earnestly she begged for mercy, and the beautiful dress was carefully thrown over her head and hooked and buttoned into place.

"There," Alice said with great satisfaction, pulling the skirt down over the crinoline. "But look at your face, miss. Whatever are you thinking?"

"I'm thinking—about my stepmother," Amanda said with what little wind she had left that Alice hadn't squeezed out of her. "She always—said—when somebody who doesn't like you—starts being nice to you—you can be sure of one thing."

"What's that, miss?"

"They are . . . getting ready to . . . *skin you*. Alice, I'm going to—faint."

"Oh, no, you're not, miss. Your color's too good for that. You'll get used to it, really you will."

"Then—I'm going to—die."

"No, miss, you'll be *fine*. You're just letting yourself worry too much about going downstairs with the family.

Captain Howe will be there. He won't let anybody skin you."

John waited in the entry hall for Amanda to come down, tugging at his uniform, the only one he'd left at home when he went on his great adventure "down South." Four years since he'd had the thing on. Four *years*. It fit him now as if he were a goddamn scarecrow.

He heard a door open and close upstairs and a brief soft laugh. Amanda. He liked to hear her laugh, though her association with him had given her scant opportunity for humor. He watched as she came carefully down the stairs.

My God, he thought. He had thought her pretty before; she was exquisite now. She looked at him warily, as if she expected the worst from him and was likely to get it. He smiled his approval of the dress and her. He was leery about actually *saying* how lovely he thought she was. She certainly hadn't taken his earlier compliment very well. Or perhaps she knew him well enough to have recognized the flagrant lust behind it. This afternoon, watching her sitting there with the sunlight on her hair, it had been all he could do to restrain himself. If Harry hadn't been there, he wouldn't have—when he knew perfectly well that his behaving honorably was the only means he had to convince his family how much he respected and admired this girl.

Respected. Admired. *Wanted.* He wanted her in the basest and most carnal of ways, regardless of his admiration and respect. He had never experienced this particular combination of feelings regarding any woman before, and it certainly made for misery—when he was miserable enough already, physically and mentally. His head ached and his eyes ached and his heart ached and his—

He offered Amanda his arm, anticipating the warm touch of her hand with pleasure. "Miss Douglas," he said with mock formality. "You're looking particularly fetching this evening."

"So are—you," she countered, giving him a little half smile. "But you still—need a barber."

He couldn't keep from grinning. No one could ever accuse her of not saying whatever was on her mind, even if she hadn't commented about the uniform.

"Are you all right?" he asked, because she was so breathless.

"No," she answered without hesitation.

"No?"

"Can't—breathe," she advised him as he led her into the drawing room.

"Anything I can do to help?"

"Keep your... pocket knife... handy so you can... cut these wretched laces... if I need it...."

He was still smiling when he led her to a chair. He was immensely pleased that she'd come downstairs. After the difficulty he'd had just getting her inside the house, he'd half expected her not to make an appearance tonight for dinner, regardless of the fact that his mother had learned her lesson from his first night home and not put either of them on display again for a roomful of guests.

But then he saw Amanda's determined look and the slight raising of the chin that he'd seen the first time he'd encountered her and the reverend. Amanda came from a proud and fierce people, and whether his mother knew it or not, she would have her work cut out for her if she expected to intimidate her.

"No, no. Come sit by me, my dear," Mrs. Howe said, and John dutifully led her to the couch where his mother was seated. He winked at her as she sat down, and Amanda couldn't keep from smiling at him. He could be so kind sometimes. She glanced at Mr. and Mrs. Howe. There was a decided strain in the room, but as time passed, she began

to breathe easier. Literally. Perhaps Alice had been right.
Perhaps she could grow used to being laced so tightly. The
conversation then and throughout the dinner was light and
neutral—deliberately so, Amanda thought. She was grateful for that; she had no wish to talk about the war, particularly with these people. She participated only minimally,
answering when spoken to and offering nothing extra when
the questions concerned her family and her home. Yes, her
father was a minister. Yes, her mother was dead. Yes, she
was very fond of her stepmother. Mrs. Howe's questions
were clearly based on what John had told her, and if she
knew the precise details of Amanda's true home situation,
it didn't show.

The meal passed uneventfully; the food was delicious as
always, though Amanda could only pick at it in her cor-
seted state. She frequently found John's eyes on her. She
thought at first that he might be concerned that she wouldn't
know the right fork, but it wasn't that kind of look. It was
the kind that made her nervous and fidgety and filled her
with that same bewildering urgency she couldn't begin to
name.

"Do you play the piano, Miss Douglas?" Mrs. Howe
asked when dinner was over and they walked back into the
drawing room.

"I haven't played since I was nine," Amanda said. "I was
barely past the C scale then." She had only managed to learn
what her mother could teach before the laudanum addiction overcame her.

"Perhaps sing?"

"No, Mrs. Howe," Amanda said. She was able to
breathe, more or less; there was absolutely no way she could
sing.

"Perhaps you would read for us then," Mrs. Howe suggested, taking a seat near the fire. "I have a copy of *The*

Woman in White. Are you familiar with it? It is so engrossing, but I've mislaid my reading spectacles—"

"Amanda, you don't have to perform for your supper," John cut in, and she looked at him gratefully. Actually, she could read aloud quite well, regardless of her performance the night the reverend had made her read from Deuteronomy. She had had years of practice reading Scripture before a congregation. A certain expertise in that kind of public performance was the only good thing the reverend had ever done for her—but she couldn't read in this corset!

The reason for the dinner and the requests for entertainment suddenly occurred to her. Mrs. Howe had been quite truthful about wanting to "get to know her," not because she was interested, but because she owed Amanda a certain debt and the sooner she knew what her capabilities were, the sooner she could make good her son's promise to see her "situated" and thereby get her out of the house.

"John, I wasn't asking Miss Douglas to perform," Mrs. Howe said. "I thought this might be a pleasant way to spend the evening."

"She won't be reading, Mother."

"John, do you think she might say one word at least on her own behalf without your—"

"For God's sake, Mother. Amanda's corset is laced too damned tight! She can't read!"

Mrs. Howe stiffened visibly. "And how would *you* know a thing like that?"

Amanda was still standing, her face burning. How indeed? Because she'd been ill-bred enough to actually *tell* him. Where he was concerned, she had forgotten every bit of decorum she'd ever learned. She looked at each of their faces, though it took every ounce of determination she had.

"Mrs. Howe...Mr. Howe, I thank you very much for including me this evening. With your permission, I'll go now . . . it's . . ." She glanced at John, but she couldn't manage anything more.

"Amanda, wait," he said as she abruptly headed for the door.

She kept going, closing the door firmly behind her and hurrying up the stairs as best she could. She could hear loud voices—John's loud voice—in the drawing room behind her. She kept going until she reached the landing, looking back only once before she reached her room. Once inside, she slid the bolt and leaned against the door, trying to catch her breath, trying desperately not to cry.

Someone knocked on the door almost immediately, but she made no move to open it.

The knock came again. "Miss?" Alice said. "Can I help you, miss?"

"No, Alice," she managed, wiping at her eyes.

"The dress, miss. You can't unhook it alone."

Amanda closed her eyes and shook her head. She'd rather die than be trapped in Mrs. Howe's dress. She took a small breath to steady herself and turned to open the door.

"Are you all right, miss?" Alice asked as she came inside.

"Yes. If you'd unhook me, please."

"Shall I lay out your night things?"

"No. Just get me out of the dress. That's all."

Amanda stood silently while Alice undid all the hooks and buttons down her back and lifted the dress over her head.

"I can take care of the rest," Amanda said.

She waited while Alice carefully hung up the dress in the armoire, until she'd punched up the fire and turned down the bed.

"Are you sure, miss. Isn't there . . . ?"

"Nothing else, Alice. Thank you."

"Good night, miss," Alice said, hesitating at the door for a moment before she finally left.

Amanda put her hands to her face for a moment, then began tearing at the corset laces and the rest of Mrs. Howe's clothes. Her own dress and petticoat, the ones she'd arrived in, were hanging in the armoire now, cleaned and pressed and ready. She took them out and began hunting frantically for the rest of her things. She found them in the second drawer she looked in, and she began to hurriedly put them on with no plan in mind other than to get out of this house.

Someone knocked on the door again, and it was no respectful maid's knock this time.

"Amanda!" John said on the other side of the door. "I want to talk to you."

She kept trying to get her clothes on, fumbling at the buttons in her haste.

"Did you hear me? Amanda!"

"If I wanted to talk to *you,* John Howe, I'd still be in the drawing room—"

The door burst open as she pulled the dress on over her head. She turned away from him and tried to get the bodice buttoned.

"What the hell do you think you're doing!" he yelled at her.

"I'm leaving," she said.

He grabbed her by the arm to make her look at him. "The hell you are. Look! Perhaps I was a little uncouth just now—not unsurprising, considering where I've been—"

"How could you treat your mother like that!" Amanda cried, trying to step past him.

"My mother! What has my mother got to do with it?"

Amanda shook her head in exasperation and tried harder to get around him, completely incredulous that he could be so dense and that she could have been so stupid as to not rebolt the door. "You don't understand this at all, do you! Your mother thinks I am the worst kind of woman there is,

John Howe! She is offended by whatever might be between us, and I don't blame her! A decent girl wouldn't do what I've done, even at gunpoint. But for your sake—for *your* sake—she is trying to make the best of it. Don't you understand how hard it is for her to have me here? To have me live in her house and sit at her table? And then you flaunt it in her face with your stupid remarks about personal things you've got no business knowing!"

"All right! I admit I shouldn't have made such an announcement in the drawing room, but Amanda, you *told* me you couldn't breathe—"

"Yes! That's how bad it is! I keep forgetting who you are—what you are, John Howe! I should be plotting some way to kill you, not telling you when my corset's too tight!"

He pursed his mouth to say something, then sighed heavily, looking down at the floor and then back at her. "This is the damned craziest conversation I've ever had, you know that, don't you?"

"Well, I can't help that."

"Amanda—"

"John, please. Just do what you promised. That's all I ask. This is your home. I don't want to cause any more trouble here. Please!"

He walked away from her, going to the fireplace and staring into the flames. He held out his hands in front of him toward the warmth. They were shaking. He was so goddamned tired!

He looked around at her. Her beautiful eyes were waiting, beautiful dark eyes that nearly took his breath away. "I need you to stay here."

"Why?"

"It's . . . too hard to explain."

"Try," she said, coming closer.

He shook his head. "I have to sit down—my knees are shaking."

Amanda expected him to sit down in the nearest chair, but he sat down on the floor instead, cross-legged in front of the fire, his head bowed. She went closer and knelt beside him, all her anger gone. He immediately leaned against her.

"I treat you badly, don't I? And I don't mean to. God knows I don't mean to."

She said nothing, letting him rest his head on her shoulder as she had so many times in their short association. He shifted his position, moving so he could lie down on the floor with his head in her lap.

"John—" she protested.

"No," he murmured, his eyes closing. "Stay with me...just for a while...I need you...."

She looked down at him. His eyes were closed, his breathing deep and even. She gently touched his hair, moving the long strands she had missed in her barbering debut out of his face. He stirred briefly, turning on his side and burrowing his head deeper into her lap.

"Stay with me," she thought he said again. His hand caressed her knees for a moment, then went still. He was sound asleep.

She looked up at a small noise. Mrs. Howe watched from the open doorway, but Amanda neither started guiltily nor made any attempt to move away from John. The damage had been done the day John Howe brought her into this house; his mother could never think any worse of her than she already did. Amanda's only acknowledgment of the woman was to place her finger to her lips to indicate that John finally, *finally* slept.

Mrs. Howe took a step forward, but Mr. Howe also stood by the open door.

"Let him be," he said, taking his wife by the arm.

Chapter Nine

Stay with me. She could still hear the words. It was no hardship to do what he asked. The truth was she'd do anything for him. She sat on the floor, letting him sleep with his head on her lap until her legs grew numb and her back stiff. Both Smith and Alice came to add coal to the fire, and the three of them managed to get John's head onto a pillow. Then they quietly left him to sleep on the carpet, covering him with a quilt from the bed. He lay like one dead, hardly stirring when the fire was stoked or when Mrs. Howe returned, still wanting him moved to a more "decent" location. This time it was Smith who intervened, reminding her that the captain himself had said that he had slept on the ground so long he couldn't rest in a bed. Mrs. Howe satisfied her notion of propriety by leaving Alice as a chaperon, but the girl was exhausted from her daily household duties and dozed in a nearby chair almost immediately. It was Amanda who kept vigil, hearing John's slightest movement, going to sit on the floor by him again and again when it seemed that another nightmare about Max Woodard invaded his dreams.

But, in the end, it was John who couldn't stay. In the early morning Amanda lay resting on top of the bed covers when Smith quietly knocked. She forced herself to the door, her body heavy with fatigue, glancing over her shoulder at her sleeping companions before she let him in.

"The captain will have to be awakened now, miss," Smith said.

"Why? I know how improper it looks, but surely Mrs. Howe understands—"

"A sergeant has come with a message from the military headquarters, miss. Captain Howe must report immediately. The sergeant is waiting to escort him."

"I don't understand. Why would they make him go to headquarters?"

"The army works in its own fashion, miss. The captain must be awakened. There is no help for it."

"You do it, then," she said, stepping aside. "I can't bear to wake him."

She stood out in the hall, expecting an explosion and getting one. John Howe did not suffer having his sleep disturbed gladly.

"Damn it all, Smith! I'm on furlough!"

"Yes, sir. The sergeant was advised."

"And?"

"And he's waiting, sir."

John's annoyance was brief, however, and she ventured a return. He was already on his feet.

"Amanda, come downstairs with me," he said, rubbing his hand over the stubble on his chin. Unshaven or not, Amanda found him entirely handsome. He glanced at her and then back again, probably because she was staring so. "What?" he asked. "Have I done something uncouth *again?*"

"Not to my knowledge," she said, trying to be nonchalant.

"Good. Then we'll have breakfast."

"I'm sorry, sir," Smith intervened. "The sergeant says 'immediately.' Cook is putting something together for you to take in hand."

"Does the sergeant say if I'm allowed to change my shirt at least?" John said sarcastically.

"No, but one would hope so, sir," Smith replied, leading the way, unperturbed as always.

"Amanda, whatever this is, it shouldn't take long, and it's got nothing to do with you," he added, because she had that worried frown again—and she looked lovely in spite of it. All...disheveled, her hair coming unbound. She looked the way he liked to see her, as if she'd just been tumbled in a big bed somewhere. He should go to sleep with his head in her lap more often.

"Yankee soldiers always make me nervous, John Howe. You should know that. They aren't the most reasonable people in the world."

"Well, we won't get into that. When I come back, we'll talk."

"There's nothing I need to talk about. I have to leave here—"

"No, we'll talk. You asked me a question. I'm going to try my best to answer it."

"What question?"

"We'll get to that when I come back. You'll wait? You aren't going to do anything crazy? I swear I'll have Smith lock you in—"

"I'll wait, John," she interrupted before he could elaborate on his latest threat. *As long as I have a choice.*

He looked into her eyes. The time had passed when he could bully and threaten her into submission, and they both knew it. "Your word?"

"My word."

He almost smiled. "Good. Good, then. You know, I feel halfway decent this morning."

"Don't look it," she said mischievously, and he made a grab for her the way he might have done with Harry, making her laugh. She laughed so seldom in his company, and God, he loved to hear it.

But he didn't have time to play. Duty called. He turned and gave her a little salute as he went down the hall. Amanda stood staring after him, feeling the familiar emptiness that came with his absences, however brief. She went back into her room, catching sight of herself in the mirror, and groaning. Perhaps John Howe was a gentleman after all, if he could take her barb about his appearance and not mention hers. Alice's elaborate braiding and chignon looked as if rats had been nesting. She hurriedly tried to take her hair down and brush it, but she heard John in the hallway before she was half-through.

"Amanda!" he called, and she threw the brush aside, raking through her hair with her fingers as she ran.

"What!" she cried as she reached the corridor, flinging her hair over her shoulder and trying to twist it together into some kind of order. He was standing at the head of the stairs, his uniform straight now and his shirt changed.

"You'll wait," he called to her, thinking he'd remember the way she looked now, at this moment, for the rest of his life.

She didn't come any closer.

"Please," he added with uncharacteristic decorum.

This time she nodded, and he smiled genuinely before he turned and went down the stairs. She walked to the landing, watching as he and his sergeant escort went out the front door. When she was about to go back to her room, she saw Mrs. Howe standing in the entry hall below. Incredibly, the woman looked up and smiled.

John didn't come back. Not that day or the next. Alice knew nothing—she said—except that Mr. Howe was furious at John's having to report, when there were military men loitering all over Washington who hadn't seen a day of real army service, much less imprisonment, and that the family, as far as she knew, had received no word as to the nature of John's delay. Mrs. Howe, Alice reported, was being strong for everyone.

Strong, Amanda thought, was Mrs. Howe's entirely natural state.

Amanda's greatest difficulty was that she had no way to pass the time. Alice remained suspiciously busy elsewhere; and Harry, too, seemed to be out of the house. Amanda read, slept, waited—worried. Perhaps Max Woodard's mother had caused John to be arrested. Was it treason in the Yankee army if a man couldn't save a friend?

She read the war news in the *Washington Star.* Fort Fisher on the North Carolina coast, the last protector of the last open Confederate port, had fallen. She knew only too well what that would mean. Worse shortages of food and medical supplies. Worse conditions for the civilians and the military alike. And she was *here,* eating roast chicken and drinking real China tea whenever she wanted.

Exhausted and guilt-ridden, she went to bed early, expecting not to sleep at all and waking to bright sunlight. But it wasn't morning; it was late afternoon. She'd slept nearly the whole day away.

She sat up in bed. A fire burned in the coal grate. She moved over to the side of the bed and let her legs hang. Alice was in the room before her feet touched the floor.

"Well, miss, I'm glad to see you up again," she said brightly. "You've had a fine sleep. You'll be feeling all the better for it. And you'll be wanting to tend to first things first, I'll bet, so you do that, and then I'll bring your clothes to you—your eyes are puffy, miss. I'll bring you the witch hazel, too, while I'm bringing—"

"Did Captain Howe come back this morning?" Amanda asked bluntly. Yes, she needed first things first, as Alice so delicately put it—but she needed news of him more.

"Oh, it's not morning, miss." Alice beamed at her, deliberately misunderstanding, Amanda thought. "Imagine you thinking it was morning. It's gone past five. You've not had your breakfast or your lunch or teatime. I'll be hurrying on—you'll be needing your clothes—"

"Alice," Amanda called, but she was out the door before Amanda could stop her. She crossed the room and opened the door, peering down the hallway, catching a glimpse of Alice as she disappeared down the stairs. She could have followed after her, except that "first things first" were indeed becoming a priority.

Alice returned, eventually, with Amanda's freshly pressed clothes, the same ones she'd arrived in, and the witch hazel.

"Captain Howe—" Amanda began immediately, because she was determined to know about him.

Alice blatantly ignored her. "We were wondering downstairs about these buttons, miss, with the CSA on them. Did you have a soldier sweetheart and did he give them to you to wear? You wouldn't see girls around here doing that, putting military buttons on their dresses. I think it's kind of patriotic, I guess the word would be. Of course, you don't think about the Rebels being that, no offense, miss—"

"Alice, please!" Amanda interrupted. "Tell me!" She was very near shaking the girl until her teeth rattled, but she forced down the urge. "Please," she said again. "Has something gone wrong with Captain Howe?"

Alice abruptly smiled. "Well, not that I'm aware of, miss," she said, busily brushing a piece of invisible lint from Amanda's dress. "He's not back from wherever they sent for him to come. Madam—Mrs. Howe—instructs me to inquire if you'd be so kind as to accept accommodations in another part of the house."

"I don't care where I am, Alice. I just want to know if John is all right. Are you going to tell me or not?"

"Truly, miss," she said. "I have no knowledge of the captain." And she said it as if she were reading from a printed page.

"Thank you," Amanda said after a moment. She understood now how Harry must have felt when he couldn't get any news. It seemed that the both of them were to be kept in the dark, because no one considered them of any particular consequence. "I should get dressed—if I'm moving."

She dressed quickly, clearly pleasing Alice with her haste. She braided her hair in one long braid down her back, and she made no attempt to take with her any of the clothes she'd been given since she arrived. With John's disappearance and this move to another part of the house, she wasn't sure it would be all right for her to have them anymore.

The new room was well away from the previous one. Alice took her there through a narrow, hidden back staircase that was actually built between the walls of the house. Amanda found no fault with the change of accommodations, though everything was on a much smaller scale. The bed was very narrow and placed against the wall and beside the only window, six-over-six panes of glass that looked directly out into the backyard. A small table sat under the window with both an oil lamp and a candlestick on it. A large portrait of a regal-looking woman hung over the head of the bed, and several smaller prints of hunting scenes and stylized ladies hung along the side, so low to the bed itself that a restless sleeper might knock them down. The floor was bare except for a small rug by the bed. A damask upholstered chair of undetermined color stood alongside a very plain ladder-back chair with a split oak seat in front of the small fireplace, and an oak washstand with a dim, mottled

mirror and a tall mahogany Sheraton chest lined the opposite walls. There was even a small serving table squeezed in
between. The room was quite pleasant actually, if somewhat mismatched. Heavy rose velvet drapes hung at the
window to keep out the cold wind and any prying eyes from
the backyard. She wondered for whom the room was usually intended. Poor relations? Harry's governess?

Alice left her there, and she sat down on the bed, wondering what to do with herself now and how to find out
about John. He had promised to get her to Richmond if that
was what she wanted; but, word or no word, there was a
limit to how long she could wait. She didn't have to have a
house fall on her to know that she was being very quietly
eased toward the door.

Alice returned shortly with a tray, the same kind of fare
Amanda had grown used to. She ate ravenously—in spite of
the fall of Fort Fisher—but she wasn't allowed to finish.
Cook arrived with flour on her hands.

"Alice!" she said, making the girl jump. "Smith says they
are waiting!" She didn't wait for any kind of reply and apparently didn't need to.

"Oh, miss!" Alice said. "We have to go right now! Mr.
Beale's waiting!"

"Mr. Beale wants to see *me?*" Amanda said, alarmed.
She remembered Mr. Beale—the lawyer who comes when
someone does something bad. She swallowed hard to get
down the lump of food that suddenly seemed to have nowhere to go. "Why would he want to see me?"

"Oh, you'd know that better than me, miss. I just know
he's one of those people you don't vex. Please hurry. You
don't want to keep Mr. Beale waiting. I'll show you the
way."

Alice stood with the door open, motioning vigorously.
They went again by the hidden stairs, coming out this time
in an alcove off the main entrance to the house. Amanda

could see directly into the huge marble foyer; she recognized the celestial stairway immediately.

"This way," Alice said, leading her toward the double doors opposite those of the drawing room. Smith must have been watching for their arrival through a crack in the doorway, because the doors suddenly opened.

"They're waiting," he said gravely to Amanda, not giving Alice so much as a glance. Amanda followed him—she had no choice unless she made a run for it.

These double doors led into the library, a high-ceilinged room with several breakfront mahogany bookcases of impressive proportions. Amanda could see hundreds of books behind the leaded glass doors. Three dark green velvet couches flanked a huge marble mantel, and green damask curtains hung at the windows from nearly the ceiling to the floor. A fire burned brightly on the hearth, but it did little to lighten the atmosphere of the room.

Amanda couldn't keep from looking around for John, but he was conspicuously absent. Mrs. Howe sat on one of the velvet couches, her voluminous skirts taking up nearly all of the seat. The only other person in the room was a small, bespectacled man. He, too, sat on a velvet couch, his lap full of papers he painstakingly shuffled from time to time in front of him. He didn't look up, and Amanda recognized the stratagem immediately. It was something the reverend might have done to make certain she understood who was in charge immediately.

"Please sit down, Miss Douglas," Mrs. Howe said.

Amanda resisted the impulse to remain standing. This was no social visit, and she saw no reason to behave as if it were. But in the presence of these two intimidating people, her knees seemed suddenly not to want to hold her, and she sat down heavily on the only vacant couch.

"This is Mr. Carlton Beale," Mrs. Howe said. "He has been our family lawyer for many years. He would like to ask you some questions."

In spite of Mrs. Howe's cue, Beale took his own good time. After a moment, he looked up to give Amanda a curt nod, staring at her clothes, carefully noting her shabby appearance. She sat very still, willing herself not to fidget, not to drop her eyes or twist her hands in her lap. When his eyes finally met hers, it was all she could do not to look away.

"Did you have any prior knowledge of Captain Howe?" he asked bluntly. His voice was much deeper pitched than she had expected.

She glanced at Mrs. Howe, whose face was carefully devoid of any expression. "I don't understand what you mean," she said.

"Did you know who he was before he sought refuge in your father's house?" Beale said pointedly, as if she were, at the very least, dull-witted. "Did you know his name? Anything about him?"

"No," she said, still not understanding the nature of the question. There was only one thing she understood about this meeting—that she had her back to the wall.

"Are you certain? Was there not some place in the town where you might have acquired knowledge of him or his social position?"

"I never had anything to do with the prison or the prisoners. I never met Captain Howe until he hid in the house. He didn't mention his social position, and there was absolutely nothing in his behavior that would suggest he had any manners or breeding whatsoever."

She could feel Mrs. Howe bristle at her comment, but she kept her eyes on Beale.

"And yet you still left with him?" he asked quietly. "Unchaperoned? A complete stranger? A man you never met before and an enemy of your country?"

"I did. Captain Howe threatened on any number of occasions to kill me. As he had a loaded revolver at the time, I had no reason not to believe him."

"You are a very flippant young woman!"

"No, sir, I am not. Captain Howe's escape was ill planned. He put my life in danger. He felt enough responsibility for that to try to help me. The only way he could do it was to keep me with him."

"Be that as it may," Beale said. "Captain Howe is safely home now. You understand that his family wants this entire matter resolved as soon as possible. You understand that they must be assured that there will be no...repercussions."

"What kind of 'repercussions'?"

"I assume that you consider yourself firmly established in Captain Howe's affections," Beale said, ignoring her question.

"I don't know what you mean," she said again. She hated this oblique approach to everything. Why couldn't he just *say* what he wanted?

"He means, Miss Douglas, that you would not be the first young woman to think so," Mrs. Howe said. "But I can tell you here and now, whatever aspirations you may have where he is concerned are quite impossible. If you fancy yourself seduced—" She stopped because Beale held up his hand.

"Captain Howe is no gentleman, but he didn't—" Amanda snapped.

"Nevertheless," Beale interrupted. "A doctor's examination is in order. Surely you understand that this matter can't be resolved until we determine that there is no illegitimate child who may later try to establish itself as an heir—"

"I am not carrying John Howe's child!"

Beale stared at her over his spectacles. "The question is *whether* you are carrying a child."

Amanda's face burned with humiliation. *How many times have you done this?* she thought, looking into his pale eyes. *Mr. Beale always comes when John does something bad.* How many times had he gotten John Howe out of some socially embarrassing liaison?

She stood up, her knees still trembling. "I'm going now," she said, her voice barely a whisper.

"Sit down," Beale said.

She didn't say anything more and she didn't sit down, edging around the velvet couch so she could get to the double doors.

"This discussion is not over," Beale insisted, and she whirled around to face him.

"It is for me, sir."

"The Howe family is trying to protect itself, Miss Douglas. Surely you can understand that. You mustn't think that they don't appreciate your part in the captain's safe return—"

She shook her head, too overcome to say anything more.

"What is it you want?" Mrs. Howe said sharply, throwing up her hands.

"Nothing! I want nothing from you or John Howe!"

That wasn't quite the truth. She had wanted the means to get to Richmond, but now she only wanted out of this room. She was no match for these people.

"Good!" Mrs. Howe said. "Then sign the papers."

"What papers!" Amanda cried.

"The papers absolving my son of any responsibility for you!"

"Is that what this is all about? Signing papers? Where are they? I'll sign them!"

"You'll...sign?" Beale said, as if to make sure he'd heard correctly.

"Yes!"

"Then sit down. The Howe family isn't ungrateful, Miss Douglas. You will be given money, enough to get you wherever you have a mind to go—with the understanding, of course, that you will not trouble the captain again for any reason."

"I understand," she said. She looked blindly at the papers Beale handed her. Her pride demanded that she tell Mrs. Howe what she could do with her money *and* her papers, but she was desperate and she was not stupid, regardless of the way Beale had tried to make her feel. She'd had a hard enough time getting here in the first place, not to know what it was like for those with no marketable skills and no money. She took the pen Beale offered, dipping it into the inkwell he had conveniently close by and writing her name carefully and with all the flourishes her mother had taught her, thankful for once for the hours she'd spent at the kitchen table practicing ovals and curlicues. Her mother had believed that one's penmanship was a direct reflection of one's social worth. Even with Mrs. Howe and Beale watching, Amanda's signature would not have disappointed her.

"The money will be in your hands on Monday," Beale said. "You will stay here tonight and tomorrow night. Then, on Monday morning, you will be on your way."

"I would prefer to go now—"

"No. You will be more comfortable here," Mrs. Howe said, as if Amanda's "comfort" mattered. "We are not completely heartless, Miss Douglas. You must give us some time to find some suitable possibilities for you. Neither my husband and I nor John would want you to come to a bad end. By Monday—"

"All right!" Amanda interrupted. Anything to get out of this room. "There is one thing I would like to know. Captain Howe—is he all right?"

Beale put up his hand again to keep Mrs. Howe from answering.

"Captain Howe is quite fine," he said.

"You've seen him?"

"I have. Today, as a matter of fact. Several times."

Several times. Several times.

The words echoed in her head. She hardly remembered walking back to the new room. She stood now staring at the fire in the coal grate, seeing nothing, her mind playing and replaying the meeting with Mrs. Howe and Beale. She had defended herself as best she could, and she had been totally vanquished.

Alice kept coming to the door, bringing her little tidbits to eat. Clearly, Cook knew what had happened. Amanda tried to behave as if nothing were wrong, taking the cake and the cookies and the candied fruit she'd sent. But it was going to take a good deal more than Cook's baking to make her feel better. She ate none of it, putting it all aside in a clean hand towel so that she could hoard it until the time when she would go from here.

Monday. And apparently John Howe knew. How could he have left her to Beale? She had been willing to go. She'd *wanted* to go, and he knew that.

But she had been one of many. Perhaps all his undesirable women had said that they wanted to leave and that they had no wish to cause him trouble. He was safe from her now. Legally and actually. She didn't even know where he was, and it was certain that no one in this house would tell her. Incredibly, the betrayal she felt was ten times worse than what she'd suffered from Thayer. She closed her eyes and took a deep breath. Alone. No family. No friends. And she had better get used to it. She didn't want to go to Richmond. She didn't want to go to North Carolina. There was only one thing that she wanted—and he was a cad.

The sun was nearly gone, and she had nothing but time on her hands. Alice had said that the Howes were out for the evening, so at least she didn't have to worry about another summons to the library. She drew the curtains and put more coal on the grate, and, huddling close to the fire, she used several of the containers of hot water Alice had brought to bathe and to wash her hair. The room was too cold for stripping naked and getting wet, but who knew when she'd have the opportunity to attend to her personal needs again?

When she'd finished, she put on a freshly laundered nightgown that had been left on her bed—another of Mrs. Howe's castoffs, a *robe de nuit,* Alice had called it, as if Mrs. Howe were too fine to sleep in anything less. She was cold, but she took the time to rinse out her chemise and drawers and petticoat, hanging them on the ladder-back chair near the fire to dry.

Then she threw a quilt from the bed around her shoulders and paced the perimeter of the small room, hoping to soon feel sleepy enough to go to bed. After a time, she knelt in front of the fire again to finish drying her hair. The house was growing quiet. She could hear a murmur of voices from time to time, an occasional clanging of pot lids in the kitchen or footsteps hurrying back and forth up the stairs, but for all that, she had never been more alone in her life.

She lit the lamp and the candle, then she went to the door to open it, because she thought she heard footsteps. The hallway was dark and empty. None of the lamps in this part of the house seemed to be lit.

She went back to pacing, only to think she heard the noise again. She listened intently, but there was nothing she could identify.

"The wind," she said out loud, because the wind was cold and sharp tonight, but the sound of her own voice made her uneasiness worse.

She moved back to the hearth, but when she was about to kneel, there was a loud noise in the hallway. She whirled around; it sounded as if someone had walked right into the wall. Something dropped and rolled, and someone fumbled at the doorknob. There was a faint curse, and the door suddenly opened.

John Howe stood there with a bottle and two glasses in his hands. He was in military uniform. His dark blue cavalryman's shell jacket was rumpled and unbuttoned, but the rest of him—

Amanda took a sharp intake of breath. He himself was impeccably groomed. His hair had been barbered by someone using scissors instead of a paring knife, someone who knew what he was doing. His mustache had been trimmed and he'd shaved. He was absolutely breathtaking. She'd never seen a soldier, in blue or gray, buttoned up or not, look so splendid.

He gestured toward the dark hall behind him. "There is not a damned lamp lit out there," he said, as if to explain his clumsiness.

She couldn't stop staring at him. All that time together, and he'd never really been a Yankee soldier to her until this very minute.

"What's the matter?" he asked.

"You look skinned," she said bluntly, and he laughed. But it was she who had suffered *that* procedure; it had been done in the library and it had been done by experts.

"Aren't you going to invite me in?"

"No," she said, but he came in anyway, crossing the room and setting his bottle and glasses precariously on the narrow mantel above the fireplace. The room immediately became too small with him in it. She had forgotten how tall he was, how deep his voice was. She had forgotten how being close to him made her feel.

"What are you doing down here?" he asked. "I had a devil of a time finding you—well, actually I was looking for somebody to tell me where you were, and here you are behind the only door with a light—"

"What do you want?" she interrupted rudely instead of answering. She had been relegated to her proper position now that she was no longer a danger to him—below the salt. She couldn't believe he would stand here and pretend he didn't know where she'd gone. He'd seen Beale today.

She was near enough to smell his masculine scent—soap, leather, the out-of-doors. She was nearly overwhelmed by the need to reach out to him. If she could just...touch him, one last time. She backed away from him a few steps. It didn't help.

"I want to talk to you," John said. "I told you that—"

"That was three days ago."

"I am in the army, Amanda. I *cannot* come and go as I please." But the fact of the matter was that he'd done exactly that. He was supposed to be on his way to Alexandria, but he'd taken this side trip home without anything that even faintly resembled a pass. He still wasn't quite sure how it was that he'd been ordered to report; one would have thought he was the last seasoned cavalry officer in the whole goddamned Army of the Potomac. Nor was he sure what he'd done to earn his new commanding officer's animosity. He'd been on the wrong side of men who ranked him before, usually because they were military incompetents and because he couldn't keep his performance evaluations to himself. He had never suffered fools gladly, particularly when one of them was apt to get him killed. But whatever the cause this time, he hadn't wasted time worrying about it. His only concern had been seeing Amanda before he got stuck in Alexandria or some other godforsaken place for who knew how long, before he could tell her everything she needed to know.

He had made it here without being stopped, thank God, and here she was, all fresh and clean-smelling, her hair loose and hanging down her back. It was all he could do to keep his hands off her. He still wasn't certain what she was doing down here, but his inquiry had made her touchy and he was perfectly willing to let it pass. He tried to look into her eyes, but she wouldn't let him. She definitely wasn't the merry little person he'd left three days ago.

"Could we have a truce?" he asked.

"What do you mean?"

"I mean, could you go ten damn minutes without criticizing?"

"I doubt it."

"Make the effort!"

"Why?"

He pointed a finger at her. "Now, don't start with me. I have had one hell of a day—"

"Oh, I am so sorry," she said sarcastically.

"Look! I have ridden hard in this damnable freezing weather all the way here, when I'm supposed to be halfway to Alexandria! It's cold outside! I want to talk to you, and I want a shot of whiskey to get warm. I even brought *you* a glass—yes, I know! You promised your dead mother! The thing is, I don't know when I'll get back here, and I—"

"Fine," she interrupted, sitting down on the one empty chair. "Talk."

He looked around the room. "Don't you have another chair that isn't doubling as a laundry?"

"No," she said, refusing to be driven to hiding her underclothes—wet underclothes at that—or fetching him a seat.

"Well, what the hell. I can do this standing. It's cold in here," he said abruptly, moving to shovel more coal into the grate. When he stood up, he took the bottle he'd brought with him and filled the two glasses. "I believe a toast is in order. Which one, do you think? 'Death to traitors'? 'Down with tyrants'? Surely there is one somewhere that won't offend one or the other of us."

He handed her a glass. Surprisingly, she took it.

"Are we celebrating?" she asked.

He looked up at the sarcasm in her voice. "I...think maybe we should forget the justification and simply imbibe," he said, and he downed his in one swift motion. And poured another. "I've been thinking about this all day. I want to tell you how much—how grateful I am that you—" She looked so incredulous that he lost his train of thought. "I...appreciate what you've done for me, Amanda. You know that. I owe you my sanity and very probably my life— What, for God's sake!" he suddenly asked. "Why are you looking at me like that!"

"Oh, please go on," she said, the sarcasm still intact. "What else do you want to thank me for?"

He reached over and took back the glass she was only holding. "I keep forgetting what a baby you are."

"I am not a child!" She was quite old enough for him to have to be "saved" from her.

"What is the matter with you!"

"Nothing! Say whatever you wanted to say and go!"

They stared across the room at each other. This thing was not going the way he'd planned. Time was running fast; he had to get to his post before someone decided to wonder why he was so late. And he had to make her understand.

"All right," he said pointedly. "I will. I wanted to say, too, that you have a lifetime champion in young Harry. I wanted to say thank you for being so kind to him."

"You're welcome."

He came closer to the chair. "Amanda, I..."

She made herself look up at him. His eyes roamed over her face, and she turned her head away.

"I keep forgetting how pretty you are," he said. "Don't you know how pretty you are?"

"That's not—" True, she was going to say. But she wasn't going to get into some kind of coy exchange that would make him think she wanted to be convinced of her stellar beauty. She looked the way she looked, not pretty enough to keep Thayer from forgetting his pledge to marry her and not pretty enough to interest John.

"Amanda," he said again, kneeling down by the chair. It reminded her of that first night at Shanley's when he'd come close like this to tell her what trouble she was in. But he wasn't dirty and repulsive now. *He* was the one who was so attractive, and, damn him, he mattered to her more than anything in the world.

He reached out to take her hand. She resisted for a moment, but he wouldn't let go. His fingers were warm in spite of his claim of coldness. She stared down at them.

"Are you afraid of me?" he asked.

"No."

"What then? Does the Yankee uniform bother you that much?"

"Yes," she answered, but it wasn't true. He'd slept with his head in her lap while he was wearing a Yankee uniform. She hadn't minded a bit.

"You don't ever have to be afraid of me. You know that."

She made herself look into his eyes. "I'm not afraid. I'm—"

"What?" he asked when she didn't go on. "What are you? Tell me. I want to know." He suddenly leaned closer. "I *need* to know. Are you a woman? Are you a child? Tell me so I'll know what to do."

"Please—" she said, trying to get out of the chair. He restrained her for a moment, then abruptly let go.

"I'm . . . sorry. I shouldn't have spoken to you like that. It's the whiskey talking—Dutch courage, as it were. The heart is willing, but the manner is uncouth." He stood. "Never fear, though. I'm going. I'll just say in parting that you have my undying admiration and respect and we'll let it go at that. You may trust that I will always remember you fondly."

She watched in silence as he picked up his whiskey bottle and opened the door.

I'm like my mother, she thought. But neither of them was the immoral kind of woman the reverend had always maintained. They were the kind who would dare to love, regardless of the risk, regardless of the pain. She could feel her eyes welling. In spite of herself, in spite of the papers she'd signed, she didn't want him to go. She got up from the chair.

"John Howe," she whispered as he stepped into the hallway.

He heard her, and he turned around, his eyes holding hers.

And she asked the question that was tearing her apart. "What if I never see you again?"

The question swirled around him. Child or woman or both, he didn't think it was the child who asked.

"It would matter to you?"

"Yes," she said.

The word was tremulous, barely a whisper, but he felt it deep. He held his arms out to her, and incredibly, she came to him. She was trembling, and she pressed herself against him. He could feel her against his chest and belly and thighs, this soft warm body he'd once dreamed of taking while he slept in a freezing hole in the ground. She had told him the truth. She wasn't afraid of him. She clung to him, clearly wanting this closeness as desperately as he did.

"Amanda..." he said, the sound part word, part groan. His mouth came down hard on hers. Some portion of his mind urged him to take care, but he had wanted to do this for a long time. When her lips parted under his, he responded instantly. He was past remembering how long it was since he'd had a woman, and she tasted so good to him. He slid his hands into her hair so he could keep her exactly where he wanted.

But it wasn't *a* woman he wanted; it was she. He couldn't get enough of her, and he couldn't help himself. His mouth plundered hers, tasting, devouring. He didn't want to do anything that would frighten her, but his desperate need of her drove him on.

What if I never see you again?

He bent her in to him, his hands moving now over the smooth flow of her back and hips. The quilt she had around her shoulders slid to the floor. He had already guessed that she wore nothing under the nightgown—everything was hanging wet on that chair. The feel of her, even through cloth, intensified his desire.

"Amanda," he said again, letting his mouth slide to the warmth of her neck. The delicate, woman scent of her skin, the feel and the taste of it nearly drove him wild. He took a shuddering breath.

"I can't—you'll have to—" He wasn't making any sense, and he knew it. He was aroused and aching, and he pressed her harder against the physical evidence of his need. Then, with the last ounce of strength he had, he forced himself to hold her away so he could look into her eyes. "We have to stop this," he said in a rush. "We have to stop right now. Do you understand?"

She nodded, but the stricken look she gave him only made him bring her close again. He cupped her face in his hands, covering her eyes and mouth with quick, urgent kisses.

"You aren't—helping me—" he tried to tell her before his mouth again covered hers. Her arms slid upward around his neck, and his hand covered her breast. He boldly caressed the hard bud of her nipple with his thumb. He expected yet another of her famous right-hand swings, but she made a soft mewing sound that took his breath away.

Oh, God!

He loved the way she smelled and he loved the way she felt. Sweet. She was so sweet. His desire had become almost physical pain, but he managed to put her away from him one more time, bodily picking her up and setting her down on the side of the bed.

"Stay there!" he said sharply. "Damn it all!"

She stayed where he put her, her chest rising and falling as rapidly as his. He had to pace around the room to keep from looking into her eyes again. If he did, there was no telling what he'd do.

Yes, there was. He'd have her on her back and naked on that narrow bed, and he wouldn't think twice about it.

"I want you," he said, still pacing. "I have since last August—"

She was about to interrupt, but he held up his hand.

"August," he repeated. "I was standing in the middle of a damn cornfield and I saw you walking— I'm—this can't— if you don't—well, answer me, damn it!"

"You haven't asked me anything! Why are you yelling?"

"Because this is killing me! I want to take you to bed right now! I want to—" He stopped pacing and stood directly in front of her. "Do you know about these things at all, or don't you?"

"I know," she said quietly.

"Good. Good. Then I won't have to leave just yet. You can stay over there and I can stay over here—"

"John Howe?"

"What?"

"I want you to be the one," she said, and the breath went out of him.

"The one . . . what?" he asked with what little air he had left.

She looked up at him, and to his surprise, tears suddenly spilled down her face. She bowed her head, and he sat down on the bed beside her and took her into his arms.

"Don't," he said, brushing her hair back from her face. "I didn't mean to make you cry—"

"It's all I have that's mine," she said, leaning in to him, her hands resting on his chest. "I want you to be the one."

He couldn't believe the turn this conversation had taken. He suddenly hugged her tightly. "My God, what am I going to do with you?" He sat there, holding her, both mind and body in turmoil.

Amanda wiped at her eyes and tried to stop crying, waiting for him to say something. He was so *quiet* suddenly and he stayed that way.

She moved out of his arms so she could see his face. "You know what to do with me," she said, her voice little more than a whisper.

He stared into her eyes, and he drew a long, shaky breath. He stood and drew off his jacket, letting it fall on the floor. She watched him yank his suspenders off his shoulders and let them dangle, then drag his shirttail out of his trousers. She could see that his hands trembled slightly as he slid each shirt button through the buttonhole.

But he said nothing.

He sat down on the edge of the bed and began pulling off his boots, and when he did, his shirt fell open. She could see his bare chest, the masculine hairiness, quite plainly. It occurred to her that perhaps she should be doing something, but she didn't ask. She took a deep breath and looked away. When she looked back, he had two of the buttons on his trousers undone.

"If you're going to yell, 'uncle,'" he said, "this is where you'd better do it."

"I'm not going to yell 'uncle.'" She wasn't quite sure how the decision to do this thing had come about, except that it had to do with her hurt feelings and a lifetime of loneliness and loving him even if she might never see him again. The decision had come so easily, it must have been in her mind a long time.

But she couldn't sit there with him rapidly running out of buttons and not lose her nerve. She abruptly reached to turn back the quilts on the bed and crawled under them, pulling everything up to her chin.

In her rush to get into bed, her nightgown slid too far up, and she worked hard to get it back down around her ankles where it belonged.

Ordinarily.

She realized that he was watching her maneuvering with unabashed interest, and while a query of some kind was clearly on his mind, he didn't ask. He crossed the room to blow out the lamp and the candle. Then he dropped his trousers. She tried not to look away, and she almost made it.

He sat down on the side of the bed to take off his shirt, and after a minor tug-of-war with her to get the covers back, he slid into bed beside her and stretched out. There was hardly room for both of them, but he made no attempt to touch her. He lay on his back staring at the ceiling, while she waited.

The room flickered with firelight. The only sounds she could hear were the squeak and hiss of the coal burning and the cold wind outside. She didn't know what to do, she thought desperately; surely, he did.

"Come here," he said finally, reaching for her, pulling her closer to him. She was surprised that he still had his drawers on. She had expected him to be completely naked.

"How far are you going to let this go?" he asked.

"How far?" she repeated, because she had thought *that* was already settled.

"You heard me," he said. "You're about as close to screaming your head off as I've ever seen you—"

"No, I'm not."

"Yes, you are. I told you. You don't ever have to be afraid of me."

"I'm—" She broke off. She turned her head to look at him. For all her declarations that she wasn't a child, she certainly felt like one. She was so *ignorant,* regardless of what she'd just told him. All she had were guesses and hearsay and some rather alarming animal comparisons. She had kissed Thayer Giffen, but those kisses had never led her to a willingness to do *this.* She was afraid, not of John, but of herself. He'd know. John Howe would *know* she was stupid about these things. He'd know she'd lied. She stared into his eyes. "I'm not afraid. I'm—"

"What?" he prompted, their faces very close.

"It's—you won't laugh at me, will you? Because I don't...know what to do. Don't laugh at me, John Howe. Not now. Please—" She pressed closer to him, needing to hide for a moment.

"I'd never laugh at you," he whispered against her ear. "Never."

He held her for a moment longer, then he gently kissed her forehead. And then her eyes and the tip of her nose and her chin. And when he reached her mouth, she gave it to him willingly, parting her lips for him as she had earlier because she welcomed the return of the exquisite feeling his kisses elicited in her. Her arms were crossed protectively over her breasts, and she worked to get her hands free, sliding them upward over his bare chest, savoring the feeling of strong muscle and rough hair. His body was so different from hers, so pleasantly different.

He gave a small intake of breath as her palms skimmed over his nipples, and encouraged, she reached up to lightly touch his face and his mouth with her fingertips. She loved his mouth, the shape and the taste of it. She kissed him where her fingers had been, slowly at first, watching his eyes close, letting her lips and tongue softly caress his. When he moaned, she hugged him tighter, wanting to get closer to him still, and she kissed him everywhere she could reach, the kisses becoming hungry and urgent the way he'd taught her, the way he was teaching her even now. She loved the brush of his mustache and the stubbly roughness of his jaw. She loved the scent of his skin, the essence that was *him*. She savored it; she would never forget. Never. When she was old, she would close her eyes and remember the taste and the smell and the feel of this man.

He suddenly broke away, his breath harsh against her ear. He was trembling, as she was trembling.

"Are you sure?" he asked. "Are you? I don't want to do anything that you don't—"

"I—I'm sure." *I love you,* she almost said. She looked deeply into his eyes. "Show me what to do."

"Ah, God, if I had any scruples at all, I wouldn't—"

"I want to be with you," she whispered.

He gave a ragged sigh and pressed her closer. "It won't be like what you saw through that window—when we got to Washington—like that man and woman on the bed. It won't be like that. I promise."

His mouth came down on hers again, and his hands began to move over her. She could feel their warmth through the cloth of her gown as they grazed her breasts and hips and the backs of her thighs.

In a moment, his fingers began to fumble at the buttons of the *robe de nuit,* but the buttons were tiny and numerous and stubbornly functional. He abandoned them for the hem instead, dragging it upward so that he could have access to her bare skin. The idea of his hands on her body in this intimate way was shocking to her, but the reality was too pleasurable for her to protest.

I want you to touch me.

He began kissing her eyes and cheeks and neck, skipping over the wad of nightgown to graze the swell of her breasts. She could feel the cold air of the room on her, and then acute warmth as he took a tightly budded nipple into his mouth. She stiffened and gave a little gasp, not in pain, but in surprise and pleasure. This new sensation suffused her body, making her head arch back, making her give a soft moan. Nothing had prepared her for this, nothing she'd seen through a whorehouse window, nothing she'd guessed at on a train, nothing she'd ever heard in the giggling, whispered details of friends' wedding nights. No wonder young girls were so closely guarded, she thought. What a difficult job protecting virginity would be if the word got out that ruination was like *this*.

He moved to her other breast, to kiss, to suckle, and the pleasure intensified. She couldn't be still. There was such an urgent and warm aching in her belly and between her thighs—for what, she didn't quite know. She knew only that he was both the beginning and the ultimate end of her longing.

He didn't bother with buttons again. He pulled the gown upward until he got it over her head instead, then tossed it aside. It occurred to her that she should be concerned about her nakedness, but she couldn't quite manage it, even when she realized that he was working to get out of his drawers.

It was better without clothes. It was better to be so close, to feel the heat of his muscular body against hers. Without shame, her hands moved over his back.

How different a man's body is, she thought again.

She could feel, too, the urgent press of his maleness against her belly. She wanted to see, but she didn't dare. He delivered small, biting kisses along her shoulder and downward to her breasts. His hands kneaded, caressed; his mouth encircled. And when she made a small, breathless sound, he brought her leg up over him, his fingers sliding to that most intimate place of all, quickly, gently exploring, before she had time to be alarmed, stroking, invading. She was embarrassed by the wetness she felt there, and she tried to move away.

"No, love," he whispered, holding her still. "I'm going to touch you. I'm going to touch every part of you...."

She tried to tell herself that she shouldn't allow him to do this, but his mouth covered hers again in a kiss that deepened until she seemed to feel it everywhere. And he did touch her, gently, always gently, until he found the very source of her need.

She whimpered as even more pleasure burst in upon her, but she tried to stifle the sound.

"No," he said urgently. "Let me hear you. I want to make you feel good. I want to—"

The rest of what he said was lost in another kiss. He caught her hand and moved it downward, guiding her, showing her how to touch him as he touched her.

He made a soft "oh" sound as her fingers closed around him, and she marveled at the smoothness, the hardness. She marveled that she was able to give pleasure as well as receive it and that even her lightest touch made him moan.

He moved her onto her back suddenly, positioning himself between her legs, the male part of him seeking entry where his fingers had been. She could feel the steady pressure as his body tried to penetrate hers, pressure and then pain.

She gave a small gasp.

He made her look at him. "Forgive me for this part of it," he whispered, thrusting deeper until suddenly it was done. He was inside her; she could feel him. She could feel that he filled her completely. He held himself perfectly still, his arms braced and straining on either side of her. She clung to him because it hurt. *He* hurt, his intrusion, his bigness.

She closed her eyes, impaled and afraid.

"Amanda, open your eyes. Look at me," he whispered. "Look at me." When her eyes opened, he gently kissed her mouth, lingering there, trying not to lose control, his body shaking with the effort. She was so hot and tight around him. He was awash in pleasure and in the urgent need to intensify it. He began to move then, staring into her eyes, slowly, tentatively, giving her time to adjust to him.

"Love me," he whispered. "I need you."

His mouth nibbled at hers, the thrust of his body into hers becoming more insistent, less painful. A faint spark of renewed pleasure began to glow deep inside her, and her breath caught. She closed her eyes again, but it was different this time.

He thrust deeper, and the spark ignited, making her writhe beneath him and moan softly.

"Love me!" he insisted, and she lifted her hips to meet his, feeling the pleasure intensify with each thrust. She didn't want him to stop. This was beyond anything she had ever imagined; she could hear the sounds she was making, sounds she couldn't have held back if she'd wanted to, sounds he'd said he wanted to hear.

But she thought that he was beyond hearing. They both were. There was only this incredible, wonderful joining, the raging need to make it last forever.

In a blinding flash of heat and sensation, the pleasure peaked, making her body jerk, making her cry aloud as she hadn't done before. His movements quickened until he, too, cried out and his warm breath rushed against her neck. He trembled violently as he thrust deeply into her, again, and then again, and he collapsed against her, heavy and still.

Her arms and legs went around him, holding him fast, loving him with all her heart. *So this is what it's like,* she thought, trying not to weep. She wanted desperately to believe that he was hers now, that no one and nothing could come between them.

What if I never see you again!

He was completely spent. He lay with her in the semidarkness, still inside her, listening to her quiet breathing, waiting for his mind and body to function again. All the women he'd done this to or with or for, and he'd never felt the way he did now. Never. It had been all consuming—for him, and for her. His heart soared with the knowledge that he'd been able to pleasure her as well.

You are my dearest love, he thought. Did she know that? He hadn't precisely told her; he wasn't even sure when *he* realized it. It was just suddenly there somehow, and where it had come from or when, he couldn't say.

He lifted his head to look into her eyes for a moment before he got up and walked to the washstand. It occurred to him that perhaps he should be careful of his nakedness, but he was closer to her than he'd ever been to another human being. They had no reason for false modesty now as far as he was concerned, and to pretend otherwise, even for the sake of propriety, seemed grossly hypocritical.

He poured water from the pitcher into the bowl. It was too cold for comfort, but there was nothing he could do about it. He wet the square of flannel toweling that hung over the wooden rod and brought it back to the bed.

"Let me take care of you," he said, reaching to pull back the covers. But she had them up to her chin again, and he had to pull hard to get them out of her grasp. "Don't, love," he said, and she finally let go.

As he pulled the covers back, she turned her head away and lay very still. He realized immediately how vulnerable she must be feeling.

"You have a beautiful body, Amanda," he said. "It gives me great pleasure just to look at you."

She made no reply, and he reached to move her closer.

"Let me take care of you," he said again. "You may— there might be some—"

"I understand," she whispered, and he gently began to wash between her legs with the flannel towel. She made only a minor protest when he touched her, more in surprise, he hoped, than in pain.

He could feel her watching him as he walked back to the washstand to pour more water into the bowl and dump it into the bucket underneath. He tossed the piece of flannel into the fire so that there would be less evidence of her lost virginity.

Except that she hadn't *lost* it. He had taken it. No, she had given it to him.

What was it she'd said? *It's all I have that's mine.*

He came back to the bed and lay down beside her, covering them both against the chill in the room. He realized immediately that she was crying. Making love with her had been the most splendid experience of his life. The last thing he wanted was for her to cry.

"What's wrong?" he asked after a moment. "Are you crying because you think I've ruined you?"

"I was already ruined," she said with that relentless logic of hers.

"Did I hurt you?"

"Not . . . very much."

Not very much, he thought with some remorse. Of course he had hurt her. She had been a virgin, and what had been entirely pleasurable for him, hadn't been so easy for her.

"I don't want you to be sorry this happened between us."

"I'm not sorry."

"What then? What is it?"

She took so long to answer, he thought she wasn't going to.

"I just don't want to have to do . . . *this* for a living," she said finally.

He rose on his elbow. "Well, that's a damn good thing, because I don't want you doing *this* for a living, either. What are you talking about!"

She didn't answer him.

"Amanda—" he said, but she turned away. "You know I love you with all my heart, don't you?" He was trying to make her look at him, and that remark certainly got her attention. She suddenly sat up, and for a moment, he thought she was going to hit him the way she had on the train.

"Don't!" she whispered fiercely. "You're safe from me, John Howe. You don't have to lie to me. You don't have to tell me what you think I want to hear!"

"I'm not lying to you. I love you—"

"I signed the papers," she interrupted, as if that explained everything.

"What papers?"

"Beale's papers! You know what papers!"

"No, I don't," he said, grabbing her to him, because if he hadn't, she would have been out of bed and running. "I don't know and you had damn well better tell me. I mean it!" he said, holding her away so he could see her face. "I don't have much time left, Amanda. What papers?"

"The ones that say you can't be held responsible for... anything!"

"Anything," he repeated. "Like what?"

"Like me—or my bastard child." She wiped at her eyes with the back of her hand, and she was incredibly beautiful to him, sitting there with her hair loose and falling around her shoulders and her breasts almost bare.

"And just where were you supposed to get one of those?" he asked, recent events notwithstanding.

"It doesn't matter where. The main thing is that I not try to pass it off as yours." Her mouth was trembling and she bit down on her bottom lip.

"Beale brought some legal papers—and you signed them?"

"Yes."

"Why in God's name did you do that?"

"To prove that I didn't want anything from you! To prove that I wasn't going to hurt you. You know what they think."

"They who?"

"Your family, John Howe! Your—"

"My mother," he finished for her. The reason for his abrupt posting outside of Washington suddenly became clear to him. His mother or one of her influential friends had petitioned it from a member of Meade's staff. A nice safe posting for a rich man's son—not too close to home and not too far away. Just far enough to keep him out of harm's way, though his mother was likely more worried about Amanda Lee Douglas than what he might still encounter in the war. No wonder his commanding officer despised him.

"I thought you wanted me to sign them," Amanda said. "Beale said he saw you today—"

"He's a damned liar."

"I thought the papers were routine, something Beale has to do every time you take up with some . . . piece of baggage . . . like me—"

"Don't!" he said, lying back down and making her lie down beside him. He didn't want even to think what her meeting with Beale must have been like. Useful as the man might have been in the past, he was still a son of a bitch.

"I want us to marry," he said, holding on to her so she couldn't get away from him again. My God, what a way to make a marriage proposal, he thought. But hell, he'd sit on her if he had to. "I want us to marry as soon as I can get back here long enough to do it. If I can't do that, then I'll arrange for you to come to me—"

"You don't have to marry me."

"Damn it all, Amanda, aren't you listening to me? I love you! If I didn't, I wouldn't say so. I certainly wouldn't mention marriage. I wouldn't have to if you've signed Beale's damned papers." He moved so that he could see her face. It suddenly occurred to him what a sacrifice she'd made, sharing a bed with him like this in spite of Beale's legal arrangements. "Amanda, I don't have time to talk you into anything, so just tell me. Now, before I have to go. I've said what I want. What do *you* want? Do you want to be rid of me? Do you still want to get to Richmond? What?"

She suddenly hid her face in his neck. "Don't send me away," he thought she said.

"What?"

She lifted her head to look at him. "Don't send me away."

"I'm not going to send you away! My God, there is nobody on this earth more dear to me than you are. I didn't know about Beale. I swear it. I've written down my intentions for my father—are you listening to me? I've told him I want to marry you. If anything happens to me so that I can't—I've asked him to make arrangements for you. You won't ever have to worry about going back to the reverend and begging him for charity or anything like that.

"You believe me, don't you? I want you to wait for me. I want you to promise me you'll wait. I want you to stay here with my family."

"Your mother won't—"

"My mother needs to be reminded that I am no longer a sixteen-year-old boy. I will see that she is, you can be sure of that."

"John, I don't want to cause any more trouble."

"My father is the head of this house, Amanda, regardless of how it may seem. He will do as I ask." He kissed her soft cheek, then rested his face against hers. "I don't know if I'll be staying in Alexandria or not. I don't know how long I'll be gone. The war can't last much longer. Ah, God, I'm going to miss you! I want you to write me letters. And I don't want any halfhearted 'Dear Captain Howe' kind, either. I want you to write to *me.* And I want them so damned personal I'll have to keep them under lock and key. You have to promise me, because it's the only way I can stand being away from you—especially now—are you listening to me?''

"Yes," she said, her voice tremulous.

"Then tell me. Yes or no. Will you wait for me? I can't make you do anything you don't want to do. I can only ask and I'm asking, as humbly and as urgently as I know how. I want you to wait for me."

She looked into his eyes, their faces close. "Yes," she said finally, and his heart soared. *Yes!*

He reached to brush her hair back from her face, then hugged her to him, pressing her close so that he could feel the warmth of her body against his. He was leaving and he wanted to remember, but this time, by God, he was going to remember the real thing. He still had to deal with a disgruntled commander, and his meddling mother and a bloody war, but Amanda had said yes. He gave a wavering sigh and his hand cupped her breast. She was so beautiful!

He closed his eyes against the rush of feeling. He had to leave, damn it all, and he had to stop this, or he'd forget he was in the army altogether. He forced himself to sit up and began looking for his clothes.

"You have to go right now?" she asked, moving on her knees to be closer to him, modestly trying to cover herself with a corner of a quilt. She didn't quite make it, and the effect was nearly too much for him. He gave a sharp exhalation of breath and tore his eyes away.

"I have to be in Alexandria before dawn," he said, concentrating on getting his trousers back on. He didn't tell her that he didn't have a legitimate reason to arrive in Alexandria late or a pass, not even a forged one.

She didn't say anything more, sitting quietly by him while he dressed, her eyes huge and sad.

"Tell me one more thing," he said when he stood to put on his jacket.

"What?"

He looked away from her, then back again. He had never asked this of any woman. He had never wanted to know. He took a short breath to shore up his courage. "Do you...love me at all? Tell me if you do. I need to hear it."

Amanda was immediately on her knees in the middle of the bed, reaching out for him with one hand and holding the quilt corner with the other, completely incredulous that he didn't already know. "I love you," she whispered, letting the quilt go so she could lock her arms around his neck. "I love you, John David Howe!"

His eyes stung with tears. She was so dear to him and the damned quilt had fallen down. God, he didn't want to leave her! There were still so many things she needed to know about him. For the briefest of moments, his mind went to Max Woodard. Amanda had been right; he had done for Max the best he could, and if he had it to do all over again, he would still have to come out of that prison alone.

He made himself smile. "Kiss me now. Hard. And let me go. You are my dearest love—"

Chapter Ten

"Please, miss," Alice said urgently. "Can you wake up now?"

Amanda turned over, careful to keep the covers high. She was still the way John had left her—as naked as the day she was born. She had meant to put the nightgown back on, but she'd been too miserable, and it was too late to worry about it now. "What is it?"

"Mrs. Howe wants to see you, miss. She wants to see you *now.*"

Amanda wasn't surprised. She was not nearly so certain as John was that his father was the head of this house, and she had expected another summons to the library before the day passed. She looked at the window. The day had barely started.

"Hurry, please, miss!"

"Yes, all right. You can tell her I'll be there just as soon as I'm dressed."

"Oh, good, miss. Can you find your way to the library?"

"Alice, it is permanently etched in my brain."

"Miss?"

"Never mind. I'll find my way and I'll hurry." There was no reason not to get this meeting over with. She waited until Alice had left the room before she got up, and she tried to dress quickly, but her mind kept remembering all the places John Howe had touched and kissed.

She was a fallen woman. The sorry end the reverend had always predicted had arrived, and yet she didn't feel at all badly about it. She looked into the dim mirror over the washstand and smiled. The truth of the matter was that she was happy.

Her underclothes were still damp, but she wore them anyway, and her own clean but overly mended dress. Two people she had never seen before stood waiting in the downstairs foyer—a middle-aged man in a brown-checked suit who leered at her, and a plump, perhaps older woman dressed sedately in gray merino. They both nodded, he while spinning his hat on his finger.

Amanda went immediately to the carved double doors of the library and quietly knocked.

"Come in," Mrs. Howe said after a moment, and Amanda took a deep breath to steady herself. She had acquired a whole new appreciation for the Daniel in the lion's den story since she'd been in this house.

"Make sure the door is closed tightly, please," Mrs. Howe said. "You didn't see Harry anywhere about? I don't want him listening at the keyhole."

"A man and a woman are waiting in the foyer," Amanda said. "No one else."

Mrs. Howe was sitting on the same green velvet couch. She looked pale and tired, and she gestured toward another woman in the room, who stood looking out of the library windows well away from the warmth of the fire.

"Kate," Mrs. Howe said, and the woman looked around. Amanda recognized her immediately. Kate Woodard, who brought little boys presents from Paris and who stood beside her brother Max in a *carte de visite*. She was more beautiful than a mere photograph could begin to show— pale white skin, cascading blond curls, eyes that were a brilliant violet blue. She was wearing a dress of pearl-colored silk with white lace and white satin ribbons. A corsage of silk violets at her throat added just the right touch of color to match her eyes. Her eyes flicked over Amanda, not unkindly, but still with a trace of superiority and what Amanda would have guessed was relief. Kate Woodard clearly found the Rebel baggage John had brought home with him no threat.

"This is Miss Woodard," Mrs. Howe said.

The other woman smiled at Amanda. "Please call me Kate. I see no reason for formality—not when we owe you so much. Come and sit down, won't you?"

Amanda hesitated a moment, then took the same couch she'd sat on when she'd had her meeting with Beale. At least *he* wasn't here.

"My dear," Mrs. Howe began immediately, "this really is quite difficult. It's enough to say that men rarely know what is and is not proper behavior. Oftentimes, it is up to us women to set things right, no matter how distressing it may be—"

"Please," Amanda interrupted. "Whatever you want from me, just tell me."

"I'm afraid I am the one who wants it," Kate Woodard said. "Do you know about me at all?"

"I know that you are Max Woodard's sister—"

"I told you John wouldn't have said anything to her," Mrs. Howe said. "You will have to do that."

"Amanda," Kate continued, glancing at Mrs. Howe. "I may call you that, may I not?" she asked, not waiting for any kind of permission. "I'm also—this is very hard," she said, managing a wan smile.

"Tell her," Mrs. Howe said. "It is no kindness to drag this out."

"Amanda," Kate began again. "I'm also...I am Harry's mother. His *real* mother. And John—John is Harry's father."

For a moment, the room swayed, but Amanda said nothing, holding herself rigid on the couch. The silence in the room lengthened. She knew that both Kate and Mrs. Howe were waiting for some response on her part, but she sat there, seemingly unmoved. What splendid training the reverend had given her, what a wonderful gift, this ability to endure. There was but one thought in her mind. Kate Woodard was telling the truth.

Dear God, why hadn't she realized it sooner? Alice had all but told her there had been some scandal involving John and Max Woodard's sister. And she'd seen John and Harry together, witnessed the tenderness between them, looked into their identical eyes. If she'd only let herself recognize what was plainly in front of her, she wouldn't have had to suffer *this*.

"I was very young," Kate went on quietly. "Too young for marriage. My father wouldn't hear of it. I can't marry at all until I'm twenty-four, unless I do so without his blessing. Amanda, I...need you to help me."

"How can I possibly help you?" Amanda asked, still struggling for control. She could endure this; she *would* endure it. If only she could keep from twisting her hands together, if only she could breathe.

"I love Harry very much," Kate said, and Amanda was beginning to hate that quiet, patient voice. "I think you are aware that John does, too. But he is obligated to you. He believes he owes you his very life. He believes—no, he *knows*—he wouldn't have gotten home again without you. I can't fight that, Amanda—"

"Please!" Amanda interrupted. "Just tell me what you want."

"I want you to release him from that obligation. I don't ask that you give him up—I wouldn't be so foolish as to ask that. I ask instead that you give John and me the chance to find out whether or not we want to truly become a family. How can he know if you are here? He would be constantly bound by the gratitude he feels for you—"

"It isn't *all* gratitude," Amanda said, looking into her beautiful, troubled face.

"Perhaps not," Mrs. Howe put in. "But I know my son very well, my dear. Quite bluntly, I believe the emotion he associates with you will fade once he is back in his own world. What you are to him is more a comrade in arms, not a potential wife. John has political aspirations—I'm sure he's told you that. I know Washington, my dear, and he certainly *cannot* attain them with you on his arm. But I ask you this. Can you be happy with my son knowing you are ignoring another woman's bitter unhappiness? John has indicated that he wishes to behave properly by you—but it is poor Kate here who sorely needs it."

"I can't decide this for John," Amanda said. "And neither can you."

"But that is precisely it. I want my son to decide. But I want him to be able to do it without the persuasion of your very presence. Without the, shall we say, burden of his indebtedness to you."

Amanda stared at her, the memory of lying in John Howe's arms surfacing in her mind. She had been no *burden* then. And he had asked for her promise to wait. She had willingly given it to him. Her word.

"He will be advised that you have *chosen* to leave here. He will accept it," Mrs. Howe said.

"I have promised!" Amanda said.

Kate Woodard leaned forward and grasped her by both hands. "Amanda, please. For Harry's sake. John is yours already—if you want him that way. Just give us some time together, that's all I ask."

Amanda pulled her hands free. "Why haven't you settled this before now? Why haven't you and he already planned to marry?"

"I haven't been here," Kate said, very close to tears. "I've been in Europe with my father. When I came home, John was a prisoner of war in that awful place in North Carolina. I couldn't get a letter to him—this isn't the sort of thing one discusses in a letter in any case. He doesn't know that I have sincere hopes that he and I can now take care of Harry. Amanda, all I want is for you to let him be free to decide where his duty lies."

"Can you forgive him for your brother?" Amanda asked bluntly. "Your mother doesn't—"

"I can forgive him anything," Kate said. "I have forgiven him. I know John. He wouldn't have left Maxwell behind if there had been any other way."

Amanda closed her eyes for a moment and took a deep, shaky breath. She was cornered; there was no way out. She had met these people head-on twice now, and both times she'd lost.

What if his baby is in me? she wanted to say.

But she loved John Howe; she couldn't keep him from the child he already had. How could she? She kept thinking of the afternoon she'd spent with Harry, that lonely, wonderful little boy. John's son, not his little brother. His *son*.

"I... have to do it, don't I?" she said finally, unable to keep the tremor out of her voice. "And you both know it."

"Amanda," Mrs. Howe said, incredibly calling her by her given name for the first time. "I know you must think that I am very... hard. But I'm not. Truly I'm not. A woman isn't allowed to *do* things, Amanda. Her only accomplishments must be her children. My son has great potential. He can be someone important. He can make a great contribution to this country. He must be allowed to do the right thing—for himself and for Kate. I truly *am* grateful for what you've done for him, and this family. I promise that you won't be left to fend for yourself—"

"I don't want your promises," Amanda said. It had come down to pride after all. She would take nothing from this woman. She made an attempt to get up. She didn't want to hear any more, couldn't bear to hear any more.

"Amanda, are you all right?" Kate asked solicitously.

No, Kate! I'm not all right!

"Quite all right," Amanda said, looking past her to the windows. It was snowing. Outside, everything looked as cold and bleak and frozen as she felt.

Why didn't you tell me, John Howe? How could he have been serious about a marriage and not have told her about Kate?

Liar! You and Thayer both!

"Amanda, no. Wait, please," Mrs. Howe said. "There is something else. I had asked you to stay here until Monday morning. I had a reason for that." She reached out to touch Amanda's arm, but Amanda barely heard her.

"Mr. and Mrs. Able—the man and woman in the hall," Mrs. Howe went on quickly. "They are from Mr. Pinkerton's agency. They have been South, to North Carolina, on my behalf. They only just returned this morning. My understanding from John and from the Ables is that your father is very... unforgiving. But your stepmother..."

Amanda looked down at her. "They've seen her? Is she all right? She's not sick or—"

"Your stepmother has sent you this," Mrs. Howe said, taking a letter from her pocket.

Amanda hesitated, then took it, her hands trembling. The envelope was homemade; it had been fashioned out of a piece of flowered wallpaper. Tears came into her eyes at the sight of Verillia's familiar spidery hand.

She tore it open. There was no second sheet. The letter was written on the back of the folded wallpaper envelope. "My dear sweet Amanda," the first line began. "Come home...."

John had little trouble getting out of Washington. He fell in with a train of army baggage wagons near the Chain Bridge and got across on their pass. It was one of the most heavily guarded bridges into the city, but the night was damnably cold, and the sentries weren't overly concerned about the traffic heading out. Later, when the camp sentry demanded his pass, he boldly handed over the bottle of whiskey he had stuck in his greatcoat pocket.

The sentry, an older man who wasn't about to be fooled, eyed the bottle and then him, his rifle ready and leveled at John's gut.

"This is a bribe?" the sentry wanted to know.

"It is," John said, swirling the bottle a little so the soldier could tell it wasn't empty.

"I could shoot you dead for it, Captain, right here and now."

"You could," John agreed, "but I'm apt to drop the bottle."

The man suddenly grinned. "You crazy son of a bitch," he said, snatching the whiskey out of John's hand.

John couldn't believe his luck. A man with a thirst instead of some Holy Roller like the reverend. He gave the sentry a smart salute and rode the rest of the way into camp—where his luck promptly ended. The sun was just coming up, and word of his not so impending arrival had preceded him. He spent the next hour listening to a livid colonel rant and rave about his flagrant lack of military discipline.

"You are a sorry piece of work, Howe!" the colonel said, still yelling because John offered no excuses for his delay. "Have you got anything to say!"

"My horse, sir," John said immediately. "He's a good mount and I've ridden him hard. I'd very much appreciate it if you'd give me leave to tend to him."

The colonel glared at him across the desk, incredulous to the point of bursting a vein. But John had been a cavalryman for the past four years, and old habits died hard. He'd be properly contrite *after* he'd taken care of his horse.

"Do it!" the colonel said. "And then get yourself back in here. I'm not done with you yet."

When John stepped outside, he realized immediately that his little one-sided conversation with the colonel had drawn an interested crowd of soldiers, not because a dressing down was unusual, but more probably because it wasn't one of them for a change. He didn't see his mount where he'd left it tied, and he pushed his way through them.

"Cap," someone called, and he looked around.

"Your mount's been fed and stabled, Cap," a sergeant said.

"Thank you, Sergeant . . . ?"

"Whickes. Ain't no need to go thanking me, Cap. I ain't aiming to see no animal suffer just because he's thrown in with a hell-raiser through no fault of his own."

John stared at the man for a moment, then smiled. "So how was the whiskey, Sergeant?"

"Damn fine. Only bright spot in the whole goddamned watch." He spit tobacco juice in a practiced arc. "You ought not to have come dragging in here late like that, Cap. I reckon you know that peacock colonel in there is going to have your butt."

"Couldn't be helped," John said, his mind going immediately to Amanda, sweet and loving and lying under him. He could *feel* her around him and his body responded immediately. Just the thought of her was enough to put him into exquisite discomfort.

He forced his mind back to his present situation, determined to focus his attention on Whickes, who was watching him thoughtfully.

The sergeant rolled his eyes and shook his head. "Yeah, well, Cap, I just hope to hell she was worth it."

The colonel did indeed intend to have his butt. John was attached to a cavalry unit in A. C. Gillem's division and heading South before he could get his coat off. But Whickes had been only partially correct. The colonel, sick to death of political petitions and independent-minded underlings, posted Whickes right along with him. Whickes was regular army, an old Indian fighter from the territories, who was as unimpressed by holy military ritual as any man John had ever met. The sergeant still kept his head almost shaved as if he expected to be scalped any minute, and apparently, disciplinary sentry duty on freezing-cold nights had become his permanent state. It was no wonder he'd been so receptive to an unexpected bottle of the O Be Joyful.

It took them four days to get to Knoxville, and nearly that long again to get situated in camp. The town was a sea of blue uniforms, and the bitter cold of Washington had given way to warm temperatures and heavy rain. The streets of the town had thawed into knee-deep mud. Everything was bottlenecked: men, supply wagons, horses. It seemed to John that half the Union cavalry was in northeast Tennessee—stuck.

He berated himself constantly for not having seen his mother's heavy hand in his sudden orders to report. She moved in high places, and she was not above whatever political machinations it took to get him placed where she wanted if the situation seemed dire enough. Clearly, she had been alarmed enough to do it, and the plan must have been to keep him occupied for a time outside Washington and away from Amanda. Well, he'd certainly complicated that. Even his mother wouldn't have wanted him sent to this god-awful mud hole in Tennessee.

He did manage to bribe a telegraph operator to send word to his father of his whereabouts, but there was only so much he could put in the message. He was hopeful of a letter from Amanda right away, but none came. He tried not to worry about it; there were a thousand things that could hold up the mail, and God knew he had plenty of other things to worry about.

His new company was undoubtedly the sorriest lot of men it had ever been his misfortune to encounter. They were the dregs of other decimated units who had been thrown together into one mismatched, indifferent, quarrelsome company. John doubted that half of these men knew who he was or his name—or each other's, which was worse. He had been accustomed to the Pennsylvania Sixth—the Lancers, the "turkey stickers"—all of whom had been, at the very least, social acquaintances. They had all come from the same background, gone to the same colleges and boarding schools. They knew one another's families. Until his capture, John had thrived in an atmosphere of camaraderie, no matter what hell he found himself in. Here, he was a complete outsider, merely one of a long line of replacements for dead officers. The flagrant disorganization and lack of discipline hit him the moment he arrived—a situation he did *not* intend to have continue. He had to stay alive to get back to Amanda, and he was less apt to do that with this sorry crew.

He had Whickes and whatever sergeants he could round up immediately haul the men out, rain or no rain, mud or no mud. The party was over, and the sooner these troopers understood that, the better. If John had learned nothing else in the Pennsylvania Sixth, he had learned that the first step toward being a soldier was looking like one. Colonel Richard Rush had tolerated absolutely no breach in regulations when it came to military dress, and annoying as it had been at the time, John found that he had learned the lesson well.

The one lesson he hadn't had to learn was how to command. He made his inspection down the hastily assembled line, giving orders as he went. No unbuttoned jackets, no city shoes, no sutlers' hats and no goddamn lieutenants with goddamn feathers. Then he gave them ten minutes to get themselves together, and God help the man who didn't make it back in time. He inspected equipment, horses, cook tents, water and food supplies, latrines, and by the time he finished, the company had enough chores to occupy them for a month. He gave them two hours, setting Whickes loose on them at his loud and profane best to make sure they did it.

Whickes had a wonderful time, but John was exhausted by the exertion it took to scare the hell out of his new company. His legs were as shaky as they'd been when he first got out of the prison, a fact that didn't escape one of the regimental surgeons, a major, who had come out in the rain ostensibly to watch the fun.

"You all right, Howe?" he asked around the cigar he had clamped in his teeth.

"Fine," John said with considerable effort. He could feel the major's scrutiny, and he tried to look a whole lot stronger than he felt.

"It's about time this company got somebody who wasn't afraid to kick these lazy sons of bitches in the— Are you sure you're all right?"

John stared at him, trying to decide if he could answer and still stay upright.

"Reid," the surgeon said, as if John had asked him his name. "Major Matthew Reid, at your service. Maybe you want to turn around and walk in that direction," he said, subtly gesturing with his head. "Your quarters are in that

Chapter Eleven

*W*hy?

The question was always in his mind and there was no way he could answer it. He simply did not understand. Everything had been all right between them when he left—or as right as possible under the circumstances. Amanda had given him the most precious gift she had to give *and* her word. For the first time in their tumultuous relationship, he hadn't for one minute considered that she would go anywhere, not after the night they had spent together, not after the promise she had made. And God knew it had never entered his mind that she would go back to Salisbury.

Why would she do that, damn it! Why would she go back home?

After two or three whiskeys too many one night, he'd even asked Whickes. Several times. Whickes had humored him and claimed not to know. He said that he believed the dashing Captain Howe was suffering from a bad case of nostalgia. If that was going around all the time feeling like something was going to die, then that was definitely what John had. He couldn't sleep, and when he did, he had nightmares.

I love you, John David Howe.

He remembered just the way she'd said it. He knew that things sometimes looked different in the cold light of day, but why would she say it if she hadn't meant it?

What happened? What happened!

He wrote a desperate letter home, demanding to know, but the reply that came was no more enlightening than the telegram had been. His mother had written it, filling the letter with phrases about Amanda like "her choice" and "her decision." He threw it aside, unanswered. On February 20, he got a second letter from his mother. This one had two sheets of paper in it with The Pinkerton Agency on the letterhead. The first one advised her that the "subject," Miss Amanda Lee Douglas, had been delivered safely and without incident to the "preplanned destination."

"What preplanned destination?" he said out loud, not caring that he was reading it in the mess hall and that there were a number of his fellow officers seated around him. He took a look at the second sheet, his incredulity growing as he read. It was an investigative report on Amanda Lee Douglas, her date of birth, her parents, her schooling. He skimmed down the page, one phrase catching his eye—*secret arrangement.*

. . . though there are no official records of the event, he read, *there are enough rumors, i.e., testimony from various acquaintances of the subject, to substantiate that she willingly entered into a secret arrangement with one Thayer W. Giffen, 1st Lieutenant, Company D, Tenth Regiment, N.C.S.T., "Ramsay's Battery," willfully and without her father's consent or knowledge, to marry said Lieutenant Giffen. The marriage did not take place, however, as the engagement was subsequently broken, the reason being, it is commonly acknowledged, that Lieutenant Giffen discovered that the subject was not a virgin—*

"That is a goddamned lie!" John said. And no one knew that any better than he did. He abruptly looked up. Every pair of eyes in the mess hall was on him.

"Bad news?" Major Reid, who was seated nearest to him, asked mildly.

"Mind your own damn business," John said shortly.

"Well, I would, John, if you'd learn to read your mail with your mouth shut. These provocative utterances of yours get the better of a man's curiosity—and your restless nights, of course."

"What the hell is that supposed to mean?"

"It means you talk in your sleep, John," Reid said, grinning and lifting his tin cup. "To the elusive Amanda," he said knowingly. "And her speedy return."

John was completely taken aback. He knew he'd said too much to Whickes the night he'd had too many whiskeys, but good God! His own private humiliation, and every one of them must know about it. He had thought himself miserable before, but the knowledge that he was likely the laughingstock of the regiment and the revelation that Amanda had planned to marry some bastard Reb lieutenant was more than any one man ought to have to bear.

Of course, he'd asked for the misery. He had demanded to know the why of Amanda's abrupt departure and now he apparently did. Thayer W. Giffen, a living, breathing reason why she would go back to North Carolina. Did she still love him? Hell, he didn't know. She'd never even mentioned the son of a bitch. He didn't know anything and wasn't about to as long as he was stuck here—except that he was nearly overcome with jealousy, an entirely new emotion in his experience. He vacillated back and forth between believing every word of the Pinkerton report and believing none of it. In his worst moments, he tried to convince himself that his brief love affair with Amanda Douglas was over. Their paths had crossed through no fault of their own, they'd been together for a time, and now it was ended. He could forget her if he put his mind to it, except that his mind refused to accommodate him. He kept remembering, whether he wanted to or not, the way she looked, and felt, and smelled and tasted. He had a whole heartful of memories, haunting memories that came back to him night and day. He'd seen her happy and sad, angry and afraid. He'd seen her aroused. And passionate. God, yes, passionate.

Amanda!

He had to talk to her. He had to, and there was no way in hell he could do it.

And he still had this damnable company of sorry troopers to deal with. He tried to be fair, to give praise when it was due, but he was sick to death of every damned one of them. He worked them hard—and himself. It was the only choice he had save desertion. It was the only choice he had if he wanted to stay alive. The rumors of a new campaign were rampant. Something was in the works; he could *feel* it, and he had no intention of going into battle with a bunch of misfits. He had them drill and redrill—parade formations, battle tactics, every cavalry maneuver he and Whickes could think of and a few Whickes had personally invented out of necessity as an Indian fighter. John even got the company a decent bugler, a boy from Indiana named Tobin, who could run through all the bugle calls well enough so that the men could at least tell them apart, even if they might not know what to do with them.

When the company had improved somewhat, John challenged other companies to match skills, and if his men won, he footed the bill for the celebration with money that suddenly appeared for him—courtesy of his mother's purse, no doubt—in a Knoxville bank. It seemed fitting to him that she fund the only route he had, roundabout though it might be, of getting at the truth.

More letters came from his mother. They were overly cheerful and filled with empty, meaningless prattle. He didn't care what was happening in Washington politics. He didn't care what Kate Woodard and the young ladies were wearing at the Sanitary Commission Ball. He didn't answer any of them, except to send some more lead soldiers to Harry. He missed the boy, and damn it, he missed Amanda. She was the only one he wrote to, letter after letter he stuffed into a leather pouch and kept because he had no way to send them.

The second week in March, the regiment moved from Knoxville eastward into North Carolina. John was in the right state, at least, and he took what comfort he could from that and from the fact that his company finally had some semblance of a fighting unit. He got no comfort from anything else, not from the whiskey ration and not from the camp followers who tagged along. He had no interest in either, and he resigned himself to his misery. It made him frantic to think of Amanda in that prison town with the war so nearly done. His only remedy was to continue his unrelenting physical activity. If he were completely spent, he could count on a few hours of uninterrupted and, he hoped, non-verbal sleep.

The mountainous terrain of the Blue Ridge was incredibly beautiful and damned hard going. The regiment had been traveling, in and out of the saddle, in twelve-hour stretches to cross from Boone into Wilkesboro. John was as jumpy as a first-timer on his virgin campaign, and his edginess was compounded by the men in command. Gillem, the division commander, wanted to burn everything he saw, and General Stoneman had gotten all over him after the raid through Boone for letting some of his men run wild with a torch. Both of them had been in a royal snit ever since, the result of which was that lesser officers like John lived hard. He lost track of the date, of the day of the week even. His only reality was the back of a horse, and for once he was damned glad to see a bivouac so he could get out of the saddle and sleep.

The night was dark and quiet. John lay in his blanket and tried not to think about the places that hurt. Listen, he kept telling himself. Don't feel. *Listen.*

Crickets. A canteen rattling. Blowing horses. A woman's soft moan.

Damn Lieutenant Pike and his big redheaded laundress! John thought, turning on his side. He could hear them quite plainly somewhere nearby, Pike's heavy breathing and her soft cries. Pike was fresh out of West Point and utterly delighted that the war still continued. He was all army, determined to go home carrying his shield or on it. The damned fool probably owned one, too. And, as a warrior supreme, he considered the horizontal pleasures his God-given right— but, damn it all, every single bivouac?

John sighed heavily and tried to endure, at war with himself once again to keep the memory of Amanda at bay. Pike and his laundress were *not* helping.

He shifted his position and closed his eyes tight, trying to force himself to sleep. He might have made it if Whickes had left him alone.

"Cap?" Whickes whispered outside the tent. "Oh, Cap?"

"What is it?" John asked after a moment, because he had no hope that Whickes would get tired and go away.

"The old man wants you. They're getting together for some kind of big powwow. Stoneman says to get you up there *now.*"

"Ah, damn it," John said, trying to unwind from his blanket. "Why?"

"Don't know, Cap. He's in another snit, though."

Well, fine, John thought. That ought to top off a truly wonderful day just about right.

General Stoneman was not a man to be kept waiting; even Whickes would have recognized that. John had no intention of antagonizing him, not when he was already out of sorts with Gillem. He quickly made his way in the dark to Stoneman's tent, but he was kept standing outside with most of the rest of the general's staff officers.

"Captain John D. Howe," an orderly suddenly called out. "Is Captain Howe here?"

"Yes," John said, stepping forward, as puzzled as the rest of them as to why he would be called in alone. Stoneman sat behind a camp table with a lantern on it. John wondered if the old man knew how much they had in common, that they had both been in hellhole Confederate prisons.

"I don't believe a man should be corrected in public, Captain Howe," Stoneman said, cutting through the amenities.

That was news to John, but he had the good sense not to say so.

Stoneman looked up at him, the piercing glare he was so famous for very much in evidence. "A war correspondent from the *Washington Star* has hand-delivered me a letter from a Mrs. Howe. It seems that she has had no news of her son. It seems that she—and certain members of Congress—believe that I am guilty of keeping him so busy that he cannot find the time to write home. Would you care to enlighten me about that, Captain?"

"No, sir," John said, looking Stoneman in the eye.

"*Have* you been writing home?"

"I have not."

"I see," Stoneman said, beginning to tap his fingers on the tabletop. "Why not?"

"It's a personal matter, sir. My mother knows the reason—both my parents do. I regret that the general was inconvenienced."

"Inconvenienced? Yes. Inconvenienced. I can assure you, Captain Howe, that I have more to do than chastise recalcitrant young officers about their neglected letter writing—regardless of what your mother and the congressmen think. I don't intend to be bothered this way again. Do I make myself clear?"

"Very clear, sir. Is there anything else, sir?"

"There is. When your presence is no longer required, Captain, *I* will let *you* know—Julius!"

The orderly appeared immediately, responding to Stoneman's unspoken command by letting the remaining officers file into the tent. John stood there, fuming. Part of him could not *believe* his mother's audacity; another part of him wasn't the least bit surprised. She was a strong woman; he had always admired her for that. But she had gone too far this time.

Damn it all!

He let himself be pushed into the background, only half-listening to the discussion around the camp table. Gillem, of course, was in favor of the same scorched-earth policy Sherman was using. Stoneman wanted to spend as little time as possible in the town; he would release the prisoners and leave them to their own revenge—

He suddenly realized that Stoneman was talking about the prison in Salisbury. He also realized that the general had called his name. Of course, John thought. Stoneman was a stickler for detail. He would know that he had an officer who had just escaped from there.

"Sir?" John said over the heads of the officers in front of him.

"What intelligence can you give us?"

The men in front made room for John to get by, and he knew perfectly well what Stoneman meant—troop strength, railroads, the number of prisoners and civilians. But he had just listened to them decide to sacrifice the town and the people in it in the name of expediency. He started his report well enough, but after a long awkward pause, he suddenly continued with, "My lady lives there, sir."

He hadn't known he was going to say it; he certainly wasn't prepared for the roar of laughter that followed. But he stood there anyway, with Stoneman's famous glare cutting him in two, not regretting for a moment that he'd said it.

"I...see," Stoneman said when the laughter died. "I take it, Captain Howe, she is a Secessionist."

"As Reb as they come," John admitted.

"I believe I now have insight into this letter business, Captain."

"Yes, sir."

Stoneman almost smiled. "Well, Captain Howe, you have certainly enlivened a routine strategy meeting. Perhaps we should have had you in sooner. Nevertheless, that is all."

Major Reid was waiting early next morning, grinning like an idiot.

"By God, John, I thank my lucky stars for the day you joined this regiment. I swear I don't know when I've had so much to write home about. My aged mother actually lives for my next letter. She is going to *love* this. Colonel Miller says you couldn't have shocked the old man any more if they'd paid you—"

"Oh, shut up, Reid! Leave me alone, damn it! I've got enough on my mind without you, too." John spurred his mount and rode away, knowing all the time Reid would catch up.

He did, but he didn't say anything, which annoyed John more.

"Surely to God you are not writing my private life home to your mother!" John burst out when he couldn't stand it any longer.

"Why not?" Reid asked. "She's an old lady. She needs a little spice in her life. I told her about Pike, too, and that redheaded laundress he keeps on her back all the time. All that subterfuge he goes through to get her into his tent when he thinks nobody is looking. Of course, you are Mama's favorite. And when I tell her your ladylove is Reb—"

"Damn!" John said, spurring his horse again.

On the tenth of April, Stoneman divided the column. John waited, grim-faced and filled with dread until the word came down that it was Palmer's brigade that was being dispatched to Salem and that John's company would go south with Stoneman.

On the eleventh, they were twelve miles from Salisbury and moving at a steady speed with no opposition of any kind. The colonels—Brown and Miller—didn't think the inactivity would last, and John was inclined to agree with them. He had not come all this way, through four years of fighting, to think that the Rebs were just going to hand over everything to Stoneman's cavalry. He had been in skirmishes where the Confederates had thrown rocks for lack of anything more lethal.

They crossed a river after midnight. He expected this to be the place where they would encounter some resistance, but there was nothing. It was damned eerie. Shortly before dawn, the scouts came riding in hard, and he got that familiar sinking feeling he always experienced when a battle was near at hand. The scouts stopped for a moment with Brown and Miller, then galloped down the line to Stoneman.

"What do you think, Cap?" Whickes asked at John's elbow.

"I think there's going to be hell to pay," John said.

Whickes spit a stream of tobacco juice, and he kept hovering around. "Cap? Me and the rest of the boys, we was just wondering what she looks like. Your lady. You know—just in case.''

John didn't ask "just in case what," and he didn't ignore the request.

"She's...little," he said, not caring anymore that the men knew about the torch he was carrying. "About so high." He marked the place on his shoulder where Amanda came. "Dark hair—pretty hair. And her eyes, her eyes are dark, too. And big. She's a pretty little thing—careful of her smiles, though. Not shy exactly. It's something else. When she talks to you, she looks right into you—" He broke off, suddenly mindful of Whickes's grin.

"If you don't mind me saying so, Cap, you are a lovesick fool."

"Get out of here, Whickes," John said.

Whickes obliged, but he was still grinning, and he intended, John supposed, to pass the description of Howe's runaway lady down the line.

There was no word from Stoneman; the column continued to advance, running into Confederate pickets just as the sun came up. The main body of Rebs was dug in on the other side of a small creek. John didn't know where it lay in relation to the rest of the town. He could see gun emplacements—twelve-pound Parrotts, he thought. A very bad sign.

The Rebs had taken up the boards on the one bridge—not much of a handicap, because the water didn't look too deep. He could see puffs of smoke high in the trees and hear the reports and the ensuing buzz as the Reb sharpshooters took up their sport. One of them was damned good, too, kicking up the dirt everywhere John moved. Troopers were scattering around him, and a detachment from the Eleventh Kentucky was sent upstream double time to ford the creek and get in behind. Right on cue, the Reb artillery started, toppling trees wherever the shells landed.

John could see that Gillem and Miller had their heads together, but the noise of the cannonading covered anything
they said. His experience told him they were likely planning
to storm the bridge, and he moved closer in.

"This company's ready, sir," he said.

Colonel Miller looked up and grinned. "I have no doubt
that one of the company is. How about it, boys?" he yelled
to the troop. "Can you put your captain where he needs to
go?"

The company responded immediately with loud whistles
and cheers.

"All right," Miller said, turning to Gillem. "Give me one
more company and we can do it."

There were more cheers. John couldn't say when he'd seen
such enthusiasm, from his own men and from the ones left
behind. They all seemed to see this as some kind of ad-
vancement of the course of true love, rather than a military
action.

"Give 'em hell, boys!" somebody kept yelling. "Give 'em
hell!"

John led the charge himself, intending to do exactly that.
But whoever commanded the Reb forces was no fool. He
withdrew as many men and guns as he could get away with,
leaving the decrepit home guard to set up a delaying action
until he could make another stand. It became a matter of
trying to run him down, if the cavalry could get through to
do it.

It took two hours—two damned hours! And who knew
where the Reb artillery had gotten to. John let himself
briefly wonder if Lieutenant Thayer W. Giffen was one of
the men who had straddled a caisson and made a run for it.
The son of a bitch was supposed to be an artilleryman.

Finally, the column was on the move again, this time with
Stoneman at the head. John and his company rode a short
distance behind him, not far enough away to suit John, be-

cause they were all acting like a bunch of schoolboys. And one of them, damn him, burst into song: "Our captain fell in *love* / With a lady like a *dove*...."

John kept expecting Stoneman to turn around and glare him to death, but he didn't. In any event, whatever happened, this group of men he'd worked so hard to unite wasn't going to miss a thing.

"You keep that bugle buttoned," he said to Tobin in passing. The last thing he wanted to hear was a lovesick singer with bugle accompaniment.

"Aw, Cap—"

"You heard me."

From the outskirts of Salisbury onward, they saw no living thing. No animals. No people. Everything was shut up tight. They crossed a railroad bridge. That, John knew. The cornfield where he'd first seen Amanda was nearby. He urged his mount into a canter.

He finally saw the Douglas house, and he reined in a bit, looking at the upstairs porch and the now budding wisteria vine he'd used to climb to the second story that night when the patrollers had cut across the yard.

It seemed so long ago.

He spurred his horse into taking the picket fence that enclosed the front yard, an easy enough jump.

"What is that officer doing!" someone shouted behind him, but he didn't stop. He couldn't be bothered with stupid questions. His only concern was getting at the Reverend Douglas so he could find Amanda, and by God, he'd beat the information out of him if he had to.

Surprisingly, the reverend came out of the house—because he didn't recognize the cavalryman who was about to ride onto his front porch. John leaned out and grabbed him by his shirtfront, dragging him down the steps.

"Where is she!" he demanded. "Where is your daughter!"

The reverend paled, but he stood his ground. "I have no daughter!"

John jerked his revolver out of his belt and held it an inch from the reverend's face, giving the horse his head so that he crowded the reverend into the porch railing. "Old man, you are dead where you stand if you play with me. I have asked you a question. Where is she!"

A woman came rushing out onto the porch, fearful and near weeping, one hand pressed hard into her breast.

"Tell me where she is," John said, glancing at her. "Verillia—tell me where Amanda is!"

Her eyes flickered at his use of her name, but she shook her head and backed away.

"You know her safety lies with me," John said in a rush. "I know who you are. She told me. She told me you were a good person. Verillia, please!"

"You—you won't let no harm come to her?"

"No! For God's sake, woman! Tell me where she is!"

Verillia gave a short nod. "She's...at the doctor's house. This street runs behind it. It's a big white house with iron railings—" She pointed in the direction, and John took off, jumping the fence again and bolting down the street.

A noise behind him made him turn in the saddle. The picket fence was down and the entire company followed behind him, Major Reid included, John supposed, so as not to miss any details for his elderly mother.

My God, he thought, but he kept going.

The doctor's house was not difficult to identify; there were indeed iron railings—and a yard full of wounded men. Stoneman's cavalry had taken a worse toll than John had thought. He supposed it was lucky that his company had come along with him on this detour; they could see to all these newly acquired prisoners, and he could get on with finding Amanda. Damned if he knew how long he could look before somebody ordered him shot. He almost smiled. Of course, they'd have to shoot an entire company as well, and an army surgeon.

He dismounted in the yard, his revolver still in his hand. His company swirled around him, moving quickly, doing what they'd been trained to do.

"Watch yourself, Cap," Whickes called after him.

He gave a short nod of acknowledgment, but he didn't slow down, crossing the yard through the boxwoods to the gravel path that led up to the front door. He stepped up onto the porch. There was a sharp intake of breath from a woman with a dipper in her hand who stood just inside the doorway. She stepped aside to let him pass.

The downstairs of the house was total chaos. There were men lying everywhere. Women ran back and forth carrying water and bandages and bowls. He pushed his way into the confusion, alarming one woman enough to make her drop her bucket. He saw a dark-haired girl in the room to his right, but it wasn't Amanda. She was too tall, too heavy. He was just about to yell out Amanda's name when he saw her. She was at the back of the entry hall, kneeling beside some poor devil in his death agony. The front of her dress was all bloody, and the man kept pulling on her, dragging on her with his bloody hands. She was so tired; he could see the weariness, and he wanted to grab her up and run with her, he didn't care where, anywhere as long as it was away from here.

He stepped over a soldier's legs to get to her, but someone grabbed him by the arm. Pike, damn him, and he wouldn't let go.

"Captain Howe! The general says you are relieved—"

He jerked his arm free, his eyes on Amanda. She hadn't seen him, hadn't once looked up from that dying man.

My poor love.

He couldn't get to her. People kept getting in his way. Pike was still yelling, and Reid. They both grabbed him by his arms, dragging him bodily in the other direction.

"Damn it, John!" Reid barked at him. "Do you want her to see you shot!"

He heard what Reid was saying; he just didn't care.

"Go on, damn you!" Reid cried. "Stoneman's fit to be tied! I'll take care of her! Don't be stupid, man! You're going to ruin every goddamn chance you've got! He'll have you shot, damn it!"

John looked at him.

"John!" Reid said, still hanging on to him. "Go on! Now! I'll take care of her!"

He stopped struggling, the truth of what Reid said finally penetrating.

"All right," he said, trying to get one last glimpse of Amanda before he went outside to face Stoneman. "All right—"

Chapter Twelve

Charlie Wood died.

Amanda looked down at her dress. His blood was all over her.

"Come away now, miss," someone said, and she looked up to see one of the Yankee surgeons who had been helping with the wounded. "There's nothing to be done for this man. The lady of the house—I've forgotten her name. She would like you to come upstairs with her. Can you do that?"

"Yes," she answered, but when she stood, her weak knees made her sway. She walked to the stairs, and she made it as far up as the third step past the turn before she had to sit down. She held on to the banister for support, but she just couldn't make herself stand again.

"Miss?"

She looked up again into the Yankee surgeon's face, surprised that he had come with her. He had red hair, a shade or two lighter than his beard, and very pale blue eyes. He seemed very tall from her vantage point, and lean. His nose was peeling from too much sun. He knelt by her suddenly, and she could see a rash of freckles on his face and hands.

"You mustn't sit here, miss," he said. "You're apt to get trampled." He gave her a tentative smile—she thought to soothe her in case she felt inclined to hysterics. "Do you live here?"

She nodded.

"Maybe you'd better go on to your room then. I'll tell the doctor's wife—or have we taken it?"

"I don't know."

"Is it upstairs? All those are spoken for, generals and colonels, you know." He smiled again, but she couldn't return the smile.

She looked up sharply at the sound of cannonading. She could feel her body trembling. She clenched her hands around the banister to try to stop shaking. There were rivulets of dried blood between her fingers.

"Where . . . are the cannons now?" she asked, still trying to hold her body still.

"Down at the river. It's not as close as it sounds."

She looked away from his overt kindness and leaned her head against the banister.

"It's your turn to say something," the Yankee surgeon whispered, teasing her a little, she realized, but she could only shake her head, the trembling worse.

"Get me some brandy, Whickes," he said to a second pair of legs that appeared.

"Yes, sir!"

"Untested!" he called after the soldier, apparently as an afterthought. He stood, then put his hand on her shoulder. "The worst is over. Truly. I'm going to get something to make you feel better."

Amanda wasn't listening. She had caught sight of another soldier through the front window. She could see only his profile, but her breath left her. John Howe was standing outside on the porch.

Her vision swam before her; the noise and confusion around her seemed to recede. She gripped the banister hard to keep from crying out to him. She couldn't believe it. She needed him so desperately, and he was really here.

She tried to clear her head, to make her legs work. The front door was ajar, and after a moment he and two other soldiers passed in front of it.

"John Howe!" she said out loud, but the effort was late and too feeble for him to hear her. He and the two other soldiers moved quickly past and stepped off the porch. She tried to get up, but her knees wouldn't hold her.

John!

The Yankee surgeon came back down the stairs.

"Here, drink this," he said, offering her a glass.

She turned her head away, still trying to see out the front door.

The Yankee surgeon was very persistent, putting his hand on the back of her neck to force her to drink. She caught his wrist to fend off the glass. "Why is it strange men always want to give me—whiskey?" she said in annoyance. She didn't want to drink anything. She wanted John Howe!

The Yankee surgeon laughed. "Well, I expect for any number of reasons. This time, though, it's entirely medicinal. You've got the shakes. Come on now. Just a few sips."

He was a determined man. She took a swallow. Then another. The whiskey burned all the way down.

"I don't want any—more! I have to get to—oh!" she said as the whiskey hit her empty stomach. "Oh!" Something was the matter with her face. She put up her hands to see.

"What's wrong?" the Yankee surgeon asked, his face close.

"My nose."

"Your nose?"

"It feels like it's . . . going away . . . oh!" She was having a terrible time staying upright.

"How long since you've eaten?" he asked.

"Eaten?"

"Oh, Lord. I'm too late with that question. Whickes! Come here and help me! Help me stand her up—where's your room, Miss Douglas?"

Amanda heard him perfectly. She even realized that he'd called her by name. She just couldn't answer.

"Damnation!" the Yankee surgeon said. "Don't you tell John Howe I got his lady drunk, you hear me, Whickes?"

"Major, I am a lot of things," the other soldier said, "but I ain't crazy."

"And don't you go telling it, either," the major said to her.

"What?" she managed.

"Lord," he said again. "Do you know where she belongs?"

"That little room yonder at the end of the front hall is got female things in it."

"And how the devil do you know that?"

"I just helped Mr. Pike move into it."

"Well, you just help Mr. Pike move right out again."

"Yes, sir, Major Reid. My pleasure."

Amanda wanted desperately to sit down, but neither of them would let her.

"Whickes, go get him out of there!"

"I *am*, Major—uh-oh, here comes the lady of the house—that there Reb doctor's wife."

"What have you done, sir!" the doctor's wife cried.

"Well, ma'am, I...seem to have miscalculated the dose," Major Reid said. "I'm afraid I'm used to men who have a little more tolerance for—"

"Drunkards, you mean!" she said.

"Well, yes, ma'am. That's about right."

"Honestly!" she scolded him, taking Amanda by the arm.

"I am sorry, ma'am. It wasn't intentional, I assure you. Captain Howe is apt to punch me in the nose for it—"

"You *know* Captain Howe?"

"Ah, yes, ma'am—"

"Well, where is he! My husband must talk to him. Right away!"

"He's down at the river, ma'am—"

"But they're fighting down there!"

"Yes, ma'am. Pemberton won't surrender—"

"I don't care about Pemberton! This girl needs—" She broke off. "You go talk to my husband, Major. Right now!"

"Now?"

"I said so, didn't I?" she said testily.

Amanda was being helped to bed and covered. She was so tired, too tired to worry about her soiled clothes, too tired to worry about anything except John Howe. It felt wonderful to lie down, but she fought against it. She had to get up. He was here. She had to find him. She had to tell him—

No. She couldn't tell him anything. He had a son, and a woman who needed desperately to be his wife.

"I saw him," she murmured in spite of herself. "John's here."

"I know, honey," the doctor's wife said. "And don't you worry. We'll find him for you—"

"No. No, I can't. He has to be free of me. He has to..." She covered her face with her hands.

"Now, now, honey," the doctor's wife soothed.

"What does she mean by that?" Major Reid asked.

"That, sir," the doctor's wife said, "is none of our business."

It was nearly dark outside when Amanda woke. Someone was knocking softly on the door, but she made no move to answer it. Her mind, asleep or awake, was filled with but one thought. John Howe was here.

"Could I have a word with you, please, Miss Amanda?" someone said after a moment.

She rose on an elbow. She didn't recognize the voice—only that it was no one from here. The accent was too hard and clipped. "Who is it?"

"Sergeant Whickes. It's important."

She closed her eyes and took a deep breath. Everyone in town had known the Yankees were coming for days before they got here. She hadn't slept; she had been working with everyone else in the doctor's house, trying to hide anything that might be carried off, trying to make ready for the worst, waiting for a battle to start. She didn't want to have to deal with anything else today. She just wanted John.

"Miss Amanda?"

"Wait, please," she said after a moment.

She felt terrible, but the complaints seemed to have shifted. Her head ached now, but her eyes no longer burned and her hands didn't shake.

She held her hands out in front of her. They still had blood all over them. She slid off the bed and walked a bit unsteadily to the washstand to pour water into the basin.

She had to scrub hard to get the blood off. Charlie had been so angry at the thought of dying under *their* feet. He'd wanted to get up, so that Yankee soldiers wouldn't be stepping all over him—

She closed her eyes at the memory. *Poor Charlie.* He had died and the Yankees hadn't even noticed.

She looked at herself in the mirror. She looked like some demented, wild thing. She needed to do something to her hair, but both her brushes were gone. They had belonged to her mother.

She gave a soft sigh, and leaned against the washstand.

"Are you all right, Miss Amanda?" a voice said behind her, making her jump violently. She whirled around, ready to fight off the soldier who had come uninvited into the room. He was a big man, and she was afraid, but he seemed to mean her no harm. He was carefully holding a tin cup.

"Are you all right, Miss Amanda?" he asked again.

"I...my mother's silver brushes. Someone's taken them."

"I'll see what I can do about it," he said. "Here now. I brought you a light." He rummaged in a breast pocket and brought out a candle, placing it carefully on the table by the bed, as if he didn't want to make any sudden moves that might alarm her. "And some coffee. You'll feel better if you drink it. I reckon your head's talking to you about now."

He held the cup out to her, but she hesitated before she finally took it, wondering why he was being so kind.

"Oh, it's real," she said, catching a whiff of the smell.

"Yes, ma'am."

She looked up at him. "Thank you," she said. If she could drink something she *didn't* want, because a Yankee soldier insisted, she could drink this. She took a tentative sip. She expected it to be bitter, but it was heavily sweetened. She couldn't keep from smiling. "And real sugar."

"Well, I heard you liked your coffee ruint, Miss Amanda. Captain Howe said I was to—"

She turned away from him. John had sent her this?

"But Captain Howe ain't exactly the reason I'm here," the sergeant said, apparently seeing her distress. "It's the general—General Stoneman. He wants to see you."

"No," she said, setting down the tin cup on the washstand hard. The coffee sloshed over the rim, and she didn't have anything to wipe it up. The mere task of finding something seemed overwhelming, and she abruptly bowed her head.

"Now there ain't no cause for you to be upset or scared or anything," Whickes said. "He especially wants to talk to you because of Captain Howe."

"I can't do that."

"The captain is in a bit of trouble, Miss Amanda. Might be it would help him some if you talked to Stoneman."

"What kind of trouble?"

"Well...*you,* ma'am. See, Captain Howe put his personal worries ahead of the army. And the army, well, she's a jealous woman, Miss Amanda. She expects to come first, no matter what."

"He doesn't have to worry about me. I'm—"

"You don't understand, Miss Amanda. The general is waiting. And he ain't a man who likes it."

She looked down at her bloodstained dress. "I'm not fit—"

"It's better if the general sees things the way they are. Might be he'd understand why Cap was acting such a fool— excuse me for saying so."

She sighed heavily. She couldn't think; her brain felt as if it were wrapped in wool.

"Miss Amanda?" Whickes said, holding open the door. "Come on now. Let's go get this over."

She led the way out, because she seemed to have no choice about it, regardless of the offering of sweetened coffee. She was not at all sure she was doing the right thing. What could she possibly tell General Stoneman? She didn't speak to anyone about John Howe. Ever. Everything the people in this town knew about him had come from the reverend and Jacob Shanley.

In the entry hall, she suddenly stopped. The windows at the front of the house glowed bright orange.

"What's burning! Are you burning the town!"

"That's just contraband that's been torched, Miss Amanda. That's all. The general says no private property—"

"It'll spread in the wind."

"Come along, Miss Amanda," Whickes said, taking her arm. She looked back over her shoulder. The sky was so bright. It was worse than the night of the Brick Row fire.

The house was still noisy and crowded, but it had been cleared of the wounded. Amanda saw no one she knew. A Yankee soldier poured soapy water on the bloody spots on the floor in the hallway and swept it toward the front door. A group of officers stood in conversation at the bottom of the stairs. They parted to let her and Whickes by.

"Howe's lady," one of them said, not bothering to lower his voice. She was careful not to look at any of them. *Howe's lady,* she thought. She supposed that the description could have been a lot worse. No, she knew that it could be. She had heard what the people in this town called her.

The general had set up his office in the wide upstairs hallway, his back to the front windows and the upstairs veranda and the burning. He was deep in conversation with his staff over maps and papers, and he didn't look up. Whickes had her sit down on a chair near the head of the stairs. Other people waited as well. The mayor. Several Unionists. Jacob Shanley. He pretended not to know her.

She looked around her. No one seemed to mind the men who sat on the floor around the walls, hugging their knees in sleep, or those who lay sprawled on the floor. The night was warm for April, and the Yankees had opened the windows. The lace curtains behind General Stoneman billowed outward from time to time, and Amanda could hear crickets and the noise of the soldiers still milling around in the yard below. She caught sight of herself in an armoire mirror in the room across from her. She looked like Tragedy in some dramatics society tableau.

An officer approached, his back ramrod straight, his hair in long ringlets. "All right, Sergeant. The general is *not* hearing any more petitions. Get this woman out of here."

He let his eyes travel over the bodice of Amanda's dress in a way that made her want to cross her arms over her breasts.

"Well?" he demanded, because Whickes hadn't moved.

Whickes gave a short exhalation of breath. "Miss Amanda," he said, helping her to stand, but instead of going back toward the stairs, he walked her in the direction of the general.

"Sergeant Whickes! Did you hear me!" the officer yelled.

"Yes, sir! I heard you, Lieutenant Pike, sir!" Whickes bawled, but he kept walking toward Stoneman, and he took Amanda right along with him. She was about to protest, but he gave her a big wink.

"Sergeant!" the lieutenant yelled.

"Excuse me, Miss Amanda," Whickes said politely. "I'll be right back. That boy is going to give hisself a fit."

He walked back to the now livid lieutenant. "Now, look, sir," he said, not bothering to lower his voice. "That general down there—" He pointed directly at Stoneman. "You're not looking, sir. *Right down there.* See? Well, *that* general has sent me to fetch *that* lady—" He swung his arm around to include Amanda. "And if that don't sit with you, sir, then I reckon you're just going to have to take it up with him."

Laughter rumbled around the room.

"It's all right, Mr. Pike," Stoneman called. "Do let the sergeant carry out his orders." His face was perfectly neutral, except for a faint twitching at the corner of his mouth, Amanda thought—hoped—might be the workings of a smile. He seemed such a dour man.

Whickes took her by the arm again, and she looked up at him in dismay. She didn't know what to say to a general who could level a whole town and sow the ground with salt if he wanted. She tried not to panic, taking the chair Stoneman indicated, feeling the complete attention of everyone in the room focused on her. The general looked at the papers on his desk for a moment, then rubbed a small area between his eyes with his two middle fingers.

"My compliments, Miss Douglas," he said finally. "Is there anything I can do for you?"

Amanda looked at him in surprise. "Do? No—nothing—" There were Salisbury boys dead and in their graves tonight, boys she'd known her whole life. What could he possibly do?

He drummed his fingers on the desk. "I trust you know that there are some things that can't be exempted from contraband. I have a duty, to myself and to the men who were imprisoned here. You understand?"

It wasn't quite a question. The truth was she didn't understand at all, but she fought down her natural inclination to say so.

"You must understand, too, that Captain Howe has his duty as well. He is one of my officers and he has drawn a soldier's lot. I will not accept anything less than complete allegiance to that duty, no matter how justified it may seem. Though I see now the—" He stopped, his eyes going to the bloodstains on her dress. "Well. Are you certain there is nothing you require?"

"Very certain," she said. The only thing in this world she wanted was John Howe, and she couldn't have him, even with Stoneman's permission.

"I hardly know what to say to that, Miss Douglas. You are the first townsperson I've encountered who hasn't asked me for something." His eyes went again to her bloody clothes. "Are you all right?"

"Quite all right," she said evenly.

"Good. I will see that Captain Howe knows that. He has been rather...difficult to live with of late."

"Difficult!" an officer on the sidelines said. "He's been a damned pain."

Amanda had forgotten until then what an audience they had. She had been watching the general closely. It wasn't a headache that plagued him as she'd first thought; it was something else. He was thin and pale, and he seemed to need to keep furtively touching the area just below his breast-bone.

"Should you need anything, Miss Douglas, please do see me. I will speak to Lieutenant Pike personally, so that you will be able to pass."

"I would like to say one thing to you," she said, standing up. "Privately, if I may." His eyes narrowed for a moment, but he waved those closest to him away.

"I think perhaps you're...in pain," she said quietly so that no one would hear. "A stomach ailment perhaps—"

He frowned, but he didn't interrupt.

"It isn't that obvious. I only wanted to say to you that you might want to speak to our doctor here about it. He has similar difficulty, and he is most reliable."

"Reliable, is he?"

"Yes," she said with conviction. "He will be sympathetic."

"There is a lot to be said for sympathy, Miss Douglas. Perhaps I will speak to him."

Whickes was at her elbow, and she turned to go.

"Miss Douglas," Stoneman said. "What became of the prisoners in the stockade?"

She looked back at him, and she could feel the sudden tension in the room. All the cordiality in the general's manner had abruptly gone.

"They were sent to Greensboro," she said, "then to Wilmington. In February."

"How did they get to Greensboro?" Stoneman demanded.

"The sick went on trains. The rest walked."

"How do you know that?"

"I was there. I went to the depot to find out what I could about a friend of Captain Howe's—"

"Do you know how many of them died? How many never reached Greensboro—much less arrived in Wilmington?"

"No," she said, looking into his eyes and sensing the real reason he'd asked to see her. He wanted some kind of verification of what he'd been told, and he expected her to give it.

"Do you know we have all the men from the town in the prison stockade now?"

"No," she said again.

"I consider that forced march to Greensboro murder, Miss Douglas."

She made no reply. There was nothing she could say.

He exhaled sharply and began to shuffle the papers on his desk. "Those men who had no direct part in that atrocity will be released," he said without looking at her. "You may repeat that."

"To whom?" she asked.

He looked up at her. "To your friends here."

"I have associated myself with a Yankee officer, sir. I have no friends here."

There was an abrupt silence in the room; all activity stopped. Stoneman glared at her over his papers. Whickes stood beside her, but she felt he would have been long gone if he'd had a choice about it. She had clearly offended the general, but she didn't try to make amends. The truth was the truth. All she had was a kindly doctor and his wife, who had made arrangements with Verilia and the Pinkerton Agency, so that she could come home to live rather than live on the Washington streets.

"Yes," he said finally. "I can see how that might be a handicap."

"Sir," Whickes said, taking her arm when she would have made her getaway. "This lady is missing some personal property. I would like to try to find it for her—with the general's permission."

"You have it," Stoneman said. "Providing it isn't Captain Howe."

There was a common hesitation in the room, until the men realized that their seemingly humorless commander had made a small joke and burst into laughter.

"Great God Almighty," Whickes said as they went down the stairs. "I can't wait to tell Cap that one."

The doctor's wife was waiting at the bottom of the stairs. "Amanda, you come with me. You need to eat something, honey. And then you need to rest—sleeping off an overdose of spirits is *not* resting," she said, looking at Whickes hard.

"Excuse me, ladies," Whickes said wisely. The doctor's wife was not in the least impressed by the fact that he was a soldier in the conquering army.

Amanda didn't see him again, but when she returned to her room, a flour sack lay in the middle of the bed. It was filled with silver hairbrushes.

She sat in the dark for a long time, waiting for the activity in the house to die down. It didn't. She could hear constant footsteps and voices. Eventually, she hurriedly tried to bathe and put on another dress. She didn't dare put on her nightdress. Her position in this room seemed precarious at best, and she didn't want to be removed from it in her nightclothes.

Shortly after midnight, the cannonading began in earnest at the river. She was so worried about John. She understood, from what the doctor's wife and Whickes had told her, that he must have been banished there because he'd dared look for her instead of doing what he was supposed to do. She wouldn't be able to stand it if anything happened to him. She could deal with anything else—with his marrying Kate Woodard, with never seeing him again if she had to, but not that.

Be safe, she kept thinking. *Please be safe.* A litany to keep her sanity.

She wondered what Mrs. Howe had told him about her leaving Washington. Not much, she assumed. Mrs. Howe had made it plain that it was up to "us women," to Amanda, to set things right.

She slept after a time, still dressed and sitting in a rocking chair by the window. Just before dawn, she awoke to someone tapping lightly on the glass. At first she thought it was rain, but it was Anne Giffen, Thayer's only sister and once her best friend.

She got up quickly and went to open it, surprised at this covert visit. Anne had deliberately avoided her since she'd been back.

"Amanda, get out of the way," she said, helping to raise the window. "I'm coming in—" She looked furtively over her shoulder, then came into the room headfirst, pushing Amanda's hands away when she would have helped her. Anne looked terrible. Her dress was torn on the shoulder and her hair was coming down. She didn't try to get up once she was inside; she sat with her legs folded tailor fashion in the middle of the floor.

"What's wrong? Anne, are you hurt?"

"It's not *me,*" she said, looking up sharply. "It's Thayer. He's been wounded. I can't find him."

"Thayer's here? What is he doing here?"

"Well, you'd know a lot more about that than me, Amanda."

"What are you talking about? I haven't seen Thayer since last August, when he finally got around to telling me he was married."

"You aren't going to make me believe you haven't asked him to help you out of this mess you're in, so don't even try—"

"Anne, I don't know what you're talking about!"

"I need your help! Don't you understand! The boys that were on the caisson with Charlie Wood—they saw Thayer fall. He was riding one of the artillery horses and he got caught in a cross fire just before they reached the river bridge. He wasn't brought in with Charlie and the rest of the wounded. He was never here, and he's not in the stockade. He never made it to Pemberton on the other side of the river. He has to be somewhere along the river road, but they won't let me look!"

"Anne, are you—"

"That Yankee officer you ran off with—Howe. He's in command of the soldiers guarding the river road. And don't look so shocked—everybody knows he's the one. It's the question of the hour. 'Are you Captain Howe's lady?'"

Amanda swung around, slapping Anne hard, her open palm making a loud cracking sound against her cheek. They both stood there, staring at each other, until Anne's mouth began to tremble and she hid her face in her hands.

"I'm sorry, Amanda! I don't know what to do! Mother's half-crazy with worry. And William's here—"

"Are you going to blame me for him, too?" Amanda said. William was the youngest Giffen and in the army with Thayer the last Amanda had heard.

"William goes wherever Thayer goes. You know that," Anne said, lifting her head. Tears streamed down her face. The place where Amanda had slapped her was beginning to redden. "Amanda, you have to help me! I don't know who else to ask! I'm so afraid William will try to do something and they'll kill him, too." She began to cry in earnest. "It's been raining. I keep thinking about Thayer—hurt and—lying in the dark somewhere—in the rain. Amanda, we can't leave him there! You have to ask Howe to let us look for him! Please! He'll do it for you!''

Amanda sat down heavily on the side of the bed. Would he? She didn't know. "What you're asking me to do. It's . . . very hard."

"I know that, Amanda. I know—" She sat down on the bed beside her, her head bowed. "What else can we do?"

Nothing, Amanda thought sadly. Not one thing. "All right. I'll . . . ask him."

"Thank you," Anne said, wiping her eyes. "Mother and I—and William—we won't forget it. We have to get out of here without the Yankees seeing us. I came through the back hedge. William's waiting just off the Mocksville road with a wagon."

"It's too light now to go back out the window."

"Then what are we going to do!"

"I don't know! Let me think! We're just going to have to mind our own business," Amanda said after a moment. "We'll walk out to the privy and see what kind of chance we've got of getting through the back hedge again. They may not even care if we come and go."

"Everyone is supposed to stay inside, Amanda!"

"All right! Then we'll make a run for it. Do something with your hair. They'll take one look at you and know you're up to something. Here," she said, holding open the flour sack. "Pick one."

"Where did all these come from?"

"Every house the Yankees 'visited' between here and Tennessee, I imagine." Amanda looked up. Anne was smiling.

"You haven't changed," she said.

"Yes, I have," Amanda said, looking into her eyes. What she had been when Anne Giffen thought of her as a friend, she would never be again. What grand plans they'd had when they were little girls—to marry and have houses of their own and lots of babies. Perhaps all that was still possible for Anne. "Hurry," she said.

Anne gave her hair a few token brushes and began to rapidly braid it. Amanda listened intently at the door. If anyone was on the other side of it, she couldn't tell. She opened it slightly; Whickes sat in a chair in the hall, snoring softly. A whiskey bottle sat on the floor beside him. She put her fingers to her lips as a signal to Anne. She was fairly certain of one thing. If there was any obstacle to leaving the house, it was this Yankee sergeant.

She opened the door a little wider. To her relief it didn't squeak. The two of them slipped quietly past the sleeping soldier.

The privy was some distance from the main house. There were a number of soldiers about, all of them seemingly busy. Amanda and Anne walked down the gravel path, then stood by the privy door as if they were waiting for someone to come out.

"Do you see anyone at the windows?" Amanda asked, looking down at the ground and moving the gravel around with her shoe.

"No," Anne whispered.

"How many soldiers in the yard now?"

"Too many."

"Then we'll just have to chance it. Walk with me toward the hedge—not fast! Just walk."

They started off. The sky hung heavy with gray clouds; it would rain again soon. The morning was cool, but not uncomfortably so, and the trees were just beginning to green. Ordinarily, Amanda loved this time of year, but the coming of spring this time had only seemed to heighten her misery. She gave a quiet sigh and tried to concentrate on the problem at hand. It was Thayer she should be concerned about—and this impending encounter with John.

"Don't stop when we get to the hedge," Amanda said. "Just keep going."

No one stopped them; Amanda had to force herself not to turn around to see why not. They kept walking until she was sure they were out of sight. Anne took the lead, breaking into a run as they neared the road where William waited in a decrepit wagon by a small clump of pine trees.

"I thought she wasn't going to do it," he said to Anne as they approached. "Hurry up!"

"William, it's not safe for you," Amanda said as she climbed up on the wagon. "They're locking all the men in the stockade."

"No, it's all right. I was at home when the Yankees came in. They already talked to me and let me go. I didn't have a weapon. I reckon I look more like some farmer's brat than a soldier."

To Amanda, he looked hardly more than a child, but she wouldn't have been fooled. Perhaps Yankees weren't as accustomed as she was to the sight of boy soldiers.

"I reckon Anne told you where Thayer went down," William said. "If you can just get *me* permission to look for him. I don't blame that Yankee captain for not letting her go. It ain't no place for a woman. Pemberton's guns can take the tops out of the trees all the way from the other side. You ask him, Amanda. You ask him if I can look. I ain't armed. I can't do them any harm."

She nodded, bracing herself on the wagon seat as William whipped the horse into a trot. It was too much for her to have to absorb. She was going to have to speak to John, and perhaps Thayer was dead.

They rode the rest of the way in silence, lost in their own thoughts. The countryside was very quiet, nothing but birdsong and nature. The cannons had stopped some time during the night, and that was some comfort. As they neared the river, William slowed the wagon. There were pickets up ahead.

Amanda took a deep breath.

"There's no need for *you* to be afraid," Anne whispered.

One of the pickets, a corporal, galloped toward them, not letting them get any closer with the wagon. His mount was nervous and prancing, crowding the wagon horse until it began to rear in the traces. William had to stand up to keep it from bolting.

"I've told you before, lady—" the corporal began, apparently recognizing Anne.

"I want to see Captain Howe," Amanda interrupted, gripping the wagon seat hard and trying to keep the tremor out of her voice. He stared at her for a moment, and she expected to have to explain.

But he didn't seem to need a reason. He dismounted, his nervous horse standing perfectly still the moment he dropped the reins. He offered her his hand so that she could climb down from the wagon.

"Cap is through those trees yonder," he said. "The rest of you will have to wait here."

Amanda started walking in the direction he pointed, not missing his hand signals communicating her identity to the other pickets when he thought she couldn't see. She walked on, knowing that seeing John again was going to be worse than she imagined. Clearly, the corporal knew precisely what she had been to John Howe.

She kept going, looking back at the wagon once before she passed through the trees. The ground grew uneven, and she had to pick up her skirts to keep from stumbling. She saw John almost immediately. He was directly in front of her, and he was sitting on an upturned bucket, playing chess with someone—with the Yankee surgeon, Major Reid.

John glanced in her direction, and he abruptly stood, upsetting the chessboard. She could almost, but not quite, hear the major swear.

She stopped and waited as John came striding toward her. *He's all right,* she kept thinking, her relief at finding him safe for a moment taking away the dread of asking him a favor. She couldn't read his expression—until he saw Anne and the wagon on the road behind her.

"If that's why you've come, it's a trip wasted," he said coldly. "I've already told that woman. I'm not letting any women in range of Pemberton's guns."

"John, please," Amanda said, trying to look into his eyes. She wanted to touch him so badly. "The boy—William—wants to go. Can't you let him, at least? They have to know what's happened to their brother. *I* have to know, John."

He suddenly smiled, but it was the kind of smile she hated, the kind that meant that mirth was the last thing he was feeling. "What did she do? Bring the only person in town she thought I couldn't say no to?"

"Yes," Amanda answered, because it was the truth and because she sensed how badly he wanted her to deny it. But she didn't want to fight with him. She just wanted to know he was all right—and to find Thayer.

"My God!" John said. "Can't you see those trees down there? How much of a chance do you think a wounded man had in that? Or somebody looking for him, if Pemberton starts again—"

"John, please! I've known him since I was a child. I don't want him to die alone out there! I know you've already refused permission. But I'm asking again. I'll do whatever it takes. Do you want me to beg you? Do you want me to get down on my knees? I will. I know your men are all watching. You won't lose face—dear God, John, you of all people should understand! Sometimes you can save a friend and sometimes you have to leave them behind—"

He grabbed her by both forearms, his grip hurting. "Damn you!" he said, but she didn't flinch, didn't turn away. She stared into his eyes.

"Please," she said. "You owe me this."

"For what!" he said angrily. "For saving my life? For giving me your virginity?"

"Yes!" she cried. "One of them ought to be worth something to you!"

He abruptly let go of her and stepped away. She reached out to touch his arm, but he wouldn't allow it.

"All right," he said after a moment. "The boy can go. Corporal Grady!" he yelled at the picket, and the corporal galloped toward them.

"He fell somewhere along the river road, near the bridge," Amanda said.

"Pass the word," John said to the corporal. "The boy is going down the road as far as the bridge to look for a wounded man. If he makes a run for Pemberton, shoot him."

Amanda was about to protest, but he looked at her hard. Then, without a backward glance, he walked away.

Chapter Thirteen

"Would you like a little fatherly advice?" Reid asked.

"Not from you," John said. Matthew Reid was a hell of a long way from being his father.

"Nevertheless, I feel compelled to give it." He nodded toward the trees where Amanda still waited. "I take it there was a rather sharp exchange over there."

"You might say that. Hell, I don't know why I don't just give her my damn revolver and let her *shoot* me. Be done with it! Put me out of my misery once and for all!"

"Well, what do you expect, John? These are her people. You know what it's like when the men dying are people you *know*. Why wouldn't she ask you for the privilege of trying to find one less of them dead?"

"You don't know all of it," John said stubbornly.

"I know some of it," Reid said, lighting a cigar. "I know what her association with you has done for her. Do you realize that most of the people in this town don't even speak to her? They'll cross the street to the other side to avoid the Yankee officer's whore, John—this is, if she dares to go out in the first place. I understand she's been warned not to, in case the men in town decide she's fair game."

"Damn it, Reid, she shouldn't have come back here in the first place!"

"Be that as it may—"

"I told you you don't know all of it."

"Aw, bullshit, John, what? That she was going to marry that joker the boy's gone looking for?"

John whirled around. "What did you say?"

Reid looked at him and took another puff on his cigar. "You heard me. I thought I was supposed to be the one who didn't *know* all of it."

John took a few steps, then kicked the bucket he'd been sitting on. Hard. "I knew that son of a bitch was here! I knew it!"

"Yeah, well, I don't think Amanda did—"

"Who told you all this anyway!"

"The town doctor. The one who took Amanda in when she came back here after you'd ruined her—"

"I didn't—" He broke off. Yes, he had. He'd saved his own hide, and she'd gotten in the way. "What did he say?"

"Let's see. He said her father, the reverend, was a pious, self-serving son of a bitch—but you probably already know that. He said that Amanda's stepmother asked him and his wife to take the girl in so she could come home—"

"What did he say about Giffen, damn it! You know what I mean!"

"Oh!" Reid said to annoy him. "Giffen! Well, he said the poor bastard was crazy in love with Amanda but he heard the call of the wild when he was far, far from home—you know how it is—a sweet young thing, a full moon, impending battle, next thing you know..."

"Damn it, Reid! Tell me!"

"I'm getting there. The doctor says Giffen wanted to marry Amanda—he'd asked her on the sly to keep the reverend from taking it out on her after he'd gone—but he got mixed up with some other girl while he was off fighting someplace and he married her. Doc thinks he probably had to, because he certainly wasn't the happy bridegroom when he came home to tell Amanda the wedding was off. They—

the doctor and his wife—don't know what he's doing here
now. They only heard he *was* here this morning. He's supposed to be with his artillery unit somewhere around Richmond. My guess is maybe he heard what a hell of a fix
Amanda was in because of you, and he came hotfooting it
home to help her, wife or no wife. He probably thinks he's
responsible for her troubles—you know, she was so broken
up over losing him, she took up with the first Yankee captain who came along—"

"Very funny, Reid, and I don't care about that. It's
just—"

"Just what?" Reid prompted.

"She . . . never told me about him."

"John, John, *John,*" Reid said, shaking his head. "Why
don't you walk right over there and *ask* her? Which brings
us to another thing. Time is running out. We'll be out of
here before sundown."

"You're sure?" John said, surprised. Pemberton was still
on the other side of the river.

"As sure as you can be in the army. Sherman is on Pemberton's other side. He'll get him. Stoneman says he's not
going to sacrifice any of his men trying to get across the river
so Pemberton can make it up to himself for giving us
Vicksburg. And I can't tell you the agony having that piece
of information has given me. I've wanted to tell you ever
since I came out here—but knowing your impetuous nature
and Stoneman's promise to have you shot if you dare dis-
obey any more orders—hell, I thought you'd take off to
town again—court-martial, Pemberton, and Stoneman be
damned. Which is why I'm so outdone with you now. For
God's sake, man! She's right here! What else do you want!"

I don't know! John thought, but he was staring right at
it and he knew it. He wanted her. He wanted her so badly it
hurt. He was angry because she'd broken her promise. He'd
been deliberately cruel, and God, the pain in her eyes—as if

he'd physically struck her. *Forgive me!* he'd wanted to say, but he'd walked away instead.

"Well, to hell with it," Reid said. "If you're done with it, I suppose we can stand you yelling for her every time you have those damn nightmares of yours. We have this far—"

"No, I'm not done with it," he said, walking in Amanda's direction. She still watched the road, her arms folded protectively over her breasts. It was going to rain again. A few drops were already beginning to fall. She was getting wet from it, her dress, her hair.

"I want you to answer one question," he said without prelude.

She glanced at him, then back at the road, her features set, her chin coming up ever so slightly. He had seen that look before, and the heavy weight around his heart grew heavier still at the realization that she must think she had to deal with him in the same way she dealt with the reverend.

But he intended to have his question answered. "This man—this Thayer Giffen—is he the reason you left my parents' house? Is he the reason you were so hell-bent to get to Richmond? Did you suddenly decide he was the better man? What?" He knew he was being too sarcastic, but he couldn't help it. "I know—I *know*—everything was all right between us when I left Washington. I need you to tell me, Amanda!"

She looked at him then, and it was all he could do not to follow that earlier inclination—just pick her up and run with her, as far away from here as he could get.

"Cap!" one of the pickets yelled, pointing off toward the river. The boy was in view, his body bent under the weight of his load. Lieutenant Thayer W. Giffen had been found.

Reid was going through the trees, sending two of the men hurrying ahead with a litter. John expected Amanda to go with them, but she didn't. She remained at his side, anxiously watching the road. The other woman, Giffen's sister, was off the wagon and running down the road, skirts flying. She tried to help the boy hold the wounded man, hovering about as they transferred him to the litter. John couldn't tell if Giffen was dead or not—until he saw him reach up for his sister's hand.

"I already know you were going to marry him," John said as Giffen was carried back. "Is he the reason you left me or not?"

"No," she said, looking briefly into his eyes, and she walked off toward the wagon.

John followed. Reid was already making his preliminary examination of Giffen's injuries.

"This arm's broken," he said. "There's a wound in the left upper thigh—not too bad. He's got a couple of broken fingers, maybe a cracked rib or two. Could be worse. He's going to hurt like hell." He dug around in his kit and handed a phial to Giffen's sister. "Give him a few drops of this in water when it gets too bad. And take him to your doctor in town—quietly, if you understand what I'm not able to say. He needs to be taken care of at home so he doesn't get pneumonia. It won't do him any good to be hauled off someplace for prisoner exchange." He looked around at John to see if he was going to object to this flagrant act of aiding the enemy, John supposed.

"Corporal, escort these people back to town," John said. "They are not to be detained along the way—my order." His eyes locked with Giffen's for a moment as he was lifted into the back of the wagon. *Ah, yes,* he thought. He knew who John was. Rivals never had any difficulty recognizing each other.

To hell with him.

Amanda climbed up on the wagon wheel, and Giffen said something to her. She leaned down to hear.

"Not you," John said, hauling her back down off the wheel. He set her on the ground and kept a firm hand on her shoulder. Giffen made a feeble protest and tried to sit up, but the effort made him cry out in pain. John ignored him. He had done all for this man that he would.

"Corporal, you will advise the people Miss Douglas stays with that for the time being, she'll be out here with me." He returned Corporal Grady's smart salute. The corporal was grinning from ear to ear. *He,* at least, approved of John's decision.

"This way," he said, taking Amanda by the arm and making her walk with him back through the trees.

"John," she kept saying, trying her best to get his hand off her arm. "What are you doing!"

The rain came harder, and he all but dragged her along toward his tent.

"I'm pressing an advantage. You have, by your arrival, saved me from desertion and very dire consequences. I don't intend to let this golden opportunity pass me by. My tent—" he said, holding back the flap, but he gave her no time to balk, lifting her off her feet and taking her inside. "Close the flap," he said, because he didn't dare let go of her long enough to do it. "Or leave it open. It doesn't matter a damn to me."

It was clearly a threat, and she understood it perfectly. She closed the flap, but it was by no means a gesture of surrender. She tried to get away from him immediately, and he abruptly sat down on his cot with her on his lap, burying his face in her neck, savoring the sweet woman smell that was hers.

God, he wanted her. His breathing grew heavy and his knees began to shake. He tried to kiss her, but she hid her face from him. She wouldn't let him touch the buttons on her dress front, so he went to the other end, running his hand up under her petticoat, searching for the open inside seams on her drawers so he could touch bare skin. She jumped when his fingers found the soft flesh of her inner thigh.

"John, don't!" she whispered fiercely, clamping both her hands around his wrist to keep him from going any farther. "Why are you doing this!"

"Doing what?" he asked in mock surprise. "I believe you just offered me whatever it took for that bastard's hide. Or did I misunderstand?"

"A-hem!" someone said outside the tent. "John? Oh, John."

"Go *away*, Major Reid."

"Pike's coming in with the dispatches, John—"

"You take them," John said, never taking his eyes off Amanda's face.

"I'm a doctor, John. I couldn't get them away from Pike at gunpoint."

He said something else, but a downpour of rain covered it. John could hear more voices, but it didn't matter to him whose.

"Amanda," he whispered, cupping her face in his hands. He didn't want her to be afraid of him; he wanted her *never* to be afraid of him. But damn it all, she wouldn't listen to him. She wouldn't even look at him.

"Lieutenant Pike reporting, *sir!*" Pike bawled outside the tent.

"Hell!" John said under his breath. "What!" he added out loud to keep Pike from bursting in, and "Quit that!" to Amanda, because she was trying her damnedest to get out of his lap.

"Sir!" Pike bawled. "Confidential dispatches in hand, sir!"

God, the man got on his nerves. He nearly lost Amanda altogether she stiffened so to get away from him.

"Quit!" he said to her. "Amanda—" He had a battle royal on his hands, but he was determined, as determined as she was.

"Throw them in," he said to Pike.

There was a long pause.

"Has he got a woman in there?" he heard Pike ask.

"Who?" Reid replied with an obtuseness John had to admire.

"He has, hasn't he?" Pike said.

"Well," Reid said. "I wouldn't say it was *a* woman."

"You mean he's got more than *one?*"

"No, you damn fool," Reid said. "I mean it's none of your damn business!"

"I must protest! The men—"

"Pike, if I were you, I'd throw those dispatches in there the way my commanding officer ordered. What the hell do you care who's in there? It's not your damned redheaded laundress! And then I'd go over there and stand until somebody calls me—and I wouldn't go annoying Pemberton, either!"

"I—" Pike began, but he finished with a big exhalation of breath. An arm presently worked its way into the tent opening and tossed a leather pouch.

"That take care of it, John?" Reid asked.

"Yes, Major," John said. "One other thing. You assign one of the boys to shoot anybody else who comes near this tent."

Reid laughed. "Anything you say, John."

He could hear Reid walking away, and Amanda immediately tried to get up again. She hit him hard on one ear and across the nose. He caught and pinned her arms, but she still struggled.

"What is the matter with you!" he hissed at her.

"With *me!*" she cried. "I'll tell you what's the matter with *me*. I'm not big enough to knock you down...and I don't...have any brothers...to do it! You think this is funny, don't you! Well, it's not! It's *not!*"

He had to catch her legs between his to hold on to her. She let her head fall forward, still struggling, her breathing ragged and quick. He held her roughly against him, her arms behind her back until finally, finally she was still. She stayed quiet against him, silent and unyielding in spite of his superior strength. He said nothing, and neither did she. There was only her closeness and the rain.

"You promised me," he said after a time. "You promised and you lied."

She didn't say anything. He drew a long shaky breath.

"You have caused me more pain than I ever dreamed of, and I don't even know why. I've suffered, if that's what you wanted. I've been in *hell* worrying about what happened to you. I just don't understand you. I don't know how you can be the way you are. That last night in Washington—I know you were afraid because I was the first. But you trusted me and you gave me everything you had to give. I've lived every day since remembering what it was like to be with you that way, making love with you and knowing—" He waited for a moment before he went on. "You loved me. I know you did. But you broke your promise to me anyway. You left me with no more regard for the pain it would cause me than—"

"Don't!" she said, her voice muffled in the front of his jacket.

"I don't understand any of it! I've tried. God knows, I've tried! What am I supposed to do with all these *feelings* I have for you? Tell me that! Didn't you understand how dear you are to me—or didn't you care!"

"Don't," she said again, lifting her head to look at him. He let go of her arms and she slid them around him, holding on to him for dear life, as if she could hide, disappear into his very being. He stroked her hair; it was rain-damp and coming undone. He was desperate for her to know, to feel the love and the need in him.

He reached down to gently turn her face upward, meaning to *tell* her what he felt, but he covered her mouth with his instead, all the pain and sense of betrayal translated immediately into fierce desire. Her lips parted under his. And she didn't try to keep his hands away now; she clung to him, letting him give her desperate little kisses over her face and neck.

He held her away for a moment to see her eyes, to *know* the truth. Did she love him? Or had it all been a lie? He found suddenly that he didn't want to know. He buried his face in her neck. He only wanted to forget. Everything—all the pain and the loneliness of his time away from her, of his whole life before her.

"You love me!" he insisted, his mouth again seeking hers. "I know you do!"

There was no gentleness in him; she didn't want gentleness. She had thought she would never see him again, but he was here, now, and she had this one last time to hold him, to be close to him. He would never be hers to keep; she knew that. Her memories would have to last a lifetime. She felt no hesitation, no indecision. Rightly or wrongly, she loved him, and nothing else mattered.

The rain drummed against the tent, seeped into it, dribbled down the sides. She was cold, but she made no protest when he abruptly thrust her backward on the narrow field cot. She raised her arms to him instead, raised her body to give him access. She helped him in his frantic rush—skirts up around her waist, trouser buttons undone. And when he plunged himself into her, she arched her hips to meet him. She had to be close to him. She had to *be* him, this one last time. She wanted to touch him, and her hands slid up under his shirt to his bare back.

His breath rasped against her ear, and she gave a soft whimper of pleasure as he thrust deeper. Yes! she thought. It was going to happen again, the wonderful feeling, the oneness. She responded immediately, rising to meet him, wrapping herself around him. The pleasure intensified with every thrust, and with every thrust, so did her need.

"I love you so!" she whispered against his ear. He had to know. He had to remember.

She could feel him tense, feel her own body arch in a rush of heat and acute sensation. He clamped his mouth over hers to muffle both their cries, collapsing against her, his body trembling as hers did, until at last they both lay spent.

It was still raining. And there was some commotion in the camp. He eased away from her and sat up, pulling her skirts down around her.

"I'm—"

He didn't go on. He concentrated on righting his clothes, leaving her feeling alone and shut out.

"What were you going to say?" she asked, and he finally looked at her.

"I was going to say I'm sorry. I'm sorry for tumbling you on a field cot as if you were the worst kind of camp follower. I know how it must make you feel. But I needed to be with you. I'm not sorry at all."

"Neither am I," she said, and he reached out to take her by the hand, pulling her upward so that she could sit beside him.

He gave her a painful smile. "We're going to have to do something about all these babies I keep trying to give you."

It was a feeble attempt at a joke, but she understood. It was either laugh or cry; she had been in that kind of situation with him before. She looked down at their entwined fingers. Her smaller hand was nearly lost in his.

"Amanda, if Giffen is the reason you came back here, you can say so. Anything is better than trying to guess."

"I didn't come back here because of Thayer," she said, looking up at him.

"What then? You just said you love me. If that's the truth, then tell me!"

She stared into his eyes. Yes, she thought. She had hurt him—when he was the dearest thing to her on this earth. For that, at least, she owed him an answer.

"Because of Harry," she said quietly.

He let go of her hand. "My God," he said, leaning forward on his knees, shaking his head in disbelief. She had taken him completely by surprise. "She told you," he said, looking back at her. "The Howe family skeleton she would have killed to protect, and my mother told you."

"Kate Woodard told me, John. Your mother was there."

"And you were so scandalized by my having a son I ought not have, you left, is that it? My God, Amanda. I'm only a man, not the best and not the worst. When I—when that happened, I was a *boy*. I was sixteen. I'm glad you didn't know me then. I was a hell-raiser and as careless as they come, but I wasn't a complete scoundrel. I would have married Kate Woodard. Oh, I had grand plans to make an honest woman of her—but I found out pretty quickly there is nothing a sixteen-year-old boy can do against two sets of opposed parents and a lawyer like Beale. It was a hell of a mess, and it was Kate who suffered for my carelessness. Her father would have rather seen her dead than married to a worthless pup like me—moneyed family or not. And *my* father wasn't about to let a grandchild of his be lost for the sake of propriety. My mother was still young enough to pass off the child as hers, so that's what they did. She and my father and Kate took a timely trip to Europe. My son was born there. The adoption was done there and Harry became my brother—and there wasn't a damn thing I could do about it, not if I loved him and wanted what was best for *him*."

"There is something you can do now," Amanda said, still looking into his eyes.

"What?" he asked, frowning.

"You can marry Kate. She wants to—"

"Who in the hell told you a thing like that!"

"She did."

"And you believed her?" he said incredulously.

"Of course, I believed her! Why would she lie about something like that?"

"Because my mother asked her to, that's why! I *cannot* believe this—and it's my own damned fault! I underestimated her. I thought she would understand. I thought my father would explain how things were with you and me. I thought she would *see* with her own eyes what you meant to me. Damn it to hell!"

"John—"

"Kate is a fine person, Amanda, but she'd do what my mother asked if she thought it was to *save* me. And I expect that is how it was put to her. I love Harry. You know that. But what good would it do to unravel his life now? He thinks he's my brother, and he's happy about it. He's only a little boy. You know what he's like. He's so...trusting. He'd never get over a betrayal like that. And Kate. Kate is engaged to marry a very dashing young officer in Kilpatrick's Cavalry—and has been since the war started. They're only waiting until the war is over. I would have told Kate about you myself, but I couldn't see her. Mrs. Woodard couldn't bear the sight of me after she knew about Maxwell. I'd ruined both her children and I wasn't welcome. I respected her wishes. It was the only thing I could do for her—stay out of her sight. God! I honestly thought my family would take care of you for me. They certainly did that, didn't they?"

Amanda gave a soft sigh and bowed her head, trying to digest everything he'd told her. Her mind was reeling. Had Mrs. Howe and Kate Woodard really perceived her as that much of a threat? Clearly, they had. Mrs. Howe had believed that, for John, it would be "out of sight, out of mind." She had said as much, and she had done everything in her power to make it so.

John kept waiting for her to *say* something. Her silence was killing him. "Your hair's come undone," he said finally. He put his hands on her shoulders to turn her around and gently worked his fingers through it, taking the pins out and letting her dark hair tumble down her back.

She sat very still as he gave her the pins to hold and carefully began to braid it. Where had he learned to braid a woman's hair, she wondered? Had he done it for Kate? Had he learned in some expensive Philadelphia or Washington bawdy house that catered to rich young men? Perhaps he'd learned from some mistress he'd had along the way.

"At least tell me *how* you came back here," he said as he worked.

She closed her eyes at the effort it took to condense the abject misery she'd felt since she'd left Washington into a few brief facts. "Your...mother hired some people from an agency—the Pinkerton Agency. They contacted Verillia without the reverend knowing and she—she made arrangements with the doctor and his wife for me to live with them. A man and a woman from the agency escorted me back here. I got home the same way I left—on a train and with the proper slip of paper."

"I saw Verillia," he said. "Talked to her—scared her, I'm afraid."

"Is she all right? I...don't try to see her. The reverend has forbidden it and I don't want to put her in the middle—"

"By God, I am putting an end to this once and for all," he said abruptly. "Reid!" he yelled, throwing back the tent flap. "Major Reid!"

The major came on the run. "What, John? What?"

"Go get me the chaplain."

"Right. Any particular one?" Reid asked, casting furtive glances at Amanda.

"No, Major. Now, Major."

"Right!" he said again.

John let the tent flap fall closed. "When the chaplain gets here, we're getting married. I can't stand this anymore. I love you. I want you for better or worse. Our lives have been tangled together since that night in January, and I mean for them to stay that way, my mother and the reverend be damned. I wish I had time to court you, but I don't." He took her by the hand. "You've got a lot to overlook where I'm concerned, but if you love me, too, then this is where you have to trust me. You have to trust me that I've told you the truth about Harry and Kate and that we have a future together. And if you think I want to marry you just because I might have gotten you pregnant, you're wrong—"

"John?" Reid said outside the tent.

"This is it, Amanda," John said, ignoring him. "Do or die—the frying pan or the fire—just like it's always been with us. So tell me. Which one will you choose?"

"John, I—"

"You have to decide now, Amanda. Right now. I love you with all my heart—did I say that?"

"We can't—"

"*Now*, Amanda. The war's not over yet, and it's come down to the same question you once asked me. What if I never see you again?"

She stared into his eyes; the rain drummed steadily on the tent.

"Tell me, damn it! Which one do you choose!"

"You!" she said abruptly. "I choose you!"

He gave her a fierce hug. "Thank God," he said in relief. "Now. We haven't much time." He threw open the tent flap again for the drenched chaplain and Major Reid to squeeze inside. Both of them removed their hats, the rain pouring off the brims and onto the ground. The chaplain looked as flustered as any man Amanda had ever seen.

"Captain Howe, am I to understand—what I mean is— the major here thinks—"

"This lady and I wish to be married," John interrupted. "Immediately."

The chaplain glanced at Amanda. "This is a bit unusual, Captain—"

"Unusual, be damned, sir. Stoneman is on the move again. I don't have time to do better. If I'm going in harm's way, I want to go knowing Miss Douglas is my wife. I've known her since January. We've spent enough time in each other's company for me to know I love her and I admire her, and if you don't marry us, I'll find a chaplain who will. Is that clear?"

"Quite clear, Captain Howe," the chaplain said, hunting inside a leather bag he had hooked over his shoulder. He took out a small book and several papers. "And you—Miss Douglas—is this hurried arrangement acceptable to your parents?"

"My parents are dead," Amanda said, not really knowing her legal status since the reverend had publicly disowned her.

"Is it acceptable to *you,* then? You don't enter into this arrangement against your free will?"

She looked at John and managed a smile. She had been in many situations with John Howe against her free will— but this wasn't one of them. "No. We have no choice, sir. He's going."

"Very well. I guess we can proceed. We need another witness."

"Whickes just rode in," Major Reid said.

"Get him," John said. "Hurry this along, Chaplain. I have dispatches from General Stoneman I haven't read yet."

"Yes, yes," he said absently, then, "Oh, my," as the import of John's remark registered. He got a pen and ink out of his leather bag. "Your full name," he said to Amanda, hurriedly writing. "Middle initial," he said to John. He glanced over his shoulder as Major Reid pushed his way in again, this time with Whickes in tow.

"We can begin now," the chaplain said, hastening the ceremony after only a few false starts. Amanda stood there, dazed, clinging to John's arm as if she might drown otherwise.

Suddenly, it was done.

"Congratulations, Captain Howe. My very best wishes, Mrs. Howe—if the witnesses would sign, please."

Both Whickes and Major Reid signed their names where the chaplain indicated, then shook John's hand vigorously. Whickes took the liberty of giving Amanda a little kiss on the cheek.

"Ain't no wonder you got Cap away from that prison," he whispered. "You are slicker than greased lightning, missy."

Amanda smiled. "I'm afraid I learned it from him."

"Out!" John said impatiently, shooing the three men outside. He immediately took her into his arms and held her tight. "I'll send for you as soon as I can," he said, placing a kiss against her hair. "Are you all right with this? I know you needed Verillia here with you."

"She couldn't have come no matter where we'd—" She didn't go on. The last thing she wanted to think about was the reverend.

He leaned back to see her face. "I keep promising myself to do better by you and this is the best I can manage."

"I love you," she said simply, and he kissed her hard.

Oh, God! he thought, wondering how a man could be so happy and so miserable all at the same time. Leaving her hadn't gotten any easier; the one thing that was supposed to give him peace of mind, this hasty and long-desired marriage, wasn't helping him at all.

He had to read the dispatches, and he let go of her to open the pouch Pike had tossed inside. Reid had been right; Stoneman wasn't going to waste his time trying to pry Pemberton out of the bluffs across the river.

"Pike!" he yelled through the tent opening, and Amanda could hear Pike's rapid, splashing approach.

"Sir!"

"Get them ready, Mr. Pike! We're on the move!"

"Yes, sir!"

Amanda looked up at John, trying hard not to cry, and he took her in his arms again. She could hear Pike barking orders all over camp, too busy now to worry that John might have had a woman in his tent.

"Let me see about sending you home," John said. "You can't ride with the column." He stared down at her, then kissed her one last time. As they stepped outside, he started to take her hand but thought better of it.

"Better not," he said. "This bunch of horse soldiers has been titillated enough." He could see Tobin nearby, his face beaming with approval. There would be no martial airs tonight, John thought, resigning himself to riding along with a lovestruck boy horn blower, who would likely want to serenade him with a hundred verses of "Lorena."

At their appearance, Tobin and the rest of the men abruptly began to whistle and cheer. Cries of "Here's your mule, Cap! Here's your mule!" rang all around them. John stood ramrod straight, his color high.

"What does that mean?" Amanda asked, because seeing John Howe in a full blush made it impossible not to. She had thought him completely dauntless, but that clearly wasn't the case now.

He gave her a pained look, then fought down a grin. "It...means any number of things. This time, damn their worthless hides, it means they want to help me with my husbandly duties when the time comes."

"I...understand," she said quickly, and the grin got away from him. He let his eyes travel over her face, trying to memorize every feature. Her braided hair, the calico dress—little pink and white flowers on a field of light blue. He didn't care where he was; except for her discomfort, he didn't care that the rain was pouring down. He could look at her forever. She was so dear to him!

"I have to speak to Reid," he said, forcing his attention to the matters at hand, but the major was already walking in their direction.

"John!" he called. "I'm staying behind with the wounded for a time. I will see that your lady gets safely home."

"Yes. Thank you, Major," he said gratefully. Reid was a good man. He would trust her safety with Reid. He looked down at Amanda. "You're getting all wet."

"I don't mind it," she said. She could already see the change in him, this transformation from her lover, her husband, to a military man.

"Whickes!" he suddenly yelled. "Find my letter pouch!"

Whickes disappeared briefly into John's tent, then brought out the pouch, tossing it to him from a distance so as not to intrude. "I put the marriage record in there, Cap!" he called, and John nodded.

"Amanda, there are letters for you in here. Ones I've been writing since I left Washington and couldn't mail. They're the closest thing I can give you to a courtship. When you read them, you'll know once and for all how I feel—ah, God, I hate this!'' He took a deep breath and looked over her head toward the trees, then put the letter pouch into her hands and leaned down. "I hope to God I've made you pregnant," he whispered fiercely.

"Cap!" one of his men yelled behind them. "Sir!"

"What!" John said without looking around.

"The farriers ain't done with the horses, sir!"

"Ride the ones without mounts double," John said. "And tell the farriers they'll have to catch up—or they can shoe Pemberton's artillery horses for him when he comes across the river."

"Sir!" the trooper acknowledged.

"A belated wish, John Howe," Amanda said, looking into his eyes. Then she turned and gathered up her skirts, running to where Reid waited with a wagon. Her parting from John had to be quick; she couldn't stand it otherwise. She didn't trust herself for a moment not to cling to him and beg him to take her with him, especially now. Major Reid reached down to help her into the wagon, and only then did she look back.

"Take good care of my wife, Major Reid," John called, and the major held up his hand in acknowledgment.

"Don't let him see you cry, Amanda," Major Reid said quietly.

"I won't—"

John stood and watched until the wagon was out of sight. There were things he should have said to Reid. He should have told him to make sure—make *sure*—Amanda would be safe in the town. And to see the reverend for him. To tell the son of a bitch that Amanda was his wife now, and if he dared hurt her, by word or deed, he'd answer for it.

He sighed heavily. A return visit to the reverend would have to wait for another time. He hadn't pressed Amanda about Thayer Giffen, either; that would have to wait for another time, too. Maybe when they were ninety. He didn't have to worry about Giffen now.

He abruptly grinned and returned to the problem at hand. He had to get these troopers out of here and catch up with Stoneman. But he didn't realize the import of the last thing Amanda had said to him until the company was on the road out. He thought that he must have whooped or something when the realization hit him, because Whickes was immediately at his side.

"You want something, Cap?"

"No," he said quickly. "Nothing."

He spurred his horse ahead a short distance. He couldn't keep from grinning, and out of respect for Amanda he couldn't tell anybody why.

But, by God, he wanted to. Captain Howe—married to his Reb sweetheart at last—*and* a baby on the way. Now there was a fine piece of news for Reid to write home to his aged mother. And how like Amanda to sneak the news up on him like that. He realized, too, that she would have let him go without telling him, if it had come down to it, if he had been obliged to acknowledge the child he already had. How close he and Amanda had come to not making it—but at least now they only had a war keeping them apart.

He abruptly grinned again; he didn't want to dwell on that, and he couldn't keep riding along with an idiot grin on his face. There was bound to be some kind of army regulation against it. Maybe he should ask Pike. If anybody would know, Pike would.

His mount began to sidle and prance, catching some of John's exuberance. He let him go—let him do his little equine dance. He saw the boy step out into the road in front of him—that same boy—Giffen's brother. What the hell did he want now—?

"Ah! God!"

My arm is numb! What...I can't...breathe! What? Whickes...I can't get... What is that... Blood...everywhere...it hurts so bad... Get me up, damn you! Damn horse...is going to...trample me! Whickes...

Old fool's crying....

Chapter Fourteen

Amanda heard the wagon before she saw it. It came right up to the front porch, with no regard whatsoever for the boxwoods and what little the brief Yankee occupation had left of the doctor's manicured lawn. Sergeant Whickes and two other soldiers rode alongside, and her heart sank at the sight of their grim faces and the riderless horse tied behind.

Whickes burst through the front door, and Amanda ran forward, trying to get by him to the wagon outside. He wouldn't let her go, and dear God, he had blood all over the front of his jacket.

"Is John dead?" she cried, still trying to get past him, because that was the only thing that could account for his behavior. "Tell me!"

"It's bad," Whickes said, and the room swayed. He held her on her feet. "I brought him to you. You stand back and let them get inside with him."

"Where, where is he wounded?" she said, forcing the hysteria down.

"Chest. Bleeding's bad—"

"The doctor's not here, or Major Reid—"

"We'll find them for you."

The other soldiers were bringing John inside. Amanda wheeled around, screaming for the doctor's wife and leading the way down the front hallway to the biggest down-stairs bedroom.

John was so pale—that same terrible gray color she'd seen on Charlie Wood. She reached out to touch his hand as the men carried him by. His skin was so cold! The muscles in his face fluttered and the hole in his side dropped great splatters of blood along the floor. His breathing was labored and shallow, each exhalation marked by a sharp "ah" sound.

The doctor's wife came on the run, directing the men as they placed John on the bed. Both she and Amanda grabbed pillows to stack behind him to keep his head up and to place under his arms so he wouldn't have to fight so hard to breathe.

"Turn around," the doctor's wife said to Whickes and the others.

"Ma'am?"

"Turn around! Now!"

They did as she asked, and she immediately began unlacing her stays. "Sergeant Whickes, do you know where the icehouse is? Near the Wayside Hospital down by the railroad depot?"

"I do," one of the other soldiers said.

"Good. Then please go there quickly and bring me some ice." She pulled off her stays and took them to the bed. "One of you bring the ice here and the other one look for the doctors. Help me," she said to Whickes. "Help me get his shirt and jacket off."

The two of them lifted John while Amanda got his arms out of the sleeves. The cloth on the front of his jacket was already stiffening with dried blood.

"See if the ball has gone through," the doctor's wife instructed, and Amanda ran her fingers along John's bare back, trying not to remember just a short while ago. Her fingers found the exit hole.

"It's out," she said in relief.

"Thank God for that." The doctor's wife began to tear the bed sheet, making two tightly folded wads of cloth and placing them over the wounds on John's chest and back. "Hold him," she said to Amanda, and she slid her stays around him. "Sergeant Whickes, you lace it up—tight!"

Whickes worked quickly, but the blood was coming through the cloth and John began to cough. A burst of bright red bubbled from his mouth and nose, and Amanda gave a soft cry. He was going to die, just like Charlie Wood. She wiped frantically at the blood on his face with what was left of the sheet, trying to clear his mouth and nose so he could breathe, surprised that her hands no longer trembled when she'd been so close to fainting just moments before.

She suddenly knew the only thing left to do. "Sergeant Whickes, I want you to go to my father's house. It's—"

"I know where it is, but Cap don't need that old man—"

"No, I want you to see my stepmother. Ask her to come right now. If my father forbids it, then ask her for her herb boxes. For the 'sang.' Especially for that—she'll understand."

Whickes left at a run, and one boy soldier remained. He stood miserably at the foot of the bed, moving when the doctor's wife wanted him to move and crying openly.

"Who are you?" Amanda asked him, still trying to wipe the blood from John's face.

"Private Tobin, ma'am," he said, sniffing loudly. He wiped his nose on his jacket sleeve.

"What happened to Captain Howe?"

He shook his head. "I didn't exactly see—it was over so quick. Sergeant Whickes said some boy stepped out on the road in front of Cap and he shot him before we knew what happened. He ran off into the woods—some of the boys are looking for him right now, but if he knows the land, I don't reckon they'll find him. They wouldn't find *me* if I was to home and of a mind to hide." He looked into Amanda's eyes. "If they catch him, they'll string him up on the first tree they come to, I know that."

"Come with me, son," the doctor's wife said. "I need you to carry blankets. We have to keep your captain warm."

By the time they returned with the extra bedding, a soldier had arrived with a block of ice in a burlap sack, which he immediately began pounding with a rifle butt.

"If you don't need me, ma'am, I'll be looking for Major Reid," he said when the ice was in pieces.

"Yes," Amanda said. "Do that, and please hurry."

She and the doctor's wife began to gather ice into a pillowcase, tying it shut and arranging it over John's chest and side. The blood had soaked through the wads of sheet and the stays.

"You keep that ice right on the wound," the doctor's wife said. "If we can keep him still long enough, it may be we can get the bleeding stopped. I'm going to see if I can find something else to use for bandages. And I want to make sure there is boiling water in the kitchen."

Amanda nodded, hardly noticing when the doctor's wife had gone.

"John," she said urgently, her face close to his. "Can you hear me?"

But nothing penetrated his awful struggle to breathe.

Amanda looked around sharply at a noise in the hallway. Verillia had arrived, thank God, and she came hurrying into the room, Whickes not far behind. She took one look at John and began to rummage through her herb boxes. "I need hot water," she said, "and I need it quick."

"The kitchen," Amanda said, hoping the doctor's wife had some boiling.

"I'll get it," Whickes said, and he must have run the length of the house, because he came back almost immediately with a steaming kettle.

"I brought both," he said, showing a pitcher of cold water, too. Verillia poured water from the kettle into the tin cup she'd brought with her, the one she always used to mix her herbal concoctions.

"You was right," she said matter-of-factly as she measured out the powdered ginseng root that came from her mountains. "The 'sang' is what this boy is needing." She kept glancing at Amanda as she worked. The reverend had forbidden her to have any contact with his disowned daughter, and for Verillia's sake, Amanda had made no attempt to see her since her return from Washington.

"What else can I do?" Whickes said.

"You can wrap the rest of this ice in something and get it down the well so it don't melt before we're needing it again," Verillia said. "Wrap it heavy and put it in the bucket so it don't get wet."

"Anything else, ma'am?"

"Yes. I'm going to be needing some honey. I want enough to pack the wound with it after we get that there bleeding stopped."

"Honey," Whickes repeated, as if he wasn't quite sure he'd heard right.

"That's what I said."

"All right, ma'am. If there's any in this town, I'll find it."

"That Yankee soldier there," Verillia whispered as soon as Whickes had left the room. "He went and made me ride on the same horse as him!" Her hair had come undone in the process and she tucked a loose strand behind her ear. "Right in front of everybody! I just thank the sweet Lord Jesus your daddy wasn't home."

Amanda smiled—then began to cry, hiding her face in her hands.

"All right, girl," Verillia said, putting her arms around her. Amanda sagged against her, gratefully accepting the comfort she'd done without on that January night so long ago. "Stop crying now. We got things to do. The first thing is no whiskey for him. Don't you let no doctor give that boy spirits. It'll be the first thing they want to do and with him hanging by a thread like he is, his heart'll go weak on him and that'll be the end. You hear?"

Amanda nodded, wiping her eyes.

"Do you want me to 'use' for the bleeding?" Verillia asked, and Amanda turned away.

"I don't think he believes in it."

"*I* believe," she said quietly.

Yes, Amanda thought. Verillia believed. She believed enough for both of them. "Do it. Anything. I don't want him to die."

Verillia added some cool water to her tin cup from the pitcher, then tested it and handed it and a spoon to Amanda. "Feed him this now. A little at a time. Force it into him if you have to."

Amanda climbed up onto the bed so she could get close enough, forcing a spoonful of the mixture between John's teeth. It all ran back out. She tried again, wedging the spoon farther back this time, tipping the liquid in between his labored breaths. This time he swallowed.

Verillia stood ready with her Bible. "More," she said, and Amanda gave him another spoonful. And then another.

"All right," Verillia said, opening the Bible and searching through the Book of Ezekiel for the right passage. She never left the verse that stopped bleeding to memory; she always read it directly from the Bible. "His name?" she asked, reaching out one hand to touch John's chest.

"John David Howe," Amanda said, fighting hard against the renewed urge to cry. She took John's hand and held it tightly, watching Verillia's lips form the necessary words, wanting to say them with her. She tried to take comfort from knowing how many times Verillia had been called on to do this and that it had even worked—sometimes:

*When I passed John David Howe and saw John David
Howe weltering in John David Howe's blood, I said to John
David Howe in John David Howe's blood—live!*

After a moment, Verillia closed her Bible. She gave a
quiet sigh. "I been living in a lonely house since you've been
gone. I wanted to come over here to see you, from the very
first. But when I married your daddy, I done stood up before God and vowed that vow to obey him. You know I
wanted to come, don't you? I know you needed me—the
way this town feels about you. I thought a hundred times
maybe I shouldn't have begged you to come home like I did.
You don't hold it against me, do you? Me doing that and
then leaving you to the wolves the way I done?"

Amanda reached out and hugged her tightly. "No, Verillia, no. I've been all right here." She let go of her and looked
back at John. "I'm not sorry for anything that happened—Verillia, what will I do if he dies! He—we got married today. Out at the river. A Yankee chaplain did it."

"Did you now!" Verillia said. "Then you love this boy. I
should have knowed the way he carried on at the house yesterday. Looking for you, he was, and he wasn't taking no for
an answer. He gave the reverend a turn, I can tell you—"

"Verillia—" Amanda interrupted, meaning to tell her
everything, because she might not have another chance. No
one knew about her condition but the doctor and his wife
and, she hoped, John. He hadn't said anything when she
made her oblique reference to her pregnancy out at the river.
She had been so worried about finally telling him, and if he
died without ever knowing...

She took a deep breath. She wouldn't let herself think
about that. She wanted Verillia to hear the news from her
and not from some gossip on the street. She looked into
Verillia's eyes. "I've got his baby coming."

If Verillia were scandalized, Amanda couldn't tell.

"Well!" she said without hesitation. "Here I been thinking *you* was the only baby I'd ever have—and I'm going to get me another one." She reached up to pat Amanda on the cheek. "You get to feeding John David that 'sang' again. We got to keep it up all night and tomorrow. Maybe even longer. A little bit at a time to keep him going, but not enough to strain him. And you talk to him while you do it. If you love him, tell him about it, so he'll know how much you need him here. I believe he can hear you. I believe they can always hear you, right up to the last."

Amanda knew that Verillia was giving her the only comfort she could, and once again she fought down the urge to cry. She had no time for tears now. She went back to spoonfeeding John, following Verillia's instructions to the letter, telling him in quiet whispers what had happened to him and what she was doing to help him and most particularly why.

"I love you, John Howe," she kept saying. "Don't let go. Please don't let go!"

It was dark before anyone located the doctor and Major Reid. Amanda refused to be put out of the room while they examined him. Neither of them suggested giving John whiskey. They had nothing to offer at all, no treatment, no medicine. The situation was too grave even for their combined skills. They simply let her continue to do whatever would satisfy her mind, and she could see on both their faces that they fully expected John to die.

"Major Reid," she said as he was about to leave the room, "can you get word to John's mother?"

He stared at her for a moment. "Most probably I can, Amanda. A telegraph message, hopefully, if the wires aren't cut."

"Please try. She should know. Major Reid?" she said, once again detaining him when he was about to go.

"I...think you've been a good friend to John—to us. I want to thank you."

"My dear girl," was all he said.

Amanda sat by John's bed all night, refusing to leave him when Verillia and the doctor's wife would have made her rest, keeping vigil with the ice and the herbal drink. She was vaguely aware that people came and went. Major Reid. The boy soldier, Tobin, who had wept so pitifully. Whickes. And women from the town who simply wanted to *see* this Yankee officer who had caused Amanda Lee Douglas's downfall.

But she let nothing fill her thoughts but him. If it were possible to drag him back from death, then she would do it. And she didn't unbraid her hair, because she had the superstitious notion that if she undid his handiwork, he would surely die.

On the third afternoon he finally stirred. Amanda was dozing in a chair by the bed. She opened her eyes to find him looking at her.

He was trying to say something.

"No," she said, getting up quickly and taking his hand. "Don't try to talk. It's going to be all right."

He briefly closed his eyes. "Tired," he managed, his voice barely audible.

"You'll feel better soon," she promised, as she had promised so many times in the past three days. Only this time she knew he heard her.

"Not—me," he whispered. "You. *You*—rest."

"I will," she said, trying not to cry.

"Now," he insisted.

"Yes, I will."

His fingers tapped on the bed beside him. "Lie down—here. Don't...worry me. Rest...for me. For our...baby...."

He did know, she thought joyfully. She looked into his eyes and saw his love for them both there. "All right," she said, her voice husky with unshed tears. "But drink this first."

She gave him a few small sips of Verillia's brew, then climbed up on the bed beside him, knowing the entire household—if not the entire town—would be scandalized. As far as she knew, no one but Verilia and Major Reid and Whickes knew that she and John had married, and even if it were common knowledge, her behavior was still no less brazen.

She stretched out along his good side anyway, careful of the pillow that supported his arm. She loved him, and she belonged by his side.

She pressed a kiss against the back of his hand when he reached to touch her cheek.

"Rest," he said again, and this time he managed a weak smile. "I won't go... anywhere. I... promise."

Epilogue

June 1865

He managed to keep his promise, but it had been hard going. Days and weeks of fever and terrible dreams that waited for him in the dark. He was always escaping from the prison in his nightmares, but he never made it through the tunnel. The walls collapsed directly on him, time and time again. Sometimes Max Woodard was with him, but always he suffocated under tons of dirt that filled his eyes and mouth and nose.

He remembered parts of his wounding. He remembered the boy—Giffen's brother, William—but he hadn't told anyone in authority who had shot him. He wasn't precisely sure why. Because the war was over, he supposed, and because he himself, in that boy's place and thinking that he was the only one left who could avenge a woman's honor, might have done the same. He knew the boy had gone into exile after the incident, where, no one seemed to know, or would tell. He thought it was likely common knowledge among certain of the townspeople *who* had attempted his assassination on the road that April day. For Amanda's sake, he wanted it put behind him, and if Thayer Giffen would ever come here to the doctor's house to see him as he'd asked, he would tell him so. He would tell him that—rivals or not—his brother could come home.

John remembered, too, all the talk that went on around him when his life hung so precariously. He knew that Reid and the town doctor had thought he was beyond saving and that it was Amanda who had refused to let him go. She alone had kept telling him what he had to do—lie still, suffer the ice, swallow what she gave him, *breathe!* Amanda. His dearest comrade. His wife.

It was incredible to him that he had survived. Better men than he lay dead now in their graves. Even with Amanda's good help, he hadn't been able to find out precisely what had happened to Max. There was no record of him on the prison hospital roster at all, and whether he had been buried nameless in one of the prison trenches or whether he lay in some hastily scratched-out grave between here and Wilmington, John would never know.

He tried not to ponder over it, because he knew it to be a useless and depressing pastime. To save himself, he had left Max Woodard in the prison—and he would have to live with the fact. He tried to concentrate instead on getting completely well. Reid came to see him several times a day; he could hear him now, teasing someone in the house as he made his way up the stairs to the second floor veranda. The veranda was John's favorite place to sit. He could move into sun or shade according to his preference; he could see the comings and goings of much of the occupation army. And he could hear Amanda and the other women in the household, soft female voices and their tinkling laughter when something went wrong in the kitchen. He could smell delicious home cooking, unfamiliar as some as the dishes might be. He could *know,* once and for all, that the war was over and that he had survived. He had felt and he continued to feel completely at home in the doctor's house. He had suffered not in the least from homesickness during his convalescence, and he knew precisely why. His home was with Amanda, wherever that might be.

"I got another telegram from your mother," Reid said when he came out onto the porch.

John frowned. He half expected his mother to arrive on the doorstep any day. He hadn't forgiven her for her part in his estrangement from Amanda, and while he was nearly recovered from his wound, he didn't want to have to deal with the scene she would likely make over his marriage. He couldn't deal with it without causing a permanent breach in their relationship. No. It was imperative that she stay in Washington and out of his sight if she wanted to remain his mother, even if it meant that he couldn't see Harry for a long time. "I thought you assured her I was recovering," he said, and Reid laughed.

"I have more than assured her, John—hell, if you died now, she could have me shot. I suppose she's still upset about your rather abrupt wedding?"

"Oh, yes. Why do you think you keep getting those two-page telegrams? I believe she's convinced that my wound must have been in my head. So when are you mustering out of the army? Any word yet?"

"The word is I'm not," he said, pointedly looking around for some kind of refreshments. "I get to stay here a while longer. Somebody's got to treat the hangovers and the hemorrhoids."

"For God's sake, here," John said, bringing out the tin of cookies that was under the newspaper he'd been reading. "Don't you get to eat anyplace else?"

"Yes, but I like your stuff best. Who sent these?"

"The ladies of Washington—hand-delivered by a friend of my father's. I thought you were eager to get back to the old Maryland home place?"

Reid shrugged, searching in the tin for just the right delicacy. "I'm not particularly needed there," he said, taking a big bite of the cookie that appealed to him most. "But there's something else I want to talk to you about, John. Canby—the new occupation general—he's very interested in you."

"Why?" John said suspiciously.

"Well, he wants to put you to work as soon as your army surgeon allows it."

"The hell he will. The war is over. I'm turning civilian."

"Actually, John, you're not. The general thinks your being on his staff will go a long way toward keeping things on an even keel here—because you're married to Amanda. I have to say I agree with him. It wouldn't hurt for people to think there was a sympathetic ear about, even if it's once removed."

"The occupation is going that badly?"

"Well, no. But then most of their soldiers haven't returned. There are bound to be incidents. Our men are already bored to death—and you know well enough where that leads. And I believe the general thinks you might be the least offensive officer he has to administer the oath of allegiance."

"Got the damn thing all planned out, haven't you?"

Reid grinned. "It's not *me*, John. I'm only telling you so you won't be so taken aback you'll say something stupid to the general—*again*. The war ended for the Rebs, not us. They can go on home and be about their business. You and I and any of the rest of us will man the occupation until the powers that be say otherwise. Besides that, judging by the complaints I hear in this household about your testy disposition, you're ready to have something to do."

"I'm finished with the damned army!"

"That's it, John. Get it all out of your system. I've said you can report to the general next week, by the way—a few hours a day."

"Reid, I don't want to play nursemaid to a bunch of—" He stopped because Amanda stood in the doorway. He forgot what he was about to say to Reid. He forgot everything except her. He *had* been testy of late; and perhaps she had taken the brunt of it.

He held out his hand to her, and when she came near enough, he drew her into his lap, in spite of her protests and unmindful of Reid and anyone who might be passing by. He didn't give a damn who might sniff because the Yankee captain, in broad daylight, had noticed his wife.

"You're not mad at me, are you?" he asked, nuzzling her cheek.

"If I were," she said pointedly, "you wouldn't have to ask."

He laughed. Now that was the honest truth if he'd ever heard it. She had never let him bully her, even in their early days.

"You're feeling all right today, aren't you? No trouble with the baby? No morning sickness or anything like that?"

"I'm fine, John Howe," she assured him.

"I'm going now!" Reid said loudly. "In case anybody cares—yes, that is exactly what I thought."

John barely heard him; he stared intently into Amanda's eyes. God, he loved her! He loved that she was strong and could give as good as she got. He loved that she was kinder than he was, and that he could tease her and make her laugh. He loved the quaint way she had of calling him by both his names. Most of all he loved that she was going to be the mother of his child. The depth of his regard for her never ceased to amaze him. His old comrades from the Pennsylvania Sixth would surely get a laugh seeing him so completely domesticated.

Domesticated. He was exactly that, and no one could be more happy about it than he. He loved being married—no, he loved being married to Amanda Lee Douglas.

He kissed her, a mild buss on the lips that promptly escalated until it took his breath away—literally. He stopped, trying to fight down his need to gasp for air, trying not to give in to another coughing fit. He rested his head against her shoulder. Unfortunately, his mind was far ahead of his body in the quest to end his celibacy. According to Reid, he was still supposed to content himself with brotherly touches and brazen fantasies. Purposeful kissing, the kind he wanted to enjoy with her so badly, was clearly beyond him for a while yet.

"Reid tells me I'm staying in the military," he said when his breathing became easier.

She didn't say anything, and he moved so he could see her face.

"You wanted to get away from here, didn't you?" he asked, his eyes searching hers. He knew that she still suffered from her association with him and that their marriage had done little to abate the gossip.

"I'd miss Verillia," she said. "At least if I'm here people can tell me about her—and sometimes I see her going past the house."

"I'm sorry, love. I want to fix this for you, and I can't." When he had been well enough to want to see Verillia so that he could thank her for her part in his recovery, the reverend had absolutely forbidden her to come.

"It's not your fault, John. The trouble is between me and the reverend."

He held her close to him then, because the realization was both sudden and painful. On that cold January night, he had not been the only one in need of escape. Amanda had been as much a prisoner as he.

They sat for a while in silence, content to be close like this, enjoying the fine June sunshine and the cool morning breeze. It occurred to him, too, that Reid was right. He *was* ready to do something. He was ready to be a husband and a father and an officer on General Canby's staff. He was ready to get on with his life, and he was damned happy about it.

"Kiss me," he said abruptly, his boldness making Amanda laugh.

"John Howe, you are not well enough for kissing," she admonished him.

"*I'm* not going to kiss. You are. Right here," he said, showing her a place on his cheek. "And right over here," he pointed out when she'd laughingly obliged. But that got out of hand, too, and he had to settle for tickling her and sneaking a hand up under her skirt to make her squeal.

"There are *people* around here," she whispered fiercely, trying to hold off both his inquisitive hands.

"And you know how much I care about that," he said, going back to tickling and whatever else he could get away with.

"John Howe, you are *awful!*"

"I am," he agreed mischievously. "And don't you love it!"

* * * * *

Author's Note

On April 12, 1865, three days after General Robert E. Lee's surrender at Appomattox, the town of Salisbury, North Carolina, was captured by General George Stoneman and his Union cavalry. The townspeople fully expected quick and harsh retaliation for the Confederate prison located in their midst, but for some reason Stoneman spared the town from destruction, in spite of the fact that the precedent for the wanton burning of civilian property had already been set in Atlanta and Florence and Columbia. There are numerous local legends as to why General Stoneman was so lenient: that he was persuaded by a prominent town merchant who provided him with a fine breakfast, that he was a Mason and local Masons asked him not to burn the town, that he and the mayor of Salisbury both hailed from Massachusetts and had been old schoolmates. All of these reasons are incredibly unsatisfying to a writer of romantic fiction. *The Prisoner* is my own version of why the town of Salisbury was spared.

COMING NEXT MONTH

#127   THE LADY AND THE LAIRD—Maura Seger
Forced by her grandfather's will to live in an eerie Scottish castle
for six months or lose the crumbling keep to rogue Angus Wyndham,
beautiful Katlin Sinclair discovered a tormented ghost, hidden
treasure and burning passion in the arms of the one man she could
not trust.

#128   SWEET SUSPICIONS—Julie Tetel
Intent on reentering society, Richard Worth planned to find a well-
connected wife. But he hadn't expected the murder of a stranger to
revive his scandalous past—or that his marriage of convenience to
lovely Caroline Hutton would awaken his passion and heal his
anguished soul.

#129   THE CLAIM—Lucy Elliot
A confrontation was inevitable when determined Sarah Meade and
formidable mountain man Zeke Brownell both claimed ownership of
the same land. Yet underneath their stubborn facades and cultural
differences there lay a mutual attraction neither could deny.

#130   PIRATE BRIDE—Elizabeth August
Pirate captive Kathleen James impetuously married prisoner
John Ashford to save him from certain death. But although
freedom and happiness were only a breath away, a daring escape
brought them further danger in the New World.

AVAILABLE NOW:

Harlequin®

JANELLE TAYLOR

Valley of Fire

HARLEQUIN IS PROUD TO PRESENT *VALLEY OF FIRE* BY JANELLE TAYLOR—AUTHOR OF TWENTY-TWO BOOKS, INCLUDING SIX *NEW YORK TIMES* BESTSELLERS

VALLEY OF FIRE—the warm and passionate story of Kathy Alexander, a famous romance author, and Steven Winngate, entrepreneur and owner of the magazine that intended to expose the real Kathy ''Brandy'' Alexander to her fans.

Don't miss VALLEY OF FIRE, available in May.

Take 4 bestselling love stories FREE

Plus get a FREE surprise gift!

Harlequin Regency® Romance™

WHO SAYS ROMANCE IS A THING OF THE PAST?

We do! At Harlequin Regency Romance, we offer you romance the way it was always meant to be.

What could be more romantic than to follow the adventures of a duchess or duke through the glittering assembly rooms of Regency England? Or to eavesdrop on their witty conversations or romantic interludes? The music, the costumes, the ballrooms and the dance will sweep you away to a time when pleasure was a priority and privilege a prerequisite.

If you are longing for the good old days when falling in love still meant something very special, then come to Harlequin Regency Romance—romance with a touch of class.

RRG

BIG SUMMER READ

Summer Reading At Its Best

In July, Harlequin and Silhouette bring readers the Big Summer Read Program. Heat up your summer with these four exciting new novels by top Harlequin and Silhouette authors.

SOMEWHERE IN TIME by Barbara Bretton
YESTERDAY COMES TOMORROW by Rebecca Flanders
A DAY IN APRIL by Mary Lynn Baxter
LOVE CHILD by Patricia Coughlin

From time travel to fame and fortune, this program offers something for everyone.

Available at your favorite retail outlet.

BSR

FREE GIFT OFFER

To receive your free gift, send us the specified number of proofs-of-purchase from any specially marked Free Gift Offer Harlequin or Silhouette book with the Free Gift Certificate properly completed, plus a check or money order (do not send cash) to cover postage and handling payable to Harlequin/Silhouette Free Gift Promotion Offer. We will send you the specified gift.

FREE GIFT CERTIFICATE

ITEM	A. GOLD TONE EARRINGS	B. GOLD TONE BRACELET	C. GOLD TONE NECKLACE
# of proofs-of-purchase required	3	6	9
Postage and Handling	$1.75	$2.25	$2.75
Check one	☐	☐	☐

Name: _____

Address: _____

City: _____ State: _____ Zip Code: _____

Mail this certificate, specified number of proofs-of-purchase and a check or money order for postage and handling to: HARLEQUIN/SILHOUETTE FREE GIFT OFFER 1992, P.O. Box 9057, Buffalo, NY 14269-9057. Requests must be received by July 31, 1992.

PLUS—Every time you submit a completed certificate with the correct number of proofs-of-purchase, you are automatically entered in our MILLION DOLLAR SWEEPSTAKES! No purchase or obligation necessary to enter. See below for alternate means of entry and how to obtain complete sweepstakes rules.

HH2U

ONE PROOF-OF-PURCHASE

To collect your fabulous FREE GIFT you must include the necessary FREE GIFT proofs-of-purchase with a properly completed offer certificate.

(See inside back cover for offer details)